"What's all that yelling and chanting?"

"Frimmie civilians," the Death Merchant shouted. "We'll leave here as soon as we put them to sleep. Don't fire until they're closer."

"It's like they want to commit suicide," the other man said, at the sight of the dozens of Frimmies running toward the waterworks from the northwest. Young men and women shouted, "Frimm! Frimm! Frimm!" and waved pistols, revolvers, and rifles. Not a single man or woman was making any attempt at concealment, nor was there any kind of order. The Frimmies were nothing but a crazed mob bent on vengeance, determined to kill the agents of Satan—the Death Merchant and his friends—who were invading their sacred city. And they were convinced that the power of God's Messenger on Earth, their beloved Reverend Frimm, would protect them.

But Frimm couldn't and didn't!

"Terminate!" hissed the Death Merchant.

The mentally deranged, fanatical Frimmies were destroyed faster than a wheat field in a raging fire. They jerked and jumped, screamed, twisted, and died. In less than a minute, the slaughter was over, and all that was left were scores of corpses lying in mounds . . .

THE DEATH MERCHANT SERIES:

#36 in the incredible adventures of the

DEATH MERCHANT
THE COSMIC REALITY KILL
by Joseph Rosenberger

PINNACLE BOOKS • LOS ANGELES

DEATH MERCHANT #36:
THE COSMIC REALITY KILL

Copyright © 1979 by Joseph Rosenberger

An original Pinnacle Books edition, published for the first time anywhere.

First printing, November 1979

ISBN: 0-523-40675-4

Cover illustration by Dean Cate

Printed in the United States of America

PINNACLE BOOKS, INC.
2029 Century Park East
Los Angeles, California 90067

This book is dedicated to
E.M.K.
of
El Campo, Texas

We wish to thank Mr. Michael Hoy, the publisher of *Principia Discordia*, for the quotes used by Russell Linders in this book.

Joseph R. Rosenberger

WARNING!

Let's not confuse cults with the various religious beliefs of the world, with Christianity, Judaism, Hinduism, Islam, etc. There is a world of difference between the cults and the traditional beliefs in God:

—A cult has a living leader. Cult doctrine is based on this leader's *revelations*, which either supplant or supplement traditional religious doctrine and scripture. This is to say that the cult leader twists religious doctrine and scripture for his own ends.

—The cult leader is the *sole judge* of the quality of a member's faith, and he enjoys absolute authority, like a god, over the members.

—A cult promises a system in which a convert may work "to save the world and humanity," but actually sponsors no community improvement programs.

—The daily work of nearly all cult members is demeaning and utilizes little of their potential, in terms of intelligence, training and/or education.

—In cults, members are taught to believe that they are "superior" to those outside the group.

—To be a member of a cult, a person must remove himself from society, cut himself off from a job, education, friends and family.

—Methods of ego-destruction and thought-control are part of a cult's recruiting and indoctrination practices.

—Cults discourage critical analysis by dictating the suppression of negative thoughts, thereby fostering a dependency on the cult's authority that arrests the maturation process.

—The cult's rituals and practices are psychologically unwholesome and, in some cases, physically dangerous when they involve the use of drugs or perverse sexual rites.

—Out-and-out behavior modification (brainwashing) is used by the cults, with victims not even realizing that they are being manipulated.

—Cults do have one thing in common: every single one has a recruiting program for its peculiar brand of faith, which appeals to that combination of optimism, idealism and narcissism that is present in the personalities of all prospective recruits. Some of these marketing strategies are so dishonest that if they were used in business, instead of religion, the federal government would intervene.

—Cults are very dangerous to the stability of American society, dangerous because money is power and can influence politics on the local, state, and national levels.

Richard J. Camellion
Village Mills, Texas

The Cosmic Reality Kill

Chapter One

I'm halfway between nowhere and nothing! Lying concealed among the mesquite, Richard Camellion adjusted the UFO alien mask to a more comfortable fit. Made of thin latex rubber, the mask slipped over his head and was very cleverly made, the skin so realistic-looking, it was difficult to tell that it was a mask from a distance of only a few feet.

The Death Merchant had very carefully cased the Haven of Truth camp. It was only one of the seventy-odd communities established throughout the United States by the Church of the Cosmic Reality—one of the more vicious and powerful cults in the world; certainly the largest "religious" cult in the U.S.

He stared at the chain-link fence a hundred feet ahead. Once the two guards and the dog were put to sleep, he wouldn't have any trouble getting inside the fence, then onto the office of the Minister of Light, the camp's director.

It was this camp that had been targeted by Everett Padden and Dwight Montroy. Whether the two deprogrammers had attempted to kidnap Morris Kenner and rescue him from the cult was another matter.

Everett Padden had been found dead—beaten to death.

Dwight Montroy was still missing.

The Sheriff's Police of Tarrant County had questioned the Minister of Light and his assistants at the Cosmic Reality camp; they had disclaimed any knowledge of Padden and Montroy. See the men? They didn't even know them, except by reputation—"Agents of Satan who attempt to corrupt the innocent, by pulling them from the path of righteousness and drowning their minds in a cesspool of materialism!" So the Minister of Light had thundered at the police.

As a result of Padden being found inside the city limits of Fort Worth, the homicide boys of the Fort Worth Police Department had made an investigation and still had the case

1

open on their books. All that was known was that Padden had not been beaten to death where his corpse had been found. Apparently, he had been worked over and then, somehow, had escaped his captors and had made it to the back of some billboards where he had collapsed and died.

Camellion was positive that Padden and Montroy had not been battered at the camp. In the first place, the two deprogrammers (who had national reputations for deprogramming members of crackpot cults and bringing them back to the world of common sense) would not have tried to grab young Kenner at the camp. According to the youth's distraught parents, their son often went to Fort Worth, with two other members of the *enlightened* (as the rank and file members were called), to buy supplies for the camp. It stood to reason that it was in Fort Worth that Padden and Montroy had intended to blackbag Kenner.

Young Kenner was still at the camp. His parents had attempted several times to see him, but he had refused to talk with them. He said he had found "inner peace" and "contentment" and did not wish to be "contaminated by agents of the devil!"

The camp was four miles from the city limits of western Fort Worth. If Everett had been beaten at the camp, it wasn't likely that he could have staggered that distance into Ft. Worth.

At this point, weeks later, it was all academic, however. Everett Padden had been murdered. That was fact. And Richard Camellion was not the kind of man to twiddle his thumbs and not do anything to punish the murderers of his friends, especially an old friend like Everett. As far as the Death Merchant was concerned, the Church of the Cosmic Reality was as good as out of business, and Reverend Hannibal Nigel Frimm, the founder of the cult, had been singled out by the Cosmic Lord of Death. "His Oneness and His Onlyness" was the heart and soul of the cult. Without Frimm, the "Frimmies" would be as helpless as spiders without legs. Those who couldn't climb the ladder of life back to normalcy would eventually end up on the skid rows of various cities or in mental institutions. The biggest martyr in the world, the American Taxpayer, would pay the bill. . . .

The Death Merchant looked up at the pale white sliver of moon and the scattered clouds. The early morning was not very bright and he had partial cover. Silence. The semidesert air was almost cold.

2

He looked at his watch. 3:18. Another 12 minutes.

For three days and two nights, he had surveyed the camp, not only from the low range of hills to the west, but also from higher ground to the north. From a friend of his in the Tarrant County Sheriff's Police Department, he had obtained a diagram of the camp. In the front of the camp, just beyond the fence, were the kitchen and the communal dining hall. To the east, across from the kitchen and the mess hall, was the reception center for visitors and prospective Frimmies. To the south, in front of the reception center, was the office of the Minister of Light. Next to the office was the command center of the "Protectors of the Righteous": men, and some women, highly trained in karate and the use of firearms. Each Haven of Truth and Abode of the Righteous—the latter being large houses in various cities where Frimmies lived in groups—had a squad of Protectors, which was used as much to keep the Frimmies in as to keep the "agents of Satan" out.

In the center of the camp was the parade ground. On either side of the parade ground, to the east and the west, were three one-story army-type wooden barracks. North of the parade ground was the Cosmic Temple, the church of the camp. North of the Temple were two more buildings. One was the gymnasium. The other was "The Rite of Cleansing Center." Here new Frimmies were brainwashed, their murdered minds saturated with the warped philosophy of Reverend Frimm, His Oneness and His Onlyness.

Frimm's "religious dogma" was simple, one that had been used successfully by "messiahs" throughout the ages.

The Last Days were rapidly approaching. The End of the World—yea, of the Universe itself—was just around the corner. The end of all Time, of all Matter and Space, would occur the first second of the year 2000 A.D. During that terrible moment every living thing and every single atom of the universe would be annihilated.

Except the members of the Church of the Cosmic Reality!

To His Oneness and His Onlyness and his flock, the explosion of the Universe would be as weak as the force generated by a drifting feather. Shucks, they woludn't even be singed! It was they who would "inherit a New Earth that God will create a trillionth of a second after the destruction of the Universe." A new Earth—the Second Heaven—would be theirs for all eternity. This was all truth. Reverend Hannibal Nigel Frimm had said so. And he was the "Messenger of God on Earth!"

Watching the northwest corner of the fence, Camellion thought of another aspect of Hannibal Frimm's teaching. Unlike other cult leaders, he put great emphasis on Americanism, on patriotism.

A clever man, Frimm, Camellion thought. *The press has accused him of being everything from a con artist and charlatan, to a schizophrenic with delusions of grandeur. But they've found it impossible to accuse him of being unAmerican.*

In front of every Abode of the Righteous and in the center of every Haven of Truth's parade ground was a flagpole flying the Stars and Stripes. Below the U.S. flag was the flag of the Church of the Cosmic Reality: a spiral galaxy, the various arms glowing with stars, the center of the nebula a brilliant white over which was a large blood-red cross. At the bottom of the flag were the words: FOR GOD AND COUNTRY.

A natural-born press agent, Frimm had another gimmick he used to confuse press and public. He lived a very simple life. The South Korean cult leader, Sun Myung Moon, lived on a $625,000 estate in New York state, while his Moonies worked 15 hours a day and barely got enouth to eat—so many newspapers alleged. The guru Maharaj Ji, the moon-faced 22-year-old youth who was "God" and the titular head of the Divine Light Mission, had private airplanes, diamonds as large as marbles, a million-dollar estate, and a fleet of Rolls Royces.

Reverend Frimm had none of these things. While the Church of the Cosmic Reality owned four Lear jets, Frimm lived like any average person. He was chauffeured around in a GLC Mazda station wagon and lived in a small frame house in the New Earth Community, the national headquarters of the Church of the Cosmic Reality, seven miles outside of Colorado Springs, Colorado. He was a widower. He didn't drink. He didn't smoke. In his youth, he had served six years in the Ohio State Penitentiary—and he didn't deny it. In fact, he often referred to his "evil ways" in his sermons, thundering, "I was a pawn of the Evil One, of Satan, who throws confusion over one's mind and blinds him to the will of God. But it was in prison that I began to free myself from the ways of Satan and first heard the soft, sweet whisper of the Lord."

The clever son-of-a-bitch!

Frimm was also very cunning in that he preached and published (in the *Cosmic Truth* magazine, printed in Chicago and given free to 1,210,000 subscribers) what millions of Americans wanted to hear. Namely, that the morals of the United States were more debased than those of Ancient Rome. Obscene books, motion pictures, and especially television were corrupting the minds of millions of American children!

There was pornography—"a tool of Satan!" according to Frimm, with "filthy adult bookstores proliferating throughout the land like a plague of locusts . . . operating on almost every block in every major city."

And the evil done by supposedly respectable people. Hundreds of thousands of babies murdered each year by abortion! Killed, or so Frimm said, because "Satan has hardened the hearts of millions of mothers and spread his slimy hands over them."

Of all the nations on Earth, there was only one more morally evil than the United States: the Soviet Union—"The world base of Satan on earth . . . the Fallen Angel of light whose gift to mankind is the moral cancer of communism. I tell you my friends, if the Master doesn't judge the people of the world within a very short time, He will owe Sodom and Gomorrah a humble apology. And judge He will. He has revealed His plan to me. A microsecond after midnight of January 31, 1999, the earth and the universe will be destroyed. Yet there is still time to repent and save yourselves!"

Then came the pitch—*join the Church of the Cosmic Reality*. For the Church of the Cosmic Reality was the *only* path to salvation, the *only* way to escape the roaring flames of Hell.

What astonished neutral observers was that thousands and thousands of supposedly normal Americans believed Frimm, even highly intelligent people . . . professional people . . . men and women in the arts and the sciences. A member of the U.S. House of Representatives quit politics to join the Frimmies and work in one of the Church's businesses, in this case a lumber mill in Oregon. So had a famous Hollywood actress! And a psychoanalyst who, of all people, should have known better.

Ironically, while many parents charged that the Church of the Cosmic Reality brainwashed their children, other parents actually approved of their children joining Frimm's movement, feeling that it was better to be a Frimmie than to take drugs or drift aimlessly through life like a chip in the wind.

Which is like saying that cancer of the stomach is preferable to cancer of the lung! the Death Merchant thought. *Or, what's worse?—the death of the body or the murder of the mind? Any idiot should be able to see that Frimm's sermons and his religious philosophy are like the horns of a steer—a point here, a point there, and a lot of bull in between!*

3:30! The two Protectors and the guard dog, a German shepherd, appeared on schedule. Dressed in short leather boots, hunting pants, and olive drab bushjackets, and carrying Armalite Ar-180 Sporter carbines, the two men walked slowly. One held a leash fastened to the harness of the dog.

Camellion had to work fast. If he waited until the two men and the dog were shadowed by the building housing the generator, he might miss. He had to tag them when they were out in the open and had the background light behind them. Using a Webber dart gun—the weapon was filled with 26 hollow needles, each one 1¼" long—Camellion reared up, raised the W-4B and placed the first dart into the right side of the dog. Filled with cyrexotin, one of the most powerful tranquilizers known, the needle buried itself in the side of the animal and put it to sleep in the middle of a yelp.

The two Protectors pulled up short in surprise, trying to ascertain what was happening. One man started to bend down over the unconscious dog when the W-4B hissed and the needle struck him in the shoulder. He jerked, tried to stand erect, then fell next to the dog.

The second man, deducing that he and his partner were under some kind of silent attack, tried to pull the Armalite carbine from his shoulder and drop, all at the same time. He fell, but not from his own power. The dart, imbedded in his right side, turned off his consciousness with the same rapidity with which one turns off a light.

And the unguarded shall eat the dust of the earth therof—Camellion: Chapter 1, Verse 1! Camellion got to his feet, shoved the Webber into one of the holsters on his belt and started running toward the fence, his leather Canoe Mocs crushing sand and prickly pears. When he reached the fence, he unsnapped the big wire-snips from the ring on his belt and went to work on the wire. Three point four minutes and 39 snips later, he dropped the wire-cutters on the sandy ground, put the fingers of both hands through the holes in the wire, pulled outward and parted the fence enough for him to slip through.

Directly ahead was the building that housed the generator, which supplied electric power to the camp by means of a tall wind tower on the roof of the structure. Slipping inside the fence, Camellion had a long way to go, all the way up the west side, then across the south front to the office in the southeast corner of the camp. He glanced at the unconscious men and the dog. All three would be out for the next few hours, and damned sleepy for the next few days.

Pulling a Ruger standard auto-pistol from a very long holster on his left hip, he checked to make sure that the Sionics silencer was tight on the muzzle, then headed south along the inside of the fence. *A risk? Yes! A big risk. Someone could always come outside for some reason and find the two men and the dog.* It was a risk he would have to take.

He quickly passed the gymnasium, the Rite of Cleansing Center, and the Temple, and was soon darting in back of the first barrack, which was no more than twenty feet from the inside of the fence. Some of the windows in the barrack were open and he could hear loud snoring and, now and then, coughing from the inside. All he needed now was for some fool of a Frimmie to look out a window and see him running in the moonlight. Not very likely. The Frimmies at the north Texas Haven of Truth put in a 15-hour day selling candy, plastic flowers, candles, incense, and other junk on the streets of Fort Worth. After returning to the camp and eating supper, they had to sit for an hour and listen to "Truth of His Onlyness, Dictated by God," a long-playing transcription of a sermon by Frimm. This nonsense was followed by another hour of discussion of "Satan's power in the world of man." By the time the saps hit the sack, they were too pooped to pop.

Hatred is always positive in that it is usually self-destructive and poisons the transpersonal levels of the mind. Yet anger is a normal and necessary emotion, as necessary as the warning of physical pain. It was cold, deadly anger that Camellion felt toward Hannibal Frimm. The cult leader was far more than ingenious in the brain department. He was diabolical. Unlike the other cults and even conventional religious denominations, the Church of the Cosmc Reality made public each year the amount of money collected by the cult and how each dime was spent.

Frimm didn't feed his Frimmies beans and rice either. To the contrary. The Frimmies were fed cheap but nourishing meals, a diet like prison food, starchy but adequate. The irony was that the Frimmies were more healthy than a lot of young people who ate loads of junk food. Their mental health was another story.

The Death Merchant had a theory that Frimm's cunning was what made him and his cult so very dangerous. There was no doubt that he was different from other cult leaders, who— as alleged by the media, and many psychiatrists and social

7

observers—were frauds interested only in making money. Frimm didn't even receive a salary; his needs were supplied by the church.

Hannibal Frimm was a dedicated fanatic. Like the murderous Reverend Jim Jones, who had ordered hundreds of his People's Temple followers to kill themselves, Frimm, in the grip of a Messiah complex, had come to believe his own lies. The self-proclaimed messenger of God in a polyester suit had fallen victim to his own Gantryesque oratory—*the dangerous fool had brainwashed himself!* Camellion was also convinced that there would come a time when Frimm's paranoid illusions would begin to tear him apart. When this happened, he would reach out for the one dream that no doubt dominated all his actions: godlike, he would deal out death. In his mental sickness, *he* was the Church of the Cosmic Reality.

When he went down in defeat, it would only be fitting that all the members die with him.

Camellion hurried past the second and the third barracks and the communal dining hall. He came to the northwest corner of the kitchen. Part of the wooden building was well-lighted, the workers getting ready for the six o'clock breakfast. He crept past the kitchen, hunching down as he moved below the two windows, reached the southwest corner, leaned out, and looked up the south side at the front of the camp. Sixty feet in front of the building was the fence and the double gate entrance, which was locked with a chain and padlock. South of the gate was the dirt road that led to Interstate Route 180, half a mile away. Through the numerous tornilla screwbean trees, Camellion could see car lights on the highway. Due to the lamps on each side of the gates, the front of the camp was bathed in light, including the south side of the camp's office and the command center of the Protectors, the latter 150 feet to the east.

The Death Merchant was about to proceed when he heard a screen door slam on the other side of the kitchen building. He turned, darted back to the northwest corner and waited, hearing someone humming "Roll Jordan Roll." Camellion looked around the corner and saw a Frimmie walking away from him and carrying a trash can. He ducked back to the shadows when the man put down the trash can and turned around to go back.

After Camellion heard the screen door open and close, he went to the southwest corner, looked at the front of the camp and decided that now was as good a time as any to make a fool of himself. In a deal like this you had to toss your rope over the other fellow's calf and see what happened.

Bent over almost on his hands and knees as he moved beneath the windows, he crossed in front of the kitchen, stood up when he came to the southeast corner, looked toward the north, then the south, then darted across the space to the side of the office, the building that would be his target. *But not yet!* He knew he couldn't burglarize the camp office until he had put to sleep the other Protectors in the command center. In a few minutes the other two guards he already had put down were due back. Two other Protectors would then walk the wire with the dog. Camellion was sure of the procedure. He had lain there for several nights, away from the camp, and watched the command center through a FJW Nite-Site Infrared Viewer.

He crept to the first window of the command center and looked into the small room. Two men were in the room, one sitting at a wooden desk, the other in front of the desk on a chair, leaning back against the wall. Well-muscled, the young dudes wore AMT Combat .45 autoloaders in side holsters.

Frimm isn't stingy with weapons either. He furnishes his goons with some of the best, thought the Death Merchant.

A crooked grin creasing his mouth, Camellion shoved the Ruger into a holster, pulled the Webber stinger, and walked around to the front of the building. He strode onto the tiny platform of a porch, opened the screen door and stepped into the room.

"Praise the Lord, Brothers. But to hell with Frimm!"

The man at the desk, reading the Bible, jerked up his head with surprise. The man leaning against the wall, reading a copy of the *Cosmic Truth* magazine, looked up, did a double-take, and almost fell over with shock when he saw the bulging red eyes and gray, red-streaked UFO alien mask. By the time he shifted his mind to high gear and figured out he was looking only at a mask, he was starting to slump from the effects of the cyrexotin in the dart that had struck him in the left side of the chest.

The man at the desk had half-risen and was reaching for his holstered .45 when the Webber hissed again and a dart popped him in the chest. The Protector fell forward, his own face a mask—one of absolute astonishment, as if he had just discovered that one doesn't get 40,000 miles on a brand new set of tires.

9

That's when the Death Merchant's luck changed from so-so to all bad. As the man fell over the desk, his left hand came down on the alarm button. Faster than Camellion could have said *Homoousianism* backwards, the siren on the roof started shrieking like a demented banshee.

All for nothing! The curtain had dropped before the first act even began. A block of ice in a blast furnace would have had a better chance of surviving than Camellion now had of getting inside the office. All he could do was to get out of the camp as quickly as possible. Scram outside the fence, run west, get to the souped-up Mercury and drive to Weatherford, 17 miles away.

Camellion raced out of the building, shoving the Webber into its holster and pulling the silenced Ruger as he ran. Since he had no intention of going 200 feet to the north, to the opening he had cut in the fence, he darted between the office and the visitors' reception center, pulled a special-purpose demolition grenade from the all-purpose bag he wore over one shoulder, tossed it at the fence and dropped to the ground.

There wasn't any explosion! *A damned dud! Of all the luck!*

Wishing he had brought more than one grenade, Camellion jumped up and pulled another weapon, an Auto Mag, from a shoulder holster over his hooded sweater. There was no silencer at the end of the barrel.

By now lights were being switched on all over the camp while the siren continued to scream its piercing shriek of warning.

Camellion sprinted from between the office and the reception center and started running north, somewhat comforted by the realization that he could probably get halfway to the slit in the fence before anyone spotted him.

Wrong! He was crossing the short space between the two barracks closest to the south when an Armalite carbine cracked to the west and a bullet tugged at the shoulder bag strap across his back.

Camellion spun and, jumping to the corner of the barrack ahead, saw that the shot had come from across the parade ground, fired by a Frimmie standing at the end of a barrack. Two other Frimmies, a man and a woman, were running south across the parade ground toward the first Frimmie with the Armalite carbine. The woman carried a 30-30 Savage, the man a Ruger carbine.

The Death Merchant had only one course of action. Already the Frimmie with the Armalite carbine was raising the rifle for another shot and yelling, "I see him. He's between the barracks."

Not wanting to alert the rest of the camp to his position, Camellion didn't use the Auto Mag. Instead, he took out the man with the Armalite with a .22 Ruger shot, the small missile hitting him in the pit of the stomach. Twice more, .22 projectiles hissed through the noise suppressor of the Ruger auto-pistol. The man with the Ruger carbine went down with a slug in his chest. The woman followed, a bullet, having gone through her right breast, lodged against a rib. "Oneness save me! Onlyness help me!" she muttered, then fell into unconsciousness.

The Death Merchant turned and ran past the end of the barrack, which was now fully lighted. His escape would have been simplified if he had made the cut in the northeast corner of the fence. The way things were, however, he had to go diagonally across the parade ground, or all the way in back of the gym. Across the parade ground would have been much shorter, but if he crossed it, he would have been completely exposed to gunfire. Camellion elected to take the much longer route.

He had raced past the end of the last barrack and was headed for the east side of the Temple when he was again spotted, the knowledge coming in the form of a loud shout from someone looking out a window in a barrack—"There he is! By the side of the Temple!"

Genuinely concerned, Camellion tore past the Temple, turned the northeast corner, and darted between the building and the south side of the Cleansing Center. He was almost to the west ends of the two buildings when three Protectors came charging around the side of the Rite of Cleansing building. Four more holier-than-thou goons, who had raced across the parade ground and turned the corner of the Temple, came at the Death Merchant from behind. All four were armed, but they didn't dare fire because of the three Protectors in front of Camellion.

The three men in front also hesitated, afraid that if they fired they might hit one of the Protectors to the rear of the Death Merchant, who didn't give them a chance to switch to other tactics. He slammed right into the three astonished Protectors, who tried in desperation to swing their own weapons in line with Camellion.

At a distance of less than five feet, Camellion used the Auto Mag on the man with the .38. The AMP went off like a mini-

11

cannon, the soft-nosed bullet striking the man in the lower chest with the impact of a cannonball, killing him before he had even the time to realize he had been hit.

Wanting to save ammo, Camellion quickly ducked a swinging rifle barrel and used a right-legged spin kick on the Protector who had swung the weapon. Simultaneously, he slammed the rounded side of the Ruger's silencer against the right temple of the third man, who was attempting to shove the muzzle of a rifle into Camellion's stomach. Camellion felt the temporal bones of the man's head cave in and his right heel flatten the other Protector's solar plexus. Unconscious and dying from shock, both men had not even fallen to the ground as Camellion darted to his right, spun around, and met the attack of the four Protectors who had come in behind him.

Camellion dropped and fired both the Ruger and the AMP a micromoment before two of the Protectors triggered their weapons, one man yelling, "*Back to Hell!* Back to the Pit, agent of the Evil One!"

The man could hardly believe what his own eyes told him: that both slugs of Brother Withers and Brother Knapp had burned over the agent of Satan in the hideous mask. How could that possibly be? Were they not the Righteous? Was not goodness on their side!

Worse, the agent of the Evil One had not missed. Brother Knapp was melting to the ground, an enormous bloody hole in his chest. And so was Brother Withers, dying from a .22 projectile that had zipped through his mouth and bored out the back of his neck.

Oneness! Onlyness! Save me! Brother Bridges had time only to suffer from repulsive images and twisted fears and to realize that he was doomed by the agent of the Damned, who was swinging the long barrel of the big shiny pistol toward him. He made one last despairing effort to aim at the Evil in the mask. He was far, far too slow. He heard only half the roar of the Auto Mag and felt only a flash of surpreme torture in his chest; then he was dead and falling into the endless black void of oblivion.

When surrounded, run like hell—Camellion: chapter 2, Verse 4. The Death Merchant got to his feet, shoved the Ruger into a holster, scooped up one of the Armalite AR-180 Sporters, and ran to the northwest corner of the Temple. He turned and looked behind him. No one, except the seven bodies on the ground. He shoved the Auto Mag into its special holster, checked the AR-180 to make sure the safety was off, and looked around the corner.

The north side was clear. Toward the south, however, eight people were running toward him. Fully clothed and wearing bushjackets, three were Protectors. Four were women in bathrobes. The eighth Frimmie, barefooted and bare-chested, wore only pants. But all eight carried either rifles or auto-pistols.

A young woman in a green bathrobe saw him as he leaned out from the corner of the Temple and started firing, his missile snuffing out her life as she shouted a warning and tried to lift her rifle.

Two women and the bare-chested dummy jerked to the right of the three Protectors who, being trained, dropped to the ground. One Protector got off a good shot, the bullet missing Camellion's head by only an inch. A moment later the man was dead, a hole in his forehead, his brain turned to gray-white mush from the Spitzer-shaped projectile with which Camellion had killed him.

One of the women with the bare-chested man screamed when the Death Merchant put a bullet through her stomach. She was falling to the ground at the same time Camellion killed the second Protector, then shot the third one through the face when the man reared up to target him in the rifle's sights.

The barefooted, bare-chested man, now running east across the parade ground with one of the women, was the next to go. Camellion's .223 projectile bored into his left hip, twisted his colon like a soggy pretzel, and knocked him to the ground. Camellion could have easily scratched out the woman if it hadn't been for the eighth Frimmie, who had just gotten off a shot with a rifle. But in spite of her nervousness, the bullet came so close to the Death Merchant that it cut across the right epaulet of his bushjacket. Camellion fired, his bullet stabbing the woman high in the chest and killing her instantly. Without a sound, she fell flat on her face, next to one of the dead Protectors. By now, the last of the group, the fourth woman, was gone. Just the same, Camellion knew he was far from safe. From where he stood, the distance to the cut in the fence was a hundred feet. The odds were against his reaching the opening, as long as the camp was lighted. *Ah-ha! The generator house was only fifty feet away.*

He threw down the Armalite rifle, pulled out the Auto Mag, took out the magazine, shoved in a full one and jerked back the slide, putting a cartridge into the firing chamber. He pulled the Ruger auto-pistol and, somehow warned by instinct, spun around, dropped and fired the Ruger blindly as he went down. Three cracks! Two of the .22 slugs missed. The third one struck a man in the pit of the stomach, doubling him over. The second man attempted to throw himself to the side of the Cleansing Center. It was a mistake. He should have fired his weapon while he had the chance. But Camellion cut loose with the AMP, hit the foolish Frimmie under the chin, bored through his mouth and blew off the top of his head.

Camellion got up, turned around and sprayed six shots into the front of the small generator house, hoping that one of the powerful missiles would find a vital spot and "kill" the generator. The fifth one did. The generator made a loud whining sound, sputtered and died. The camp lights flickered. A moment later the camp was plunged into total darkness.

Do it! Camellion darted to the northwest corner of the fence and soon was squeezing through the opening. Expecting slugs to start buzzing around him like angry hornets, he kept low and started running across the sandy ground. He had failed, but he was alive and unharmed.

All I've succeeding in doing, Camellion thought as he hurried away, *is warning Reverend Frimm!*

Chapter Two

An imposing figure of a man was Hannibal Nigel Frimm. Six feet three inches tall and as solid as an iron anvil, Frimm was the kind of man whose mere presence dominated a room and whose face could lend itself to any and every mood or occasion. The intelligent gray eyes could twinkle warmly or burn with hell-and-damnation fury, his mouth could twist into a big smile or become a slit of rage and determination—as Frimm's mouth was now, while he read the evening edition of the *Colorado Springs Democrat*. A naturally fast reader, he scanned rapidly the long article about the tragedy that had befallen the Haven of Truth outside Fort Worth, early in the morning of that very day.

The camp had been attacked by a mysterious man in a hideous mask. More than half a dozen of the Righteous had been brutally murdered. The murderer had escaped, and no one knew who he was or why he had attacked the camp. The Sheriff's Police were "continuing to investigate the murders."

Frimm was enraged by the second half of the article, which gave a brief history of the Church of the Cosmic Truth, stating that it was the largest "cult" in the United States and "has often been sued by irate parents who maintain that the cult uses brainwashing techniques on their children."

Brother Elmer Peek and Brother Matthew Hinkley, two of the six Ministers of Light at New Earth Community, saw a heavy vein on the side of Frimm's neck begin to throb and his mouth become more compressed as his eyes neared the bottom of the page. Having read the article before coming down to the private meditation room of His Oneness and His Onlyness, they knew he was reading the paragraphs that referred to him as a "Prophet of Doom whose main theme is that the end of the world is only twenty years away—too far in the future for anyone to call him either a liar or a crackpot."

Frimm tossed the paper to the table and leaned back in the plain wooden chair, a cloud of black fury drifting across his face. His skin was surprisingly clear and smooth for a man of 58 summers. And for a man who was self-educated—he had quit school in the sixth grade—he used excellent English, devoid of slang and colloquialisms.

"The stinking press!" he thundered. "Words that are formed from the ink of evil and inspired by the Fallen Angel!" He calmed down and lowered his voice. "We can be certain that the attacker was not a deprogrammer. None of them operate in such a savage and expert manner."

"Could revenge have been the motive?" offered Hinkley.

A man of medium height, with small features and nervous hands perpetually in motion, Hinkley had been a boxer until 11 years before, when he happened to wander into a large tent on the outskirts of Joplin, Missouri, where Frimm was scaring the devil out of listeners with a hellfire sermon.

"I don't think revenge was the motive," Frimm said, his eyes very thoughtful. "If all he had wanted to do was kill, he could have remained outside the fence and have thrown hand grenades into the barracks. The police did find the grenade that failed to explode. He must have had others with him."

Brother Hinkley nodded slowly. Brother Elmer Peek stirred uncomfortably on his chair.

"He came into the Haven to search the office," continued Frimm. "I am certain of it. We know he was in the vicinity of the office because he rendered the two Protectors inside the command center unconscious with darts. He wanted to be sure that they couldn't interfere with him while he searched the office for whatever he came to find."

The theory did not appeal to Hinkley—Frimm could tell from the way Hinkley clenched his fist on the table. There was not the least doubt in Frimm's mind, for he had discovered years ago that he had an amazing talent for reading body language and that this talent enabled him to be a good judge of people, to predict how they would react, what they would think and do and feel. It was this ability that had helped him build the Church of the Cosmic Reality.

It was Brother Peek who orally but politely dissented. "I can't agree, Reverend. There is little money in any of the Havens' safes."

"Both of you are forgetting the two deprogrammers, Everett Padden and Dwight Montroy. Thanks to Brother Kenner, the Protectors were able to kidnap those two agents of Hell at

16

their motel. Therein lies the answer to the attack on the Haven. The Lord has inspired me with the truth."

Brother Peek moistened his dry lips, remembering the report that, as the church's Director of Security, he had read. Padden and Montroy had been taken to the Haven and physically punished in a Chamber of Chastisement. But men had died from the punishment, at least the Protectors had thought they had. The Protectors were driving the two corpses toward Fort Worth, to dispose of them in a landfill, when Padden had revived, crawled from the back of the truck and escaped. The Protectors had never found him. The police had—dead.

"But Reverend, if revenge wasn't the reason. . . ." Hinkley let his voice trail off and looked searchingly at Frimm.

"Not revenge, not as such." Frimm's low tone was sly. "Whoever came to the Haven was seeking legal evidence that might incriminate the church in the disappearance of the two deprogrammers. We can conclude that the man who attacked was either a good friend of Padden or Montroy or else was hired by their families. I am sure of it."

"Fortunately it's over," Peek said heavily. "What is done can't be undone. We'll easily survive the bad publicity. We always have." His square face brightened. "No doubt we'll even gain new members by the—shall I say?—'bad press reviews' "

"We will endure because it is the will of the Lord," Frimm said curtly. "For all eternity we will exist. But don't think that we've seen the last of the man who attacked the Haven in Texas. Such a man sits beside the throne of Lucifer and cannot accept defeat. He will attack again, perhaps even here, the New Earth Community!"

Somewhat stunned by Frimm's macabre prophecy, Brothers Peek and Hinkley hesitated, the impact of Frimm's foretelling of danger making them feel vaguely uneasy.

Peek, suddenly having the urge to turn in his chair and look behind him, suddenly felt ridiculous, like a small child afraid of the dark. He wondered why he felt a premonition of doom, especially in this room, Frimm's own personal meditation room, which was thirty feet below the ground and could be reached only by a special elevator to the rear of the Temple. There were a score of other rooms on the underground level, soundproof rooms where recalcitrant members of the church were taken for spiritual purging, often being confined for months in the cells, depending on the power and resistance of the Evil Spirit possessing the Righteous. No one above

17

ground, or in the private meditation room of His Oneness, could hear the cries and screams of those being purged.

Hinkley broke the short silence. "Why, he wouldn't dare come here, to the New Earth Community. We're a city of three thousand people! We have three hundred Protectors here, every one an expert in Cos-do, the church's version of karate. Even if this Antichrist should be foolish enough to set foot on holy ground, I ask you, what could he do? He is only one man."

Hinkley stared at Frimm and once again experienced an inner tingling, as odd sensation as if someone alien had entered his mind. He sensed that His Oneness was appraising him and, perhaps, reading his every thought. With effort, he broke free of those hypnotic gray eyes and looked down at the polished surface of the table, his own reflection a stranger to him.

"It is not the unwatered tree that gives ripe fruit," Frimm, who had folded his arms, said quietly. "The man who so boldly attacked the Haven in Texas is an expert in firearms. He also has tremendous nerve and daring and is very resourceful. We have proof of that. We can conclude he is not an ordinary man and that we can expect another visit from him." Frimm's eyes fastened on Brother Peek, who looked definitely disconcerted, his expression crumpled, his eyes clouded with concern.

"Brother Peek, I realize you know what you must do," Frimm said.

A former corporation lawyer, Peek thought he did but he wasn't sure. For the past year, Reverend Frimm had changed, becoming more secretive and suspicious. At times he spoke in parables, so that often it was difficult to understand the true meaning of what he said.

Peek cleared his throat. "I'll have Steinhoff make an immediate check," he said. "His agency is very effective, and he has informants all over the country, including Texas. It shouldn't take him and his people more than a week or two to discover who Padden and Montroy's closest friends are. By a process of elimination, we might be able to deduce the identity of the lone assailant."

Reverend Frimm's head of white hair jerked in a nod. "Fine. And inform Brother Sessons to put his men in full alert, day and night. But he and the other Protectors are not to mention a word to the other residents of New Earth."

"I'll attend to it as soon as we go upstairs," Peek answered.

Matthew Hinkley glanced briefly at Peek, then looked cautiously at Reverend Frimm. "Let's say this man does attack. What assurance do we have that he'll strike here. We have Havens and Abodes in every state. He could attack one of them . . ."

Frimm smiled. "True enough. But Padden and Montroy didn't disappear in Illinois or Florida or Maine. Our headquarters and the national center of the church are here at New Earth. For those reasons, he will strike in the West." His cold eyes swung to an apprehensive Peek. "I also want you to notify the Ministers of all Protectors at all the Havens and Abodes within a radius of five hundred miles and warn them to be on full alert. To be fully prepared is half of the victory."

Dark shadows of doubt and anxiety drifted across Brother Hinkley's mind. Basically a moral man, his conscience had nagged him for several years. Lately, the sense of guilt and wrongdoing had grown worse, like a raw, open wound. A tiny voice continued to whisper: murder is murder.

At first, years ago, during the early 1970s, the deprogrammers who had attempted to kidnap youthful members of the church were only beaten. Then, as more and more deprogrammers began to succeed in their attempts, Hannibal Frimm had become more determined. The crisis occurred when a young woman, who had been kidnapped and deprogrammed, wrote a long article for a national magazine, "exposing" Reverend Frimm and the church, proving to the public at large that the cult was using techniques of brainwashing. Fortunately for the church, the Chamber of Chastisement was not yet in use, or she would also have written about it.

God whispered to Reverend Frimm, and Frimm revealed his words: "Had not the Lord God in His anger destroyed Sodom and Gomorrah with fire and brimstone? To free the Hebrews, had not the Lord God killed the first born of the Egyptians? And had not Jacob's sons, selected by God as the fighting progenitors of His chosen race, slain the Schechemites and even stolen their wives?" All these things were true, as revealed in the Holy Bible.

"God can do as He pleases because He is the 'I Am Who I Am,' " Frimm had thundered at the Ministers of Light and a selected group of the Protectors. "He is the Alpha and the Omega, the beginning and the end. He is His own law. He killed His enemies for the good of humanity, for the good of the Righteous. We must follow His example. These men of evil, who call themselves deprogrammers, are filled with the

19

foul spirit of Satan. These men must be killed for the Children of Righteousness. By killing them we strike at the Evil One."

At the time, no one had disagreed with His Oneness and His Onlyness. No one had been quite that foolish. Or brave. But from that moment on, Hinkley's faith had wavered, and he had begun to doubt not only Hannibal Frimm but God. How could one be sure that it was God who spoke to Frimm? For that matter, even if God did speak to Frimm, how could a just God kill innocent people or be a party to murder?

Wisely, Hinkley had not voiced his own growing doubts to anyone, not even to his own wife, who was a fanatical believer in Hannbial Frimm. Should his doubts become known and should he be denounced, where could he go, what could he do? Sixteen years earlier, he and Mavis had signed over their house and bank account to the church. All new members signed over their assets to the Church of the Cosmic Reality.

There was further agony of soul. During those rare moments when Hinkley could be brutally honest with himself, he realized that, should he be denounced, Frimm would never permit him to leave the organization. As the Minister of Finance, he knew too much. He could tell the press too much. Hinkley knew that Frimm would have him killed—an "accident," a fine funeral, and that would be the end of him.

Now and then Hinkley wondered how he and Mavis could have been so stupid as to believe the religious philosophy of Hannibal Frimm. How could they? Because the man was a spellbinder! That's why. He was brilliant and so charismatic that no one could resist him.

Then, there was the purging of souls, which Frimm had begun many years ago. Derived from Frimm's own voracious reading—notably Freud, Emerson, and Hitler—this technique involved hard manual labor, carefully applied mutual support and, at the hub of the religious wheel, the purging that later came to be known as the Rite of Cleansing. This purging consisted of prolonged group encounter sessions, during which personalities were broken down and defenses stripped bare. During the Cleansing, it was not only acceptable to criticize the mistakes and stupidities of others or to reveal one's negative reactions to someone else's behavior, it was the entire purpose. The Cleansing was the battlefield in which strong emotions were displayed, individuals learned to react to their behavior, and demands were made to correct errors in thinking that was non-spiritual.

Very cleverly, Frimm had patterned the Cleansing on his

knowledge of human behavior, knowing that the Cleansing had an aggressive tone, since it proceeded on the basis of indictments in which one participant would point out the defects, transgressions, or errors of another, a technique first utilized by the Chinese Communists. The norms of the Cleansing called for the group to support the indictment, and unless the indicted individual could quickly fend off the attack, he would find himself opposed by the entire group, with various members adding their observations in support of the original charge. And it worked! The Righteous believed.

Yet this was only a part of the Cleansing . . .

Yes, because he was a spellbinder! thought Hinkley. The force of Frimm's personality was overwhelming, hypnotic. Hinkley remembered what one defector had written about His Oneness: "You can't imagine how intoxicating he is! You could walk into those sessions ready to challenge him and then walk out without saying a word. You knew he had control over your life. You knew he could do with you what he wanted to do."

But, quietly and gradually, Frimm began to change. The number of backsliders, those men and women who left the church, was a carefully guarded secret that was never divulged to the world. Hinkley knew what had happened. Frimm began to brood about the rate of "recidivism to evil." The more he dwelt on the problem, the more convinced he became that goodness and morality could only be found within the Church of the Cosmic Reality.

It was then that God began to speak directly to Frimm. *It was then that God revealed to Frimm the exact time and date of the end of the world!*

The Righteous believed.

Frimm began to take on the status of a secular god. The Church of the Cosmic Reality grew and prospered, and with it the adulation of Hannibal Nigel Frimm. Frimm aphorisms were plastered on the walls like so much Mao-thought. A microphone was hung above his place at the dinner table to catch his every word, for who could tell when God might speak directly through His Oneness and His Onlyness?

Lest someone should miss a particle of "Frimm Wisdom," a radio system was installed in the New Earth Community and later in every Haven and Abode, and Frimm's musings and sayings were piped 24 hours a day over the wire. Listening was compulsory, even in the privacy of the bedroom.

Hannibal Nigel Frimm became a dictator, controlling his

Frimmies by the same diabolical efficiency with which Adolf Hitler had controlled Nazi Germany. Only the Frimmies adored Frimm far more than the Nazis had ever worshiped Hitler.

At first, Frimm's obsessions and eccentricities were harmless enough. He gave up smoking, so everyone else stopped smoking. He kept his head shaved for seven months, so for seven months thousands of Frimmies went around with bald heads. Frimm next decided that milk was the work of Satan. Milk then became as rare as hens' teeth. Frimm took to whittling, which led to 30 minutes a night of Hobby Lobby, with everyone whittling.

But not everyone remained a brainwashed idiot. With each new bit of caprice and pronouncement by His Oneness, more and more members abandoned the church, their departures only increasing Frimm's special brand of religious insanity.

The crisis came in March of 1977 when Mr. and Mrs. Charles LeMay, who had been members of the church for nine years and residents of New Earth Community for seven, decided that they had had enough. Wanting to sever their ties with the cult as gracefully as possible, the LeMays went to Frimm's office to tell him goodbye.

They didn't expect what they got. In a wild rage, Frimm cursed them and accused them of being tools of the devil. They were possessed by Satan, controlled by the Supreme Evil and the origin of all sin. He called in half a dozen Protectors and had Mr. and Mrs. LeMay beaten senseless.

"Take away everything they have!" Frimm screamed after the couple had revived. "Don't let them leave with one suitcase. Throw them out the gates with only the clothes on their backs!"

Brother Wilbur Sessons, the head of the Protectors at New Earth, had prudently pointed out to Frimm that since the LeMays looked as though they had been run over twice with a steamroller, it might be wiser to keep the couple at New Earth until they recovered.

"Absolutely not!" Frimm had screamed. "I don't want such moral trash polluting the Righteous. Throw them out right now!"

"Your Oneness, they can barely walk," Sessons had said in just the right tone of voice. "People will wonder what happened to them."

"I said, *throw them out!* The Almighty will protect us!"

The Almighty didn't!

The LeMays were shoved roughly through the gates of the community, to the jeers and curses of the Frimmies. Their clothes caked with dirt and blood, the couple was stumbling down the highway when a Colorado state patrolman spotted them.

Rushed to a hospital in Colorado Springs, the LeMays told the police what had happened.

Every major newspaper in the United States carried the story of how Reverend Frimm, Brother Sessons and four other Protectors were arrested and charged with aggravated assault. Sunday supplement magazines carried articles on the history of the cult and the eccentricities of Frimm and his "Cult of Crazies."

His Oneness and His Holyness paid a thousand-dollar fine and was given a suspended sentence. Brother Sessons and the four Protectors got six months in the county jail.

Mr. and Mrs. LeMay sued the church and Frimm for $5,000,000, but settled out of court for $473,000, which the church foundation paid. . . .

Lost in his thoughts, Hinkley faced the fact that Frimm's arrest, three years ago, had been the turning point. Since then, the decline had been slow but steady. More and more Frimmies had backslid. During the spring recruiting in 1979, some college students had even sneered and laughed at teams of recruiters.

"Brother Hinkley, your mind seems to be on the other side of the world."

Hinkley was suddenly aware that Reverend Frimm was speaking and regarding him with suspicious eyes.

"Your Oneness, I was considering what you said about the attacker looking for legal evidence." Hinkley was surprised at the rapidity of his excuse and the calmness in his voice. "Could he have been looking for financial evidence, trying to steal records?"

"Our finances are in order, are they not?" Frimm said severely.

"To the penny. Very recently I received a letter from the home office of the accounting firm, reassuring me that everything balanced. There isn't any problem there."

Elmer Peek spread his hands on the table. "Reverend, what about those federal agents from the Bureau of Alcohol, Tobacco and Firearms. They still want to know why we need fifteen submachine guns here at New Earth. I told them we wanted the guns for protection, but they were very skeptical."

"I would assume you consulted with our attorneys in Denver?" asked Frimm, gathering his robe around him—still another one of his eccentricities. Until a year before, he had worn his robe only during religious services in the Temple. From then on, he began wearing it constantly, even at the dinner table. Furthermore, he had ordered the Ministers of Light at New Earth to wear theirs, except when they left the confines of the community.

"Yes, I did," Peek replied. "They said that buying the machine guns was one of those 'spotty' things as far as the Federal Government was concerned. Legally, the ATF can't prevent us from buying the weapons. Machine guns are legal as long as the yearly ownership tax is paid. But Finebaum suggested that we give up the purchase. He said the Treasury Department could resort to all kinds of legal tactics to slow the purchase." Peek hesitated, as if expecting a reprimand. "Finebaum said that it would be too time-consuming to legally battle the ATF."

Both Peek and Hinkley were mildly astonished at Frimm's reply.

"Louis Finebaum is Jewish, and the Jews are the chosen people of God. It is written in the Old Testament. But the Lord does not speak to Finebaum as He speaks to me. The Lord has told me to buy the machine guns. Buy them."

Peek only nodded. Reverend Frimm quickly added, "Now leave me, both of you. I want to talk to God . . ."

Chapter Three

Twenty-two days after the Death Merchant had attacked the Haven of Truth in northern Texas, he was at the Warm Rest Trailer Park off Highway 122, a mile west of Broadmoor. Broadmoor was less than five miles southwest of Colorado Springs, Colorado. He couldn't have cared less about sightseeing. Colorado Springs, near the foot of the massive 14,110-foot-high Pikes Peak, was just another pleasure resort. Gaping and gawking had never been one of Camellion's favorite sports. If you've seen one mountain, you've seen them all, especially after you've spent time in the high Himalayas.

The 14 mineral springs were located in nearby Manitou Springs, which was considered part of the same area. Colorado Springs was also famous for the nearby Pike National Forest and the United States Air Force Academy—as well as the national headquarters of the Church of the Cosmic Reality. The New Earth Community was seven miles due east of Colorado Springs. Actually the headquarters of the cult was closer to the little town of Ellicott than to Colorado Springs.

The Death Merchant had been at the trailer park for several days, passing the time by reading and doing special Yoga breathing exercises in his small Vulcan trailer. There was plenty of time. Linders wouldn't telephone from Mesa, Arizona, until the night of the third day. In an emergency, however, Camellion could phone another number in Mesa. Linders's sister would take the message.

During the middle of the hot afternoon of the third day, Camellion decided it was time to size up the New Earth Community. Visitors were always welcome at the headquarters of the Church of the Cosmic Reality. There were even regularly conducted tours of the settlement, one in the morning and one in the afternoon. It didn't make any difference to Camellion. He had no intention of entering the small community, which could accurately be described as a small town of 1,750 people—deluded fools, every one of them. But he could check out the highways, look over the area surrounding New Earth Community, and perhaps spark an idea as to how he could get to Reverend Frimm, who was better guarded than the President of the United States. In addition, since the LeMay incident, county and state police were keeping a close watch on the community. Protectors patrolled by jeep and on foot, day and night, not only on the various "streets" of New Earth, but along the inside of the fence. On the surface, gaining access to Hannibal Frimm seemed impossible.

Even if I get to him and manage to get him out of camp, Camellion thought, what then? I can't just blow his head off. That wouldn't be cricket!

Camellion checked a road map. He could go east on Highway 122, turn off onto 83, and at the interchange hit 94, the highway that would take him past the New Earth Community.

He put away the map and set the tear-gas traps inside the trailer. He wasn't at all concerned that someone might find the weapons section in the floor. Experts wouldn't be able to find the compartment, not even with metal detectors, since the entire bottom of the trailer was metal. Anyhow, the Auto Mag and the Ruger he had used in Texas were not inside the compartment. First he had destroyed the riflings of the barrels of the auto-pistols. He had then taken the weapons apart and had dropped them into quicksand in the Big Thicket. The termination of the Frimmies in Texas could never be pinned on him. Besides, he had been somewhere else during the attack. . . .

The Death Merchant left the trailer, locked the door, got into the Pontiac Grand Prix and drove out of the trailer park, the bright sunlight flashing on his dark glasses as he made the turn onto the highway.

He analyzed the overall situation as he drove. Part of the problem was that, with Russell Linders, he was working with an unknown quality, even if trusted people in the CIA had recommended him, including George F. McAulay. On vacation, Linders had met with Camellion a week before the Death Merchant had made the strike against the Frimmie camp in north Texas. The two had arrived at an agreement and had mapped out a first level strategy, Linders agreeing to help, he said, because "I hate those damned cults," and became Camellion had offered him $25,000 cash for two months' work.

By the time Camellion attacked the Texas settlement, Linders was in Mesa, and Roger Zettker was becoming a member

26

of the Church of the Cosmic Reality, in a Haven of Truth a few miles from Mesa.

Zettker wasn't an unknown quality. He was a 22-year-old headstrong hotdog. Against Camellion's advice, he had insisted on going through with his scheme to join the church and try to learn something of importance from the inside. He had chosen to join the Frimmies in Mesa, because he had a brother in that Arizona city. He could tell the Frimmies that he happened to be in the general area of their settlement to visit his brother. Zettker had been a very good friend of Dwight Montroy and wanted revenge.

The Death Merchant frowned. The trouble with Zettker was that he didn't know his own ignorance. He had taken a correspondence course in "How To Be A Detective" and thought he was J. Edgar Hoover II.

His own overconfidence will get him into trouble! mused the Death Merchant. *A little knowledge has killed many a good man—and quite a few bad ones.*

At least his security was safe. Neither Linders nor Zettker had known that Camellion planned to burglarize the office of the Frimmie camp in Texas. Linders didn't count; he was a pro.

But even if young Zettker did make a fool of himself and was caught, he couldn't tell what he didn't know!

So far Zettker had not done too badly. During the past two weeks, he had managed to phone Linders four times and make reports. He had been accepted as a member of the church, was undergoing intensive training in Frimmian theology and, at night, was working in the kitchen—until two o'clock in the morning. The only reason that he was able to phone was that, during the only morning hours, he was able to slip out of the large kitchen and use a phone in a dark hallway.

Linders had called the Death Merchant in Texas the day before Camellion had started the drive to Colorado Springs, reporting that for several days he had not heard from Zettker.

"No telling what kind of a mess he's gotten himself into," Linders had said in his faintly Southern drawl.

Camellion had then given him a specific date and time to phone the manager's office at the Warm Rest Trailer Park.

Another four and a half hours. . . .

Traffic became heavy in the southern part of Colorado Springs, with most of the cars bearing out-of-state license

27

plates, belonging to tourists. But Camellion was able to speed up once he turned north and was on the multilaned 83.

It was a perfect day for driving. A clear sky, a smooth freeway, and an engine in excellent working order. The only thing Camellion lacked was a firearm. He felt that he didn't need one. Too, he didn't have a permit to carry a gun in Colorado. Should the state or county police stop him for any reason and find a weapon he'd have a lot of explaining to do. Why take such a foolish chance?

Automatically, he always watched the cars behind him, not so much in the manner of an average driver, but with all the caution of a man who knows that certain people would like to see him dead. Assassination on the highway was always a possibility.

He was a mile or so north on 83 when, glancing in the rear-view mirror, he noticed a red Chevy Malibu Wagon 50 feet behind him. The vehicle seemed to be keeping pace with him. He glanced again in the mirror. Four men were in the car—young men.

A coincidence? Possibly. If not, Camellion knew he was playing against a stacked deck. The only physical protection he had was a Paralyzer, a tube of CS tear gas, legal to carry in Colorado.

He pushed down on the gas pedal and soon was hitting 65 m.p.h. The driver of the Chevy Malibu increased his speed, but didn't attempt to pass Camellion. Instead, he kept the Malibu 40 feet behind the Death Merchant.

Camellion gradually slowed to 50. So did the driver of the Malibu.

Mercy, Mercy! cried Mrs. Percy. I think I have trouble!

Camellion pushed down on the gas, and soon the Grand Prix was racing at 70 m.p.h., the tires eating up the hot concrete. Quickly, Camellion passed four other cars. And so did the Malibu, hanging onto him like a giant red leech.

Camellion no longer had any doubts. Someone had picked up his trail, either from the trailer park or sometime later. The intention of the men was obvious. If they had merely wanted to find out where he might be going, they wouldn't have remained with him after he speeded up. Knowing he had spotted them, they would have dropped back to avoid suspicion. They had not.

They had to be Frimmies, and they meant to kill him!

Camellion passed two more cars and saw that he had several miles of clear highway ahead of him. He speeded up to

80, determined to outrun the red death behind him. If he couldn't, sooner or later he'd zip past a state or county cop, who would get into the act because of his outrageous driving.

He closed in on the vehicle ahead, a blue-and-white Dodge Colt Wagon. As he was about to pass, the driver of the Dodge increased speed and swung to the left, blocking the Pontiac, preventing Camellion from passing.

That's it! Two of them working the old squeeze play!

The Death Merchant swung back to the right. So did the Dodge. Behind him, the Chevy came up fast but did not attempt to pass, remaining 25 feet to the rear.

Why were they waiting? With the Dodge preventing Camellion from passing, the Chevy Malibu should have been trying to move up, to come alongside and blast away.

Once more Camellion turned to the left and attempted to swing around the Dodge Colt. Once again the driver of the other vehicle jerked to the left and prevented him from passing. Camellion turned sharply back to the right and speeded up. But the driver of the Dodge was not to be tricked so easily. Every bit as fast as the Death Merchant, the man swung back to the right. Again Camellion was blocked.

The Death Merchant could not be certain, but he thought there were three or four men in the Dodge. All of them! Protectors from the New Earth Community! Who else?

But how could Frimm and his freaks have traced me from Texas to the trailer park? Camellion wondered.

Never hesitate. When in a bind, do the unexpected. Confuse the enemy. Camellion gauged the distance, relaxed, increased speed and aimed at the back of the Dodge. His front bumper slammed into the rear end of the Dodge Colt, shoving the car ahead six feet and causing the driver to lose some control over the wheel. For half a second, the Dodge wavered, Camellion smiling when two frightened faces turned and looked at him from the rear seat.

You want to play with Death! I'll show you how!

The driver of the Dodge speeded up slightly.

His hands firm on the steering wheel, Camellion pushed down on the gas and again rammed the rear end of the Dodge, this time much harder. Metal screamed and bumpers crumpled, metal smashing metal, the crash as loud as the report of a pistol, the impact of such momentum that the tires of the Dodge screamed on the concrete as the car rocketed forward. It was only with effort that the driver managed to control the vehicle.

29

Another bit of the unexpected. Camellion rapidly slackened off, his decreasing speed increasing the distance between him and the Dodge, but just as quickly narrowing the length between him and the Chevy Malibu, whose driver also slowed in order to remain behind Camellion.

The once-friendly highway was now Camellion's bitter enemy. Although there was flat, open country on both sides of the road, Camellion couldn't pull off to the side, to the right. The embankment was much too steep. Also, to protect motorists, a foot-high concrete retaining wall was at the right edge of the highway, at the top of the embankment.

To the left? A ten-foot-wide parkway divided the two lanes of northbound traffic from the two lanes on the south side, a retaining wall at the east and the west edges of the wide strip. Even if Camellion could have scooted over to the southbound lanes, he wouldn't have taken the chance. He would have been slammed by cars going in the opposite direction and have caused a pile up for half a mile or more.

The Chevy Malibu was still there, 75 feet behind him. The Dodge Colt had slowed and was now a hundred feet ahead. Camellion was debating whether to put on speed and once more slam into the Dodge, when he glanced up in the rearview mirror and saw the motorcycle roaring past the Chevy.

Camellion knew. Now the whole business made sense. The Protectors in the two cars were not supposed to whack him out. Their job was only to set him up, to "steady the target."

The two jokers on the Honda had the job of terminating him.

The Honda came up fast, like a big, black streak. The driver, hunched down behind the handlebar faring, stared straight ahead through the clear acrylic windscreen. Like Enos Hawkins, the second Protector also wore a full-face helmet. There was one slight difference between Hawkins and Brother Lybrand Wittenborn. Brother Wittenborn, leaning back against the Sissy bar, had a Smith and Wesson .41 Magnum revolver in his right hand. He brought up the big weapon and swung it directly at Camellion as the Honda roared past.

The Death Merchant slowed and turned slightly to the left, a micromoment before Brother Wittenborn pulled the trigger. The weapon exploded, the shot a roar even against the background thunder of the Honda. There was a plink of glass breaking, and a bullet passed an inch to the rear of Camellion's head. The big slug popped through the glass of the door on the right side and sped on its way.

Camellion immediately slowed slightly. Brother Wittenborn got off another quick shot when the rear wheel of the Honda was parallel to the left front tire of the Grand Prix. This bullet, coming in at a steep angle and slightly downward, bored through the thick laminated windshield on the left side. Chips of glass struck Camellion's face and pinged against his amber-colored sunglasses. He was lucky in that the bullet missed the underside of his right forearm; yet it did cut through the sleeve of his Madras blazer before going all the way through the back of the seat and finally burying itself in the rear seat.

As quickly as the Honda had roared in, it was gone, passing the Dodge Colt ahead of the Death Merchant, who now was convinced that he had about as much chance as a grasshopper in a hen house—*especially if the driver of the Honda is daring enough to turn around and come back,* he thought.

It was the Frimmie with the .41 Magnum that worried Camellion. The Protector was not a beginner. Any person who could handle a .41 Mag with only one hand was plenty good! Both shots had missed only because Camellion had accurately judged when Wittenborn would fire and had turned and then slowed at the precise time.

Highly concerned, Camellion searched for a solution to his dilemma. He was still trying to find the answer when he saw several cars moving transversely to his own position—a mile up ahead, to his right. The cars were moving west.

A side road! Either it passes underneath the highway or intersects it. I wonder which?

He saw the Honda roaring back from the north. The two damn-fool Frimmies were going to make another try at burning him.

Camellion realized that this time the Frimmie gunman would be more determined. This time he would be very cautious and wouldn't fire until the Honda was almost even with his car.

He weighed the odds. The greater danger lay in the .41 Magnum.

There was a way out, Camellion realized. *But if I miscalculate a fraction of a second, we'll both go up in smoke. The hell with it!*

Camellion turned to the left and headed the Grand Prix straight at the roaring Honda, a move Brother Hawkins had neither expected nor anticipated. For four seconds the front of the Pontiac Grand Prix was pointed directly at the motorcycle, and Camellion could see the wide, terrified eyes of Haw-

31

kins through the helmet the man wore. All he could see of the shooter—of Wittenborn—was the arm and hand holding the .41 Magnum.

Instinctively, Brother Hawkins turned sharply to his right to avoid what he thought must be an inevitable collision. At the same time, Camellion swung the Grand Prix back to the proper side of the road.

The Honda was going too fast for Hawkins to control it. The side of the front wheel struck the foot-high wall at the edge of the parkway. Hawkins lost all control of the machine. The Honda flipped over a second after Camellion's car had sped by. Hawkins and Wittenborn didn't go flying or diving to the concrete. The Brothers couldn't. They had fallen with the Honda, and their left legs were pinned by the high-speed machine.

At 50 m.p.h., the Honda skidded over the concrete, taking the two screaming men with it. The sheer speed of the cycle, its weight on Hawkins and Wittenborn's legs, and the terrible friction, burned away clothing and melted flesh the way wax flows under a Death Valley sun in August.

The Protector driving the Chevy Malibu twisted the steering wheel, sending the car sharply to the left to avoid the Honda and the two howling men skidding to the right at a long, slanting angle. The right front wheel of the Malibu narrowly missed hitting the heads of the two men, although it really wouldn't have made any difference to Wittenborn and Hawkins.

The Chevy weaved and rocked, the tires burning rubber. The vehicle then skidded slightly as the radial tires rolled through the wide streaks of blood and gore left in the wake of the skidding motorcycle. Somehow the driver retained control and increased his speed, intending to catch up with the Death Merchant.

Behind the Chevy, the runaway Honda hit the protective wall at the edge of the road. For several seconds it skidded along the side of the wall, then came to a stop with its two unconscious Protectors. Hawkins and Wittenborn were dying, the flesh of their left legs shredded to the bone, the exposed femoral arteries and veins pumping out blood. All at once the Honda exploded in a bright flash of red and orange flame, and just as quickly began to burn. By the time Hawkins and Wittenborn were dead, they'd be a blackened mess of burnt flesh.

* * *

32

The Death Merchant had increased his speed, as had the driver of the Dodge Colt.

At once, Camellion assumed that the intensified effort of the Dodge's driver to outrun him involved the crossroad—evidence that the two-laner intersected the four-ribboned highway. But now that the Honda was out of the chase, Camellion assumed he had a fifty-fifty chance. He was also certain that the goons in the Dodge Colt were not about to permit him to go around them.

Due to Camellion's speed, the Protectors in the Dodge had time only to park the car at an angle across the road, so that its front was pointed toward the northwest and its rear to the southeast. Just as Camellion had assumed, the driver had stopped in front of the east-west intersection road. Hurriedly, the man next to the driver jumped out, got down in front of the Dodge and pointed a shotgun in Camellion's direction.

To make matters worse, the Chevy Malibu was right on his tail, at a distance of only forty feet.

Camellion had seven seconds to make up his mind. He could stop and take his chances. Against a shotgun the odds were nil.

Or I can ram the side of the Dodge, Camellion thought, *in which case I'll succeed in killing myself. If they don't succeed in terminating me!*

He saw that there was still a third choice. By putting the Dodge Colt across the double lane, the driver had parked more to the west than to the east, wanting to make sure that Camellion could not turn left, go against the lights—should he be willing to take the chance—and escape by driving west on the intersecting road.

Camellion had one small chance. There was almost enough space between the rear of the Dodge and the protective retaining wall on the east side of the north-south highway.

The Pontiac Grand-Prix was a more powerful car than the Dodge Colt.

Fiddle-faddle! Time, Life, Death—all relative! Let's do it!

At 70 m.p.h., Camellion headed straight for the space between the back of the Dodge and the retaining wall. The three Protectors inside the Dodge and the Frimmie with the scattergun stared in fear and disbelief.

Impossible! Almighty God was on their side. Reverend Frimm had said so. The agent of Satan was supposed to stop. Why hadn't he? Yes! That had to be the answer—the Evil One in the Pit was forcing him to drive at suicidal speed.

Brothers Oscar Moore and Paul Vinten tried to leave the back seat by throwing open the right rear door, while Brother Walter Cley, the driver, attempted to escape via the right front door. The Frimmie freak with the shotgun had time only to fire both barrels and jump back from the front of the car. But he had fired much too quickly, while Camellion was still too far away. The pellets pinged against the windshield and the left side of the Grand Prix, but didn't do any damage.

The Death Merchant slammed through the open space at 74 m.p.h. The right front wheel of the Pontiac missed the side of the foot-high wall by only a scant inch. The left side of the already crumpled bumper and the grill crashed into the left rear of the Dodge Colt.

Bang! There was the ear-splitting sound of metal smashing into metal, of metal ripping metal. Most of the bumper of much of the grill of the Grand Prix crumpled into unrecognizable junk, the same terrific impact crushing the left rear fender of the Dodge and knocking the car around in a half-circle. The right rear door of the Dodge Colt slammed against Moore and pitched him against Brother Vinten. Both men yelled in alarm and fell half on the back seat, their knees hitting the floor. Brother Cley, one foot on the concrete, felt the right front door slam against his leg. He fell to his back on the front seat, the agony in his right leg intense.

With not even one hair of his head out of place, Camellion drove the Grand Prix toward the two-laned crossroad. To avoid hitting the short protective wall across from, and to the north of, the road that intersected 83, he turned the steering wheel to the left.

Camellion was aware that he could have continued to the north, confident that he could outrun the Chevy Malibu, whose driver had jammed on the brakes and screeched to a halt ten feet to the south of the Dodge Colt. He didn't go north because he didn't know how thick the traffic might be two or three miles ahead. Four or five miles north was the Interchange and the turnoff to 94. Traffic at the Interchange would be thick, especially with visitors going to and coming from New Earth Community. A crash at the Interchange could kill—how many innocent people?

The Protectors are fanatics, every bit as crazy as the members of Hitler's SS, Camellion realized. *To kill me, they might be willing to commit suicide and take any number of innocent people with them. They have to be candidates for the funny farm to have attacked me on the highway.*

34

The instant the Grand Prix was clear of the end of the protective wall at the edge of the road, Camellion turned slightly more to the left and slammed on the brakes, which caused the Pontiac to slide into the classic "bootleggers' turn," the rear end skidding to the front from the right, and the front spinning around to the south from the left.

Instantly the Death Merchant fed gas to the carburetor, straightened out the wheels and sent the Pontiac zooming forward, a section of the bumper dragging on the concrete and sending up a shower of sparks.

Brothers Moore and Vinten, half-falling out of the right rear of the Dodge, stared in horror at the oncoming car, thinking Camellion was going to ram them. Brother Cley, raising up from the front seat, also gaped in amazement.

At the very last moment, when it seemed that a crash was inevitable, Camellion expertly turned the steering wheel and drove the car to the left onto the east-west intersect road. He saw how the traffic had piled up. Dozens of vehicles were stopped to the south on 83, the driver of the first car 150 feet behind the Chevy Malibu, the frightened man not wanting to get any closer to the strange battle going on in front of him. On the east-west intersect road, one driver had stopped at the edge of the two lanes of traffic flowing south on 83. When the lights changed to green, and the north-to-south traffic would halt. But the driver to the west did not move. Behind him other cars had set up a furious honking, not realizing what was happening. To the east, the first car in a line of vehicles headed west had stopped 50 feet from the edge of the four-lane north-south highway.

The Death Merchant turned onto the intersect road, the tires of the Pontiac screaming in protest on the concrete. He jammed down on the gas pedal and headed east.

In the meanwhile, Brother Henry Koil, a .45 Colt autoloader in one hand, had jumped from the right front seat of the Chevy Malibu and Brother Albert Sulberry from the back seat on the right side. Brother Sulberry had a nine-millimeter Thomas DA auto-pistol. Standing beside the car, the two Protectors began firing at Camellion's tires.

Zinggggg-zinggggg-zinggggg! Projectiles ricocheted from the rims of the Grand Prix on the right side. Then missiles found the tires. *BANG! BANG!* Both tires blew at the same time.

Helpless, there wasn't anything Camellion could do. As he lost control of the car, he took his foot off the gas and felt the

Pontiac lurch heavily to the right. All he could do was hope to heaven, keep loose and hang on. The world started to turn upside down as the Grand Prix began to roll over. Camellion closed his eyes, pressed his chin against his chest, pulled up his legs and hung on for dear life to the steering wheel. The car rolled over on its right side. Camellion heard metal being crushed and glass breaking. His shoulder slammed against the insulated dash mat, his right hip striking the back of the front seat. The Pontiac slid for a few feet on the grass and weeds of the dry field, then stopped. Except for an ache in his left shoulder, he was unhurt. He stood up as best as he could, his feet on the broken glass of the right front door. He reached up, opened the left front door, swung it back and hoisted himself out of the Pontiac, angry as a wild bull over losing the car. He became twice as annoyed when he saw the Chevy Malibu had left the highway, turned onto the side road, and was coming straight at him, the Frimmies totally ignoring the several dozen parked vehicles on the road, whose occupants, afraid of gunfire, had gotten out and were on the other side of the vehicles.

Camellion's left hand dove to the inside of his coat pocket and he pulled out the Paralyzer. Again he resorted to the unexpected because he had to. By the time the Chevy screeched to a halt six feet behind the overturned Pontiac, Camellion had sprinted to the right side of the vehicle.

"Shoot! Kill the agent of Satan!" screamed Brother Rodney Elwyn, the driver. "Kill him! Kill him!" He couldn't fire at Camellion because the Death Merchant was racing to the right of the hood.

Brother Norman DeGasper, in the left rear seat, didn't know what to do—get out or stay inside. Brothers Sulberry and Koil did their best to kill Camellion. Sulberry's Colt roared as a slower Brother Koil raised the Thomas DA autoloader.

At the same instant as the Colt roared, Camellion ducked to the right, paralyzer in his left hand, and simultaneously, he reached out with his right hand.

The .45 Colt projectile streaked across the top of Camellion's left shoulder, the hot slug raking the material of his Madras blazer. The stream of liquid tear gas hit Brother Sulberry full in the face, the fierce burning instantly blinding him. During the same several seconds, Camellion's right hand grabbed the left wrist of Brother Koil. Viciously Camellion pushed the arm upward, just as the Thomas DA autoloader

36

cracked, the 9mm slug going upward and passing an inch over Camellion's head. Camellion slammed Koil's hand against the top of the window and forced him to drop his weapon.

The Death Merchant ducked to pick up the Thomas DA as Elwyn fired around Brother Koil and Brother DeGasper got out of the car and ran around to the back. By then the Death Merchant was beginning to worry, not only about DeGasper but Brother Elwyn, who had also gotten out of the car.

Camellion jumped back and fired at DeGasper as DeGasper pulled the trigger of his revolver. The Death Merchant's bullet struck DeGasper low in the stomach. The Protector's bullet cut through Camellion's flowing white Galahad shirt, then bored through the back of his open blazer.

Spinning around, Camellion jerked to the left, heard Brother Elwyn's gun explode, and felt a bullet burn along his rib cage, the pain as intense as if he'd been touched with a redhot poker.

Camellion fired twice. His first bullet hit Brother Elwyn high in the chest and knocked him back, just as his finger pulled the trigger of the Diamondback a second time. The second slug, going slightly awry, struck Elwyn's chin, glanced downward, went through his throat, and bored out the back of his neck.

"*Freeze!* Drop the gun!" The loud, authoritative voice came from behind and to the left of Camellion.

The Death Merchant let the Thomas DA slip from his hand and raised both arms—the cavalry had arrived!

"Hands on your head. *Turn around!*

Camellion turned and saw a Colorado state trooper in a shooting stance, his hands wrapped around a .357 Colt trooper revolver. His car was parked ten feet down the road.

From the corner of his eye, Camellion saw that two other state police cars were parked on the highway and that troops, with drawn guns, were handcuffing the Protectors who had been in the Dodge Colt.

The Death Merchant smiled. He had won.

Chapter Four

As thin as a whisper, Captain Marvin Dowdy, the commander of Colorado State Police Station Number 7, looked at the circle of faces in front of his desk. It was cut and dried in regard to William and Marion Dempsey. They were what they claimed to be: tourists from Rhode Island. So were the other two couples, the Cranes, from Chester, Illinois, and the Taylors, from some tiny spit-in-the-road town in Nebraska. Both couples were still shaken from the battle they had witnessed and were afraid that appearing in court would interfere with their vacations.

The tall, lean Texan with the strange blue eyes and the expensive clothes was something else—but what? Twenty-four years in the Colorado State Police had taught Dowdy a lot about life and people, and he was convinced that Richard Camellion was no ordinary man—no way. Camellion was too calm, too sure of himself, too composed. For a man who had just killed four persons, he acted as if killing was all in a day's work. It wasn't normal.

"All right. Let's go over it again," Dowdy said with a sigh, his eyes on Camellion, who sat on a wooden chair, his hands folded in his lap, his legs crossed, his eyes calmly regarding the police official. "Mr. Camellion, you're certain you didn't know any of the men in either car, or the two men on the motorcycle?"

"I never saw them before this afternoon," Camellion replied, "and I don't know why they tried to kill me. I can only assume they mistook me for someone else."

"And you haven't any connection with that kooky Reality church?"

"None whatsoever."

"You've never had an argument with any of those men, either the ones you killed or the ones taken into custody?"

38

"Never. I've told you what happened. I was driving along and the men in the Malibu began to keep pace with me. Fearing a robbery, I attempted to outdistance them. The next thing I knew, the men in the Dodge Colt tried to stop me. A few minutes later, two men roared by on a Honda and one of them tried to kill me. They turned around, came back and tried a second time. I managed to turn off onto the side road and the men in the Malibu shot out my tires. My car overturned. You know the rest. I only defended myself."

"That's the way it happened," J.S. Crane said quickly. A plump individual in his late forties, with small, hooded eyes, he spoke sincerely. "Mrs. Crane and I were behind the Malibu and saw the whole thing. It happened just like Mr. Camellion said. They attacked him. It's a miracle that he wasn't killed."

"And you didn't try to pass the Malibu?" observed Dowdy, toying with a pencil on his desk. "You stayed behind to watch?"

Mr. Crane looked angry. "I thought of passing, but changed my mind when I saw what was happening," he said, his tone indicating resentment. "I certainly wasn't going to involve my wife and me in some kind of dangerous highway game. Then the motorcycle came by and one of the men fired shots at Mr. Camellion. After that, I decided that the best thing I could do to protect ourselves was to stay where I was."

Captain Dowdy nodded. "I see."

"That's why we stayed parked on the side road," Bill Dempsey cut in. "We didn't dare try to cross when we saw what was going on—I mean how the group in the Dodge blocked the road and tried to prevent this man"—he turned and looked at Camellion—"from passing." He paused and mopped his brow with a white handkerchief. "Later when he crashed through, spun around and turned off onto the road we were on, I tell you, sir, we were plenty scared."

Dowdy's cool eyes swung back to Mr. and Mrs. Crane. "Earlier you mentioned that Mr. Camellion rammed the rear end of the Dodge several times."

"I did," J.W. Crane promptly answered. "Mr. Camellion rammed the Dodge several times. At the time, we thought he had lost his temper and was trying to force them to let him go around. But they wouldn't give an inch. What they did, they raced ahead and turned their car sideways on the road. I've never seen anything quite like it."

"My husband and I saw the men in the Malibu shoot at Mr. Camellion," Edwina Taylor said nervously. "Two of

39

them. After they shot out his tires, they got back into the car and the driver drove the car onto the side road. I'm positive because we were parked behind the Dempseys and saw it all. It's like he said—I mean Mr. Camellion. They tried to kill him. He only defended himself."

For a moment, Captain Dowdy studied Mrs. Taylor, who was in her early fifties, and wore too much makeup and too much Indian jewelry. She reminded Dowdy of a walking, talking advertisement for turquoise.

Dowdy's next question, directed at Camellion, didn't faze the Death Merchant. "Are you a veteran, Mr. Camellion? You don't look old enough to have been in World War Two."

"I was in the Korean War," Camellion said, knowing that the police officer was trying to establish where he had acquired his coolness under fire. "I was a cook."

If Marvin Dowdy was disappointed with Camellion's reply, his expression didn't show it. All he did was scratch behind his left ear, clear his throat and lean back in the swivel chair, slowly turning the pencil in his hands.

"Mr. Camellion, I believe you said you were a rancher, down in the Big Thicket in Texas?"

"I did," Camellion said quietly. "This is the third time I've told you." He glanced at the tape recorder on one side of Dowdy's desk. "It's all there on tape."

"How large is your spread?"

"Ranching is only a hobby with me."

Dowdy's eyebrows raised. "You must have an occupation?"

"I play the stock market, and I'm very successful at it. Right now, Consolidated Mining of Arizona is a good buy. It's copper, and copper is on the rise."

"I'm not interested in mining stock, Mr. Camellion," Dowdy said evenly. He then looked at the three couples. "The rest of you are free to go. However, you'll have to testify at the inquest. It will be two or three days from now, at the courthouse in Colorado Springs." He glanced down at a writing pad on his deck. He then looked from the Taylors to the Dempseys. "You're staying at the addresses you gave and are vacationing in this area?"

"We're at the Holiday Inn close to Austin Bluffs," Bill Dempsey said uncomfortably.

"We're at Sullivan's Lodge," Harvey Taylor said in disgust.

"But we're only passing through Colorado!" protested J.W. Crane. "We didn't plan to remain in this area."

"We're going to visit our daughter and her family in Cedar

City, Utah," Mrs. Crane said in a small voice, getting to her feet with her husband.

"I'm sorry," Dowdy said sympathetically. "I can't change the law. As witnesses, you must testify at the inquest. The only thing you can do is go to a motel in this area." He got to his feet, took a card from a holder on the desk, leaned over and handed the card to Mr. Crane. "Call me at this number and give me your address when you get settled."

"I suppose we'll have to testify at the trial of those men?" Harvey Taylor said bitterly.

Captain Dowdy walked around to the front of his desk and leaned against the front edge of it.

"Yes, you will. That's part of the law. Of course, I can't tell you when the trial will be. Based on the testimony you folks have given, we've charged the men with reckless driving and assault with a deadly weapon. At this point, I can't even say for sure that there will be a trial."

"No trial?" J.W. Crane appeared not only confused but indignant. "Why not? After all, those men tried to murder Mr. Camellion!"

"They could plead guilty," Dowdy explained patiently. "They could plea bargain for a lesser sentence. Who knows? At this point there are a lot of *if*s."

J.W. Crane almost glared at Captain Dowdy. "But if there is a trial, all six of us—seven with Mr. Camellion—will have to testify. That means that a month or so from now, after we're back home, we'll have to come clear across the United States!"

Dowdy sighed again. "The state will pay all travel expenses and the cost of your lodgings. And don't blame the Colorado State Highway Patrol. We only enforce the laws.

"Now I understand why people don't want to get involved," Edwina Taylor grumbled, turning to go with her husband and the others.

"Mr. and Mrs. Crane," called out Captain Dowdy, "you will phone as soon as you're settled?"

Mr. Crane turned and nodded. "Sometime later tonight."

"Tomorrow will be fine," Dowdy said politely.

The highway patrolman across the room opened the door for the three couples, and soon the Death Merchant was in the room with only Captain Dowdy and the other officer.

The Death Merchant realized that Dowdy suspected there was much more to the murder attempt than what Camellion had told him. *But he can't disprove my story*, he thought, *and*

41

that's the cause of his frustration. It's time I put on the pressure.

"Captain, I have been here for three hours," he said, with a deliberate tone of annoyance. "How much longer is this going to take? I've told you what happened. The Cranes and the Taylors and the Dempseys have confirmed my story. What else is there?"

Leaning against his desk, Dowdy folded his arms and looked at Camellion. "A few more questions, Mr. Camellion. Then you can go. You said you came to Colorado for a few weeks vacation and that you didn't know any members of the Church of the Cosmic Reality?"

"Correct."

"You're not one of those so-called deprogrammers, are you?"

Camellion smiled. "I couldn't care less about a bunch of brainwashed fools. As far as I'm concerned, the followers of Reverend Frimm are the results of test tube experiments that went sour."

"Why choose Colorado for a vacation?" Dowdy picked at his left nostril. "Why not some other state?"

"I wanted to look at the stars from the top of Pikes Peak," drawled Camellion. He locked eyes with Captain Dowdy. "I didn't expect to be assaulted on one of your highways by a gang of goofs who may or may not belong to the New Earth Community."

Too smart a cop to be riled by Camellion's curt answers, Dowdy only stared at the Death Merchant. He knew a hardcase when he saw one. Professional experience told him that he could have kept Camellion in his office until the Second Coming and still not get a particle of truth out of him . . . the real facts.

"I don't suppose you know any Frimmies in or around Fort Worth?" Dowdy asked, fully expecting Camellion to say that he didn't.

"Not a single one, Captain. I don't associate with kooks."

"Uh-huh." Dowdy adjusted his rimless glasses to a higher position on his nose. "Tell me, Mr. Camellion. Don't you find it rather odd that a gang of Frimmies should single you out—an innocent stranger—for an assassination? Are you curious as to why they tried to murder you?"

"A case of mistaken identity," Camellion said. "What else?"

"I guess you know that I could hold you for investigation, at least for forty-eight hours?"

"I guess you know that I could sue for defamation of character—and I would, Captain." The Death Merchant didn't smile. "I don't think your boss, the Superintendent of Public Safety, would appreciate the publicity."

It was with some effort that Dowdy managed to control his temper. He was getting ready to tell Camellion to get the hell out when the phone on his desk rang. He picked up the receiver, said "Dowdy here," and listened intently. "But you didn't find anything incriminating?" He listened some more. "Fine. All right. We can't. We've got to let them out on bail."

He replaced the telephone on its cradle and stared severely at the Death Merchant, who remained as calm as a tombstone.

"I also find it unusual for anyone to use tear gas as traps in a trailer," Dowdy said suspiciously. "And before you start quoting the law to me"—he walked behind his desk and sat down—"let me tell you that we had a search warrant and enough probable cause to obtain the warrant. The troopers left the warrant in your trailer. Any questions?"

Without any change of expression, Camellion got to his feet, yawned, and politely put the tips of his fingers over his mouth.

"My car was towed in. When will I be able to get it?"

Dowdy smiled indulgently. "The photographers should be done with their work by tomorrow afternoon. Call in first to make sure we're finished with the vehicle. You'll have to come with the men in the tow truck. We can give the release only to you. Another thing, I'd be careful if I were you. The men we arrested are going to be released on bond. A man's on his way right now with the cash. Reverend Frimm is a fast worker, but I know you wouldn't know anything about that."

"From what I've heard and read about Frimm, he's got a one-half horsepower brain running a three-ton mouth," Camellion said.

Dowdy called across the room to the state highway patrolman standing by the door, "Difford, have someone drive Mr. Camellion back to his trailer park—and Camellion, make sure you show up for the inquest."

Walking toward the door, Camellion didn't look back. "All you have to do is phone and let me know when, Captain. I'll be there."

The Death Merchant could tell that the police had done a thorough job of searching the trailer. Small items he had arranged a certain way in his drawers were out of place. The

43

police had even looked into the small butane-gas stove and utility cabinets. They hadn't, however, discovered his secret compartment filled with arms and other equipment. He would have been astonished if they had.

The search warrant was on the table. He was reading it when a loud knocking sounded on the side door of the trailer. Camellion put down the document, turned and looked through the one-way viewer in the center of the door. The man doing the knocking was Nathan Harrison, the owner/manager of the Warm Rest Trailer Park. *Chances are, he's going to ask me to move,* Camellion thought.

Camellion threw open the door and gave Harrison his best irascible scowl. Harrison, who was at least sixty but dressed like a man in his twenties, was nervous and embarrassed, his hands fumbling first with his gray Apache tie, then dropping to the enormous brass belt buckle, on which was engraved a Brittany spaniel.

"What is it?" Camellion growled. "I'm very busy."

"Mr. Camellion, as you know, the state police were here and searched your trailer. I had to permit it. They had a search warrant." The man tried to sound gruff and speak in an authoritative voice, but failed in the attempt. "Tear gas went off in your trailer, and,"—his pudgy face twisted with uncertainty and his hands fluttered like the broken wings of a bird—"and this is a respectable trailer park. It was all very upsetting to the other occupants. We heard on the news about your being attacked, and I'm sorry for what happened. But I must ask you to move. I'm sure you understand."

Camellion treated Harrison to a nod of appreciation. "Naturally I understand. I'm sure that you understand there's to be an inquest and that I'm one of the principal witnesses?

Harrison blinked suspiciously. "But . . . what does that have to do with your moving?"

"The police have ordered me to stay put," Camellion lied. "I'm afraid, Mr. Harrison, that you'll have to put up with me for the next three or four days, until after the inquest. After that, I'll be moving on."

Harrison's face almost fell to his ankles. The man simply didn't know what to say. "Well," he began.

The Death Merchant wanted to ask him if he had received any phone calls for him. He didn't because he assumed that the police had told the man to keep track of his movements and to report any calls. To remind Harrison of Linders's telephone call—if Linders had called!—would only cause the man to attach importance to the incident.

"Was there anything else you wanted to ask, or tell me, Mr. Harrison?"

The man's hands went again to the knot of his Apache tie. "Come to think of it, there was a telephone call for you at the office. With all this exictement, I almost forgot it. A man asked to speak to you. When I said you weren't here, he hung up."

The Death Merchant nodded lazily, acting disinterested.

"Thank you, Mr. Harrison. Rest assured, as soon as the inquest is over, I'll be moving."

Without giving the man time to even say good night, Camellion closed the door, locked it, went over to the kitchen section, filled a small copper kettle with water and put it on the stove to boil.

A short time later—drinking tea and eating sardines and banana jello—he analyzed all the components within his computer-like mind. For now, he had been rendered totally impotent. But Reverend Frimm and his Protectors were equally powerless. There had to be at least two Colorado Investigation Bureau agents watching the trailer and a dozen more keeping both eyes on the New Earth Community.

Frimm had tried and failed. The next round would be Camellion's.

He tossed an empty sardine tin into the garbage disposal. There were several ways that Frimm and his freaks could have learned of his identity. A smooth-working detective agency was one answer, and the Church of the Cosmic Reality was known to employ the Sentinel Detective Agency, an outfit based in Los Angeles and bossed by a creep named Ralph Steinhoff, one of the best private eyes in the business—as crooked as a pretzel but very good at his job.

There was another answer: the Frimmies in Mesa, Arizona, could have discovered that Roger Zettker was a spy and forced the young man to reveal all he knew. Camellion gave the Frimmies a lot of credit for efficiency. Either way, they had reacted very quickly in tracing him from Texas to Colorado Springs.

Still another danger! Roger Zettker knew about Russell Linders, although Zettker didn't know that Linders was a "company" man. But Camellion could not ignore the obvious: if Zettker had been caught and tortured into telling everything he knew, then Frimm and his group of lunatics knew about

Linders, and he was also in danger of becoming the target of an assassination attempt.

Be that as it may, the Death Merchant was not concerned for Linders's well-being. Linders was a member of Q and knew every dirty trick in the book. Anyhow, he would have heard on the news broadcasts what had happened on Interstate 83. His own logical conclusions would put him on constant alert.

Camellion finished the jello. Calling Linders at his sister's home in Mesa would have to wait until the next day. To phone now from Harrison's office would only arouse the already suspicious Captain Dodwy and complicate the matter and, if Dowdy had placed a tap on Harrison's line, involved Linders's sister and her husband.

Having forseen just such an emergency, the Death Merchant and Linders had worked out a very simple oral code, and since Mrs. Raine, Linders's sister, and her husband knew that Linders worked for "some government agency" and suspected it was the CIA, neither one would be surprised at any coded message. They would assume it was government business and faithfully transmit the message to Linders.

The Death Merchant thought of the next day. No problem. It would be a simple exercise to call a cab, lose Dowdy's men in downtown Colorado Springs, go to a public phone booth, and contact Linders's sister in Mesa, Arizona.

Dowdy's a good cop. He already suspects me of the Frimmie wipe-out in Texas. At this very moment, Dowdy was no doubt on a private line conferring with either the cops in Fort Worth or the Sheriff's Police of Tarrant County.

Another annoying complication. Investigators from Fort Worth would tag Camellion for questioning even before the inquest.

The Death Merchant was not unduly worried. He had a steel-encased alibi and could prove that when the Haven of Truth outside Fort Worth was attacked, he was far away, playing cards with five good friends, one of whom was the chief of police of a small town in the Big Thicket area. All five would swear on a stack of Bibles as high as the Empire State building that he had been with them that night.

Camellion smiled to himself as he cleared the table. Dowdy had him pegged as a sharp operator—*they'll probably use the A-B-C method of surveillance,* he thought. *The mere fact that I'll be able to give them the slip will convince Dowdy that I have something to hide.*

The Death Merchant went to bed with a nine-milimeter

MAB autoloader, thinking of Persig's Postulate: The number of rational hypotheses that can explain any given phenomenon is infinite. It was also his conclusion that in a short while he would become a "secret alcoholic" and have to undergo "treatment" in a certain clinic in Dallas.

I'll have to get myself arrested for public drunkenness to-morrow night, he thought before drifting off to sleep.

Chapter Five

The Tower of Consolation and Heavenly Communication stood in the exact center of New Earth Community. There wasn't anything complicated about its structure. One hundred and seventy-six feet tall and twenty-eight feet on each side, the Needle, as the tower was commonly called by non-Frimmies, was simply a framework of girders covered with stainless steel sheeting that caught the rays of the sun and, at times, almost blinded one with flashing, shimmering rays. There weren't any steel-cable guy wires to spoil the overall effect. They weren't needed. The foundation of the Needle rested on bedrock.

Inside the tower was a small elevator by which one could be taken twenty-one feet below the flat roof of the tower. From the inside, a stairway rose to the roof, to the Consolation Chamber.

Like an enormous bubble, a dome of crystal-clear plastic covered the entire roof. However, from the top of the dome, an eight-foot circular portion could be opened by means of small motors. Shutters inside the door could be closed to prevent light from entering.

Reverend Frimm often sat inside the dome, especially when problems of great weight were on his mind. Almighty God used the burning rays of the sun and the yellow, mellow light of the moon as mediums by which His words could be transmitted more easily to Reverend Frimm, His mouthpiece on earth.

The Tower of Consolation and Heavenly Communication was used also for special meetings, such as the meeting His Oneness and His Onlyness was now presiding over at 3:30 in the morning. With him were three men: Brother Peek, Brother Wilbur Sessons, the Minister of Light of the Protectors, and Ralph Steinhoff.

The light of a full moon shone only through the eight-foot

circular opening around the top of the plastic dome. The rest of the dome had been shuttered as a preventative against the authorities listening with long-range parabolic mikes from nearby mountains. There was even a "white sound" generator in the dome to prevent any bug from transmitting conversations. Brother Qualls, the Minister of Light of food supplies had installed the WS generator. Before becoming a member of the Church of the Cosmic Reality, Nils Qualls had been an electronic engineer in the research department of General Electric in Schenectady, New York.

Brother Wilbur Sessons stared in anger at Ralph Steinhoff.

"We pay you a yearly retainer of seventy-five thousand dollars," he said tightly, "and all you can tell us is that you don't know where Camellion is. Or that guy named Linders."

"It's been six weeks since the inquest and since Camellion returned to Texas," Brother Peek reminded the private detective.

"A man can't just vanish off the face of the earth!" Sessons said loudly. "And from the way Camellion handled himself on the highway, he's some kind of expert. A man like that doesn't give up. He won't quit!"

"Correct on all counts," Steinhoff said unconcernedly. "No, Camellion didn't vanish. He managed to give my men the slip. Those things happen. My men are good, but they're human. They make mistakes like anyone else."

An expensive but conservative dresser, the carefully groomed Steinhoff had the appearance of a diplomat who was very careful of his weight and health; and he had the manners to match, an ingratiating manner that would have made a board member of the Cosa Nostra trust him—or religious fanatics like the Reverend Frimm and his group of special crazies. Steinhoff worshiped only at the Church of the Almighty Dollar and wasn't the least bit impressed with Frimm in his blood-red hooded monk's robe and the two Ministers of Light in their pink robes. They were nuts today and they'd be fruitcakes ten years from now, especially the hulking Sessons, who had been a "sanitary engineer" before joining the church of selected crackpots. Piss on him! Piss on Frimm. Piss on all of them!

His Oneness and His Onlyness sat on a white plastic chair, his hands, as if in prayer, against his chest. Wisely, he listened and said little.

The beefy Sessons had a lot to say. After all, it had been his Protectors that Camellion had made fools of on Interstate 83.

Those who hadn't been killed by Camellion had pleaded guilty to assault with a deadly weapon and had been sentenced to three to ten years in the Colorado state penitentiary. There had been no appeal. His Oneness and His Onlyness didn't want anymore adverse publicity.

"See here, Steinhoff. We can't accept that kind of inefficiency!" Sessions's voice was definite. "Your own report on that man Camellion proves he's not a deprogrammer and that there's something not right about him. He's got that little old ranch, but is seldom there, and nobody knows where he goes or what he does. All you found out was that he was a friend of Everett Padden."

"It's the same with that man Linders." Brother Peek's voice acquired a thin edge as he cut in. "He's supposed to work for the U.S. government, and that's all you know about him."

"Not quite." Steinhoff fingered his close-clipped mustache. "We do know that Linders's sister and her husband are not connected in any way with whatever his real business might be."

"We're discussing Linders, not Mr. and Mrs. Raine," Peek said patiently. "Tell us what we *don't* know."

"My boys scored zero on Linders. He dresses well and seems to have plenty of money. He might be a government man working for one of Uncle Sam's law enforcement agencies. I hope he isn't. If he is, it could mean that Washington is trying to put you people out of business."

"Hogwash," growled Sessions. "The only agencies in the government that'd be interested in us are the IRA or the BATF. The tax people don't operate the way Linders does, and all the BATF does is batter down doors and entrap innocent gun dealers. Anyhow, we complied with all the federal laws when we bought them submachine guns." He pointed a long, thick finger at the calm Steinhoff who was clipping the end from a slim panatela. "It's your inefficiency that caused us to lose Camellion—and Linders, too!"

"Mr. Steinhoff, you know you're not allowed to smoke up here," Peek said.

"No law against chewing on it, is there?" Not the least bit ruffled, Steinhoff turned to Sessions. "Speaking of inefficiency, I think you have a lot of shorts in your wires. It was I who discovered that Camellion was a good friend of Padden's, I and my agency that kept a watch on him down in the Big Thicket. It was my operatives who trailed him from Texas to Colorado Springs. Then you and your Protectors were to take off. Well, *Brother* Sessons"—he put an insulting emphasis on the "Brother"—"your 'Protectors' couldn't even protect themselves. Christ! They had him all—"

"Do not use the name of the Lord in vain!" intoned Reverend Frimm solemnly. "Profanity is a bitter fruit poisoning not only the mouth but the soul."

"Your men had Camellion all bottled up on the highway," Steinhoff said to Sessons, "and he made fools of them. He drove circles around them. He killed the two men on the Honda, and without even a pistol, he blew up two of them—with one of their own guns! I don't mind telling you, I never want that son of a—I never want him looking for me!"

"I admit he's some kind of expert," backtracked Sessons sullenly. "But the next time he tries anything the story will have a far different ending. I don't care how good he is, he's still only one man."

Reverend Frimm spoke in a voice barely above a whisper. "Is there not some way we can manufacture evidence to place the blame of the murders in Texas on him? God has revealed to me that Camellion was the Agent of Satan who destroyed the Righteous Ones at the Haven of Truth."

"Your Oneness, that is not possible," Peek said, in a tone that one would use to a retarded child.

"Impossible," Steinhoff said flatly. He wanted to laugh and ask "His Oneness" why it was that God hadn't told him how to destroy Camellion. God told him everything else! But Steinhoff knew there was a definite boundary beyond which he dare not go. "If we tried a scheme like that, it would backfire on us. Camellion could account for his time when the Texas camp was attacked."

"An alibi can be faked," Sessons said dourly.

"Right. But the police accepted his alibi and that's what matters," Steinhoff said. For a moment he looked at Reverend Frimm, then moved his eyes to Brother Peek and Brother Sessons. "Saving the world is your business, but you don't know anything about security."

Sessons made an angry face and started to speak, but Reverend Frimm raised a restraining hand. "The Lord helps those who help themselves, Mr. Steinhoff. We have helped ourselves. Our security at New Earth is excellent. We have the latest electronic alarm devices. Our people keep careful track of visitors. No one can pose as a visitor and remain within the community after the gates are closed. The vehicles of our people who leave at night on business are carefully checked when the Righteous return. The Protectors are constantly patrolling, even in the daytime. And we have God watching over us."

Steinhoff wanted to say that the guards—and *God!*—had not done such a good job in Texas. Instead, he said, "I didn't mean physical security at New Earth, or in any of the other communities."

"Get to the point!" Sessons cracked the knuckles of his left hand.

"Termites burrow from the inside." Steinhoff's voice was smug with satisfaction. "Camellion's been exposed. We know he's our enemy. The police know it, but they can't prove the connection. He's helpless. He can't move against you."

"Infiltrators! You mean infiltrators," Peek said, watching Steinhoff carefully.

"Exactly. For all you know, your entire chain of Havens of Truth and Abodes could be riddled with informers working for Camellion, or for whom Camellion might be working."

Steinhoff threw a swift glance at Frimm, but couldn't detect any particular reaction in the expression of the crackpot. Not that it mattered. It was always difficult, if not impossible, to know what the religious fanatic was thinking.

"The spy in Mesa didn't fool us," Sessons said, emerging from his brief silence. "He's—" Sessons caught himself and stopped speaking. Why tell Steinhoff where Roger Zettker was buried? The Superstition Mountains, outside of Mesa and Tempe, in Arizona, held a lot of black secrets. Roger Zettker—that devil's disciple—was only one of them. "He'll no longer be a threat to us," Sessons concluded. "To anyone."

"Yet he wasn't caught by any deductive reasoning on your part." Steinhoff shifted his weight in the chair. "As I understand it, Zettker was caught in the act of phoning a report to someone on the outside, presumably Russell Linders, since he was in Mesa at the time."

"As His Oneness said, God does protect us," Sessons replied, cleverly evading the slur on his efficiency. "The Lord . God will not permit Agents of Satan to exist in our midst, not for long. Being an unbeliever you would not know that."

"Brother Sessons is absolutely correct," Reverend Frimm declared briskly. He got to his feet and held up his arms in the manner of one who was the victim of a holdup. "The Lord has spread His protective cloak over New Earth Community. We are safe here from all evil."

His Oneness suddenly turned his head to one side and held

it at an odd angle. The expectancy on his face was one of bliss and expectancy.

"Listen! Do you hear it?"

Sessons glanced at Peek. Ralph Steinhoff faced remained fixed and noncommital. Brothers Sessons and Peek looked fearfully at Frimm, who had raised his arms over his head and walked to the center of the floor, so that he stood beneath the circular opening in the top of the dome.

All Peek and Sessons and Steinhoff could hear was the wind blowing in through the circular opening from Pikes Peak and the Rocky Mountains eighty-five miles to the west.

"The sweet voice of God!" whispered Reverend Frimm. "I hear His words!" His voice, quivering with bliss, rose in volume until it became a near shriek. *"Yes, dear Lord! Yes! yes! I hear! I believe, Lord! Ohhhhhh Thank You, Lord. Yes! The Church of the Cosmic Reality will spread throughout the United States before the final conflagration of time and the universe! Yes, God! I hear. I shall obey. I Shall rulé from the White House and spread the Word throughout the land. The Evil Ones shall be made to suffer and will be damned in the Pit of Worms and Eternal Misery. Oh, thank you, Dear Lord!"*

Shaken, for psychotic people made him nervous, Ralph Steinhoff looked at Peek and Sessons, whose own faces reflected a fanaticism that was chilling . . . expressions of maniacal fervor that made Steinhoff want to jump up and run from the dome.

For years, he had assumed that "Reverend" Frimm—who had never attended any theological institute—and his aides were nothing more than very clever con-artists.

Now he knew better, and the truth staggered him.

Reverend Hannibal Frimm and his Ministers of Light were stark, raving mad!

Chapter Six

"I'll say this for you, Camellion. You think big! Crazy, but big!" Linders said, a touch of amusement in his voice. "I've been in on some crazy stunts, but this one has to top them all."

"We'll know more once we take a tour of New Earth Community," the Death Merchant said. Sitting in a plush tower-back seat next to the CIA man, Camellion admired the way Linders handled the Silver Ranch motor home, driving it as though the big vehicle were a part of him. Camellion felt an acute sense of loss every time he thought of the sleek house on wheels. Even though he had gotten the Silver Ranch deal at a discount, he hadn't enjoyed buying it. Every cent for this mission was coming out of his own pocket. Weeks ago he had concluded that the total bill might be as high as 250 grand. To Camellion's way of thinking, the cost was equal to two and a half missions for the CIA.

Tired of looking through the window at the monotonous stretch of highway, he swiveled around in the thickly cushioned chair and looked at the woman who was preparing iced tea. In her early thirties, Janet was certainly worth looking at. She always smelled wonderfully of French scent and today was wearing a short dress of a creamy color, very simple but elegant, leaving her arms and neck bare. Her auburn hair was done up high in an Empire bun. She reminded Camellion of a model, the kind you see on magazine covers, only heavier and more shapely. Unlike models, she wasn't the least bit flat-chested.

An ex-policewoman, Janet Minnick was Russell Linders's girl friend.

Every time Camellion looked at her, he thought of the 15 grand he was paying her to play the role of his daughter-in-law. He hoped she'd be worth it.

Janet brought three tall glasses of iced tea on a tray to the front of the motorhome, handed one to Camellion, put one on the tiny swing-out table between the two seats and took the third glass for herself. She sat down on a blue velvet convertible sofa-bed in back of Linders's seat and doubled up her legs beneath her.

"How's the schedule holding?" She looked at Camellion. "We'll still pull into Colorado Springs about nine?"

"Sure thing, sweets," Linders answered. "We'll turn off at Limon. Highway 24 will take us straight in. Then we'll swing north on 83." He glanced at the Death Merchant and grinned. "Your own personal target range, right?" When Camellion didn't reply, Linders finished with, "We'll be at the Diamond-T no later than ten-thirty."

Janet stirred the ice in her glass with a long-handled spoon.

"In that case, we'll be able to take tomorrow's afternoon tour of Frimmie land. I'm rather anxious to see what New Earth Community looks like up close. I've read so much about the place."

"We'll rest up tomorrow," Camellion said firmly. He had swung around to face Janet and Linders. "Russ can use the afternoon to contact his friends and find out about the helicopters."

Another thirty grand! thought Camellion. *But they'd be fools to risk their lives and twenty-five years in prison for less.*

The woman's voice was reflective. "You know, guys. I've been thinking about religion and cults ever since I got involved with this project. I can understand how the average person belongs to some faith. You're born into, say, a Baptist family, so you grow up to become a Baptist—or a Catholic, or Jewish or Methodist or whatever your parents were. But a member of a cult? It doesn't make sense."

"It makes a lot of sense," Camellion said. "Cults emerge when groups lose faith and withdraw from prevailing religious practices. Members then commit themselves to the leadership of charismatic and highly authoritarian figures. It's a fact of life that most people need faith in something."

Linders made a noise of disapproval. "A realist needs faith only in himself. I don't need another man to tell me his version about God."

"What the general public doesn't know is that most cults know exactly what kind of recruits they want," Camellion said. "Jim Jones sought out the oppressed—especially poor blacks, whores and other outcasts—who would believe his

55

message of egalitarianism and his offer of a communal home. But religious cults such as the Moonies—and the Frimmies—prefer college students of above-average intelligence and idealism who, they think, would be a credit to the cult.

"The Frimmies and the Moonies are alike in many other respects," the Death Merchant said. "Both cults use psychological methods like a trained surgeon. Isolation—from family, friends and all contact with the outside world—is the first step. Next, recruits are made to feel guilty about their past lives and recognize their need to be reborn like their all-knowing 'brothers and sisters' in the new family of the cult. Several cults, such as the Children of God and Hare Krishna, even give recruits new names or devise private measurements of time to underscore the cult's *new reality*. But the development of a new personality is gradual. It requires various forms of sense deprivation, inculcated through loss of sleep, low-protein diets and exhausting rounds of chanting, praying, and indoctrination in the thought of the new father figure.

"It's actually very simple when you stop to think about it. The entire idea is that converts have to believe only what they are told. They don't have to think, and this relieves tremendous tensions. Inside Moon's camps independent thought is considered a tool of Satan. It's the same way in Frimm's Havens of Truth and his Abodes."

Janet put down her glass of iced tea and reached for her cigarettes in a pocket of her dress. "Well, I'm not a psychologist, but I'm inclined to think that such people have basically weak personalities."

Russell Linders, who had slowed the motorhome for traffic ahead, chuckled, "I'll buy that. I don't believe that any truly intelligent person can become a cult follower. All cults demand blind faith and damn the man or woman whose inquiring mind prompts them to question *dogma* founded on half-truths, myths, and just plain nonsense."

Janet's eyes went to Camellion. "In these cults, isn't there some critical point, some turning of the road?"

The Death Merchant put down his own glass, thinking that she made tea too weak for his liking.

"The critical point in the coversion process occurs when recruits are forced to make a major commitment to the cult. This may mean signing over one's bank account, property or children to the group, or even joining in drug or sex orgies, as Charles Manson demanded of his half-witted 'family.' "

"My God!" said Janet. "What insanity."

"Who said the human race had any sense?" Linders said with a low laugh.

Camellion shrugged. "It follows that once you've done something—turned over your bank account or your house and kids to some fruitcake cult, it becomes more and more difficult to admit even to yourself that you've made a mistake, that you've made a fool of yourself. Subconsciously you will then go to great lengths to rationalize the whole process, and the cult leaders know it. Once this process of rationalization begins, the mind is open to all sorts of beliefs, no matter how ridiculous."

"Incredible!" Janet murmured, exhaling cigarette smoke as she talked.

"Life is incredible, and that's why it's interesting," laughed Camellion.

Russell Linders shifted gears and increased the speed of the motorhome. The highway ahead was several miles of straight-as-an-arrow asphalt. "Unless we ignore the rumors Zettker heard and reported to me," said Linders, "Frimm is using out-and-out psychological torture of the worst kind to gain converts."

"What about sex?" Janet brought up, a wicked little gleam in her brown eyes. "Sex has got to play a leading role. Even a lunatic like Reverend Frimm can't ignore the sex drive."

"He hasn't," the Death Merchant said, hooking his thumbs over the belt of his white gabardine jumpsuit. "In virtually all cults, sex is a central means of controlling members' lives. Some cult leaders, like Charles Manson and Jim Jones, used some of their followers, both male and female, for their own pleasure. But most cults rigidly segregate males and famales and teach that sex is an instrument of the devil. Moon not only arranges all marriages but also demands such powerful repression of sexual feelings that, it is believed, many members actually revert to pre-puberty innocence. Women stop having their periods and men often find that they do not have to shave as often."

"What about Reverend Frimm?" asked Janet, her voice very intense and curious. She noticed that the twilight had grown deeper and that Russell had turned on the headlights of the motor home.

"Frimm's not the same kind of nut as Moon, at least not about sex," explained Camellion. "He segregates the unmarried Frimmies, which is natural and normal enough. Married couples have their own cottages. There aren't any sex orgies or promiscuity. We can't accuse him of perverting the sexual drive, at least not in the sense that he makes perversion or suppression a part of the indoctrination process."

"We don't have to discuss young Zettker," said Linders with finality. "He's dead and no doubt buried. So unless we're wrong, we can be sure that Frimm and his Protectors are not adverse to murder. And if they terminated Zettker, how many others have they murdered?"

"We don't have any conclusive evidence that Zettker was killed," Janet said airily. "We're only assuming."

"Like we're assuming that the sun will rise tomorrow." Linders voice was like a low animal growl. "I was talking to him at one in the morning. Suddenly I heard sounds like scuffling. Then someone hung up the phone. That's enough for me."

Camellion said, "We can say with certainty that the Frimmies caught him. I'd say he's dead."

"When his parents inquired about him," Linders said, "they were told that he had left the camp, had quit the Reality church, and that no one knew where he had gone. The Mesa police went out to the camp and investigated, but they didn't get anywhere. That means that Zettker has become just another statistic in the realm of disappearances. How about some dinner, sweets?"

Janet Minnick got off the sofa-bed. "How does steak strike you?"

Linders nodded. "Sounds all right."

"With fried potatoes and salad," Camellion said.

"Okay, guys. Using the microwave oven, it won't take long."

Janet turned and went back to the kitchen section of the motor home, wishing that Camellion and Linders didn't have such different preferences. Linders liked his steak rare. Camellion preferred his well-done, almost burnt.

"After dinner, I'll drive us in the rest of the way," Camellion said. "You've been at it the past four hours."

"Did you see the sign we just passed?" Linders said. "There's a recreational area a few miles ahead. I'm going to pull off there and we can eat together."

"Why not? There's plenty of time. We made reservations at the park a week ago; we can get there any time we want."

There were other vehicles in the large rest area, several cars, two vans, and another motorhome. The night was quiet, the moonless sky a black carpet dotted with diamonds of stars. The air was cool, and Camellion had turned off the air conditioner. He had opened one of the four sun roofs and the Dynamic air scoop, which would let in fresh air but keep dirt and water out, should it be open during a rain shower.

They talked of cults while they ate, the Death Merchant explaining that cults were neither foreign to time or to history, and that drawing a fine line between cults and religion was not an easy matter. He went on to say that, over the years, the world has seen any number of strange religious cults, such as the I am, the Shakers, the Church of Zion, the Agapemonites, and the Oneida Community. These cults were either gone and forgotten or, like the Shakers, nearly all dead.

There had been cults of pure racism, some well known and still very powerful, such as the Ku Klux Klan. Others were almost totally unknown but had been very powerful and very dangerous during their existence. The violently anti-Semitic Order of the New Templars had been founded in Austria about the term of the century.

Adolf Hitler had been a member of the Austrian New Templars. . . .

Camellion, who had finished eating, pushing back his plate. He rubbed the left cheek; the mastoplastic "flesh" itched. "A lot of people don't realize it," he said, "but long before modern America became a playground for all sorts of gurus, swamis, and yogis, the U.S. had an Eastern religion that never made any headlines. This was the Vedanta Society, which was introduced to the West in 1893 by a young Indian named Vivekananda. By 1916 the Vedanta Society had branches in every major American city. It's still in existence . . . a harmless cult whose members bother no one."

Russel Linders leaned back and lit a cigarette. On the verge of being handsome, he spoke with the accent of a cosmopolite who somehow had retained those certain inflections common to New England. His curly black hair showed only a faint touch of gray, while his high cheekbones and dark complexion at first glance suggested American-Indian blood, but the short military mustache and the urbane twinkle in his wide-set, blue-green eyes, were Caucasian.

He smiled and said, "It seems to me that people have to have two things in this life—sex and religion."

"It's sex that has made Tantrism popular in Western nations," Camellion said. "It's a Hindu cult that so far hasn't generated much publicity, and it's not a part of any of the major American cults, as far as I know."

"I never heard of it," Janet said, leaning to one side to let Linders light her cigarette.

"Tantric rituals," explained the Death Merchant, "always culminate with sexual intercourse between the worshipers. Apart from this ritualized sex—it's called *maithuna*—Tantrists are encouraged to break society's sexual code as frequently as possible. Group sex, incest, and other bizarre sexual practices are considered valuable in helping the Tantrist to transcend conventional ideas of good and evil."

"At least we can't accuse Reverend Frimm of being a Tantrist," said Linders. "In Zettker's reports, he said there wasn't the least bit of hanky-panky at the Mesa camp." He paused and frowned. "I keep thinking about that Spanish friend of yours in New Mexico. You sure he'll show up?"

"Carlós Martinez* is a man of his word; he'll be at the trailer park in time. And he knows what he's getting into."

Janet Minnick said, "Speaking of sex, there isn't any wild sex at the Moonie camps either. I suppose Moon and Frimm think alike in this respect."

"I consider Frimm to be ten times more dangerous than Moon," Camellion offered. "The Frimmies outnumber the Moonies nine to one. Another way of putting it is to say that the Frimmies are a small army. With every member trained in the use of firearms."

Linders's eyes narrowed. "As far as I know, Washington doesn't consider the Frimmies a threat to national security, if that's what you're getting at!"

"It was only a passing thought," Camellion said. "It's rather terrifying to think of a couple of hundred thousand loonies blindly following a madman with dreams of glory; and no one uses the fear the way Frimm does. He's a master at the art."

"The brainwashing process," Linders said.

"There's more to it than that. Christians don't feel guilty about hating atheists because they're convinced that atheists are on a greasy slide to hell. Whether it's conventional religion or one of the cults, the framework of belief operates in a *closed* system, in the sense that any proper self-criticism is denied. Anyone who questions the dogma is obviously being put up to it by the devil himself. We know this to be 'true' because the dogma tells us so. What is the most sacred and authoritative book ever written in the world? The Bible. How do you know? It says so in the Bible. Who is God's messenger

*See Death Merchant #32, *The Deadly Manhunt*.

on earth? Why Reverend Frimm, of course. How do you know? Because Reverend Frimm says so."

"You mean that cults make hate 'respectable,' " Janet asked.

"Yes, in that cults allow people to hate without feeling guilty. Not only that, but cults provide a safe, group-sanctioned outlet for aggression against the common enemy. Cult leaders also convince members that they will die, either at the hands of enemies or cult loyalists, if they defect. The Children of God tell defectors that either God or Satan will strike them dead."

"The Frimmies have had their share of defectors," said Linders. "But from what I've heard, they never defect directly from one of the camps or so-called *Abodes*. They wait until they're away from the group and then simply walk away and don't return. I'm inclined to think that those who tip their plans about leaving, while still inside the camp, end up in Cells of Attrition."

"We'll know for sure within the next two weeks," Camellion said. He got to his feet. "It's time we made tracks. . . ."

A few miles from the Diamond-T Trailer Ranch, the Death Merchant pulled off to the side of the road and had Linders take over the driving, remarking that it would seem a bit odd if a seventy-five-year-old man wheeled in the big motorhome like an expert.

"It would be more out of place if they saw me in this jumpsuit. I'd better put on clothes closer to my bygone generation."

Camellion went to the rear of the motorhome to change while Linders, with Janet sitting next to him, drove the remaining few miles. By the time Linders was turning into the Diamond-T, Camellion had changed into a short-sleeved white shirt, blue slacks, white socks and open-toed slip-on casual knit kickers. He had also put on a hearing aid, the kind with a plug in the ear and a wire, which ran from the plug to the mike and amplifier, clipped to his shirt-front.

The hearing aid was as phony as Camellion's appearance of age, as the deep wrinkles in the skin mottled with faint blotches of red and blue, as the bags under the rheumy eyes, over which he now wore glasses. With plastic putty, he had broadened his nose, and with putty and liners had made his mouth smaller. Even his arms and neck had the aged skin effect.

To complete the disguise, he had a shaved skull and wore a latex hairpiece that had only tufts of white hair on each side. It had taken him six hours to get his new face and he was very pleased with the result. Furthermore, the new kind of masto-plastic putty enabled the skin to "breathe," and was of such durability that for several weeks one could leave it on and wash over it. The only problem was shaving. A special chemical solution, concocted by CIA chemists, was injected daily; this solution would prevent the beard from growing for a period of two weeks. The chemical could not be used for more than two weeks, without running the risk of serious damage to the male hormones.

Leaning on a plain wooden cane with a curved handle, Camellion saw at once that the Diamond-T Trailer Ranch was one of those vacation areas that believed in security, which explained the high price of a lot. The high cost explained why "Mr. and Mrs. Barry Robbinette" had been able to get a lot reserved on such short notice.

A young man, in white slacks and white sport shirt, was at the entrance, in front of the fancy iron gates in the white brick wall. Behind the wall, tall elms and beech trees swayed gently with the night wind.

Linders stopped ten feet in front of the gate and turned off the headlights. The young man at the gate waved a hand. Another young man—he, too, was dressed in white—came out of a small office to the left, carrying a metal clipboard in his hand.

"Have we come to a trailer park or a fancy concentration camp?" cracked Janet, watching the young man with the clipboard approach the motorhome from the driver's side.

"Good evening, good evening. Welcome to Diamond-T Trailer Ranch." He oozed friendliness. "May I have your names, sir?" he said to Linders.

"Mr. and Mrs. Barry Robbinette, and Mr. Andrew Robbinette, my father," Linders said heartily.

"Tell him, son," Camellion cackled in a weak voice, thumping the tip of his cane on the floor. "Tell him about that young friend of yours you're expecting."

Janet turned, looked consolingly at Camellion, and said gently, "Don't you worry, Paw. Barry's friend won't be here until day after tomorrow."

"We finally talked my father into taking a vacation," Linders explained, his tone and expression indicating he was placating the old man. "He's speaking of a friend of mine, Mr. Martinez, who will be stopping by to visit us."

"I understand perfectly, sir," the security man said. He looked past Linders and raised his voice. "Don't worry, Mr.

Robbinette. We'll make sure that Mr. Martinez finds your trailer."

The security man then told Linders to drive in and park by the small building to the left. There he'd give them their name plates, which would be used as identification tags while in the park and especially when entering. "I'll then take you to the main office. Mr. Higgins, our manager, will take you to your lot."

He stepped back from the motorhome and waved Linders ahead.

"What do you think—*Paw?*" Linders asked with a chuckle, as he drove through the gates the other security man had opened.

"We wouldn't want a place more respectable," Camellion said in a low voice. "This is the last place in the world that the Frimmies or Captain Dowdy would expect us to be. It's perfect."

"It's too quiet," Janet surprised them both. "It's like a mortuary that makes you feel guilty because you're still alive."

The Death Merchant didn't say what he was thinking. *If something goes wrong, something unexpected, none of us will be alive. . . .*

Chapter Seven

Convinced he was right, Captain Marvin Dowdy put his feet on the bottom projections of the swivel chair, leaned back, opened the blue folder marked *Richard J. Camellion: 647-D-8* and read the last report he had received from the Colorado Bureau of Investigation. The report had been written by the two C.B.I. agents who had been watching the motels and trailer parks in and around the Colorado Springs area. During all these weeks, the two agents had not seen anything of Richard Camellion. They had spotted several men resembling him, but none of the men had been the tall, lean Texan.

Another report, this one from three C.B.I. agents keeping tabs on New Earth Community, indicated that there had not been any unusual activity in the area of the Church of the Cosmic Reality.

Dowdy rubbed his chin in frustration. A lawman of the old school that stressed instinct and common sense over modern laboratory methods, he didn't like to think he had been wrong about Richard Camellion. No, by God, he wasn't! He was positive that Richard Camellion was not the kind of man to quit.

Dowdy readily admitted that he had a problem because he didn't have any hard evidence that Camellion had been trying to do anything in connection with the Church of the Cosmic Reality. There wasn't any evidence that he was a deprogrammer. Nevertheless, there had to be some kind of connection between Camellion and the Frimmies. Why else had those fanatical Protectors tried to kill him? True, the Protectors were all psychopaths, but they didn't attack people for the fun of it. They had attacked Camellion for a very specific reason.

"Damn it," Dowdy muttered, his bafflement getting the better of him for the moment. Even more disconcerting and

64

equally as defeating as his lack of evidence was the phone call he had received from C.B.I. headquarters a few days earlier. The C.B.I. was taking its men off the case. Dowdy bitterly remembered the conversation.

"Marv, we don't have a case against Camellion. We never did," Amos Mull, the director of the C.B.I. had said. "And we don't have the manpower to keep following hunches. Hell, the only reason we checked on Camellion in the first place was because the Governor got mad over all the publicity the state received from that ruckus on 83."

"I suppose Camellion's being a good friend of Everett Padden doesn't count?" Dowdy had responded angrily.

"It never did, and you know it." Mull had become angry. "Padden had a lot of friends, and you don't arrest a man or keep tabs on him for the rest of his life because a good friend is murdered. When that shootout at the church camp took place, Camellion proved he was nowhere in the vicinity. The Texas police say Camellion's clean."

"Now listen. I—"

"You listen, Marv! You're trying to skin the wrong rabbit. What happened out there on 83 is that the goons of the Reality organization got Camellion mixed up with another bird."

"Then how come Camellion's disappeared again in Texas? Or haven't you people heard that he's nowhere to be found?"

"What else is new? We understand he's been doing that for years. Okay. The guy's some kind of loner with weird habits. Who knows what he does when he's not around? Hell, maybe he shacks up with some woman. Who cares? It's not a crime to be a privacy nut. Hell, we even checked him out with the FBI—nothing. I'm sorry, Marv. I can't justify my men continuing to chase shadows and assumptions on your part."

Dowdy swung around in the chair and slammed the blue folder to his desk. He told himself he was acting rather childish. After all, Amos was only doing his job and calling the shots as he saw fit.

He frowned and sucked in his lower lip. There was the possibility that he was wrong about Richard Camellion. But he didn't think so. His instincts had served him too well over the years. By God, there was something not right about Richard Camellion. The way he had handled himself out on 83! Incredible! Only a man very much at home with violent death could have been that cool. And where had he acquired all that kill-talent? Damn it to hell, if the state police hadn't stopped him, he would have killed every man in that car.

An even bigger puzzle was what had happened a few days after the death chase and battle on the cutoff road. Drinking in the Yucca Lounge, a downtown Colorado bar, Camellion had gotten plastered and become abusive when the bartender refused to serve him. When Camellion had refused to leave the establishment, the management had called the police—after Camellion had knocked out the bouncer with some kind of a karate punch. Camellion had spent the night in jail. In court the next day he had paid a $200 fine and received a stern warning from Judge Harkess.

Bull! Who in hell did Camellion think he was fooling? He wasn't the kind of man to get plastered in private, much less in public. Why had he done it? What did he have to gain? There had to be a reason.

Dowdy made up his mind to find out. By God, he'd use his own men.

He leaned over his desk and pushed a button.

"Yes sir?"

"Baker, come in here."

Chapter Eight

Mr. and Mrs. Barry Robbinette, Mr. Andrew Robbinette, and Señor Carlos Martinez waited until Friday before driving out to New Earth Community in a rented car and taking the afternoon tour. It was on the first Friday of every month that the Church of the Cosmic Reality held an early evening service for the benefit of visitors, with His Oneness and His Onlyness himself giving the sermon and, inspired by Almighty God, speaking in tongues.

The Death Merchant wanted to see "God's Messenger on Earth" in action, although he had another reason for going to New Earth Community.

He intended to kill Reverend Hannibal Frimm.

Even at a distance, Camellion and his people could see that the area occupied by New Earth Community was immense.

"I'd say more than a mile and a half square," said Janet Minnick. Sitting next to Linders, who was driving, she watched the string of cars, all of them going to the center of the Church of the Cosmic Reality.

"I think you're right, sweets," Linders said. "When you think of all that land in terms of shopping malls, you're talking about millions of dollars.

The Death Merchant, in the back seat with Carlos Martinez, remained silent. Without a firearm, he felt decidedly uncomfortable. But none of them carried an autoloader, for two very good reasons: except for Camellion, everyone wore walking shorts and sport shirts—except Janet with her thin blouse and skimpy bra. It's not easy to hide an autoloader in walking shorts.

Elderly men also wear shorts, but Camellion had not wanted to take the time to change the healthy skin of his legs to the dried-out parchment of a man in the ice-age years of his life. He couldn't if he had wanted. His legs were knotted with muscles. All the cosmetics in the world could not reduce the actual size of those muscles and make them appear to be withered with age.

Walking shorts would also have interfered with his technique of decreasing his height and appearing to be shorter than he actually was. He walked hunched over, leaning heavily on the cane, as though crippled with arthritis. The shirt he wore made his chest, back, and shoulders appear to be thinner. The shirt was not merely several sizes too large, or it would have simply hung on him, the deliberate bagginess obvious. Instead, the shirt had been very carefully tailored to sag around every muscle bulge of his particular torso. The pants, cut a bit too large, drooped just right.

The second reason why Camellion and the other three did not carry hand guns—even ones as small as a .22 auto-pistols—was that each person entering the Cosmic Temple was subjected to metal detectors, a precaution adopted by the Protectors to prevent anyone from trying to assassinate His Oneness and His Onlyness. All over the United States, Frimmies were constantly warning that Agents of Satan, especially in the form of Communists, were everywhere and were constantly plotting to kill God's Messenger on Earth.

Despite his lack of a hand gun, the Death Merchant was not helpless. He had enough death hidden on his person to kill hundreds!

"Listen Camellion. There's still time to call off your scheme," Linders said very seriously. "We have a better chance with the helicopters. Buttons and Hardtack flew in 'Nam and are experts with choppers. Who do it the hard way? Why not fly in, drop packets of TNT on every building in sight and blow up the whole community. We'd be almost certain to get Frimm."

Janet stirred uneasily and drew in a few quick breaths, the fact that Linders was speaking so casually about mass murder amazing her.

The Death Merchant shook his head. "No, hundreds of innocent people would be killed, and if we didn't terminate Frimm, we'd never get a second chance. Anyhow, we'd generate nationwide sympathy for the Frimmies if we killed most of them."

Linders disagreed. "I don't think so. The American people are used to death and violence."

"Possibly you are right," Camellion said without expression. "The world is governed by men dedicated to ideas, not to people. If I fail to neutralize Reverend Frimm in this first at-

68

tempt, we'll use the choppers, but definitely not to bomb the settlement."

"It's your neck. But what makes you think you'll come out alive if you fail?" enjoined Linders, some slight sarcasm to his voice.

I looked in a full-length mirror and saw an aura of soft green! That's how I know! thought Camellion, but only said, "Just a hunch. A feeling that I won't die today or next week, or even during this year."

Linders hunched his shoulders. "Like I said, it's your throat you're sticking under the blade."

By this time they were very close to the main entrance of New Earth Community and Linders slowed the station wagon. The cars ahead were barely moving now, the slowness necessitated by the loops of bright red ribbon the Frimmies at the gate were handing out to the occupants of each vehicle that entered the community. These were identification ribbons, to be worn around the neck as a means of letting the Frimmies know who the visitors were.

"We're in the wrong business," Russell Linders said. "When this is over, I'm going to get out of the insurance business and start a new religion. There's money to be made in myth and man-made magic."

Carlos Martinez, smiling slightly, glanced at the Death Merchant. Camellion hadn't told him anything about Linders, anymore than he had divulged information about Carlos. Yet not for a moment did Carlos believe that Linders was in the insurance business. An insurance man wouldn't be the type to be helping Richard Camellion. Carlos did not know that Camellion was the Death Merchant . . . only that he was an adventurer who always seemed to have plenty of money.

"I'll be your high priestess," cracked Janet with a little laugh.

Linders chuckled. "We'll call it The Church of the Laughing Community of Linders. We'll worship Eris, the Greek goddess of chaos and confusion." He laughed heartily. "That way we can devote ourselves to the doctrines of Utter Chaos and Discordianism."

"More than fitting for what I intend to do once we're inside New Earth Community," Camellion exclaimed.

"The Laughing Community of Linders will need a bible," Jane said.

His hands relaxed on the steering wheel, Linders thought for a moment. "All right. We'll call it the *Principia Discordia*, and have it authored by . . . oh . . . ah, that's it! By Magnum Opiate—the Magnum Opiate of Malaclypse The Younger! How does that sound?"

"Such a religion would never succeed," Camellion said, the tone of his voice so sincere that Janet turned and scrutinized him curiously. "We might end up converting ourselves," he said seriously. "If that happened, we'd lose our civil rights."

"I'll be stupid and ask why!" Janet murmured. Amid an aura of exciting new perfume, she turned toward the front and leaned forward to peer at the Frimmies at the entrance of New Earth Community.

"Convictions cause convicts," Camellion said. "Whatever you firmly believe imprisons you."

No one laughed. Linders forced his taut nerves to behave themselves, and a broad grin appeared under his close-clipped mustache.

"Knock it off, Paw. We're coming to the gate. Look like tourists, everybody."

Carlos Martinez leaned closer to the Death Merchant. "*Mi campañero,* give up this plan. It is loco. Even if you manage to kill this Reverend Frimm, you must still escape from the community. You will be one against hundreds."

Camellion smiled crookedly. "*Amigo,* don't concern yourself. Death will not gather me in his arms this day. Just do as I have told you: have the car at the spot we marked on the map. Don't fail me."

Carlos nodded, looking dismal.

It was now Linders turn at the gate. Carefully, he turned in and stopped under the large arched entrance made of rough white limestone, the entire massive portal resembling the main passageway of a medieval castle—*the Disneyland entrance to a city of fanatics!*

All smiles and white teeth, the dozen or so Frimmies at the entrance could have been young men and women anywhere, on any street, U.S.A., the men dressed in light, cool sport clothes, the women in breezy, sleeveless dresses of cotton and polyester blends.

A young man thrust his face at Linders. "Welcome, sir, to New Earth Community, the true home of the true God on earth."

A young female Frimmie closed in on the other side of the station wagon, noted the number of occupants, then handed Janet four large loops of red ribbon.

"Please wear these around your necks at all times," she said in a pleasant voice. "We don't want any of our guests getting lost. Enjoy yourselves, Brothers and Sisters."

"Follow the other cars to the parking lot, Brother," the other Frimmie instructed Linders. "There you'll join the other guests and be met by guides who will conduct the tour of our community. Go with God, Brother."

"Thank you, Brother." Linders put the loop of ribbon around his neck, drove forward, and joined the long line of cars, following them to the parking lot where Frimmies were dividing the visitors into groups of forty.

"I will now tell you the quote on prayer from the *Principia Discordia*," he said in a low, mocking voice. "Mal-2 was once asked by one of his disciples if he often prayed to Eris. He replied with these words: 'No, we Erisians seldom pray. It is much too dangerous. Charles Fort has listed many factual incidences of people confronted with, say, a drought, praying fervently—and then getting the entire village wiped out in a torrential flood.' "

It was difficult for Janet to keep a straight face. She did manage to say, "Damn it, will you stop it? We're supposed to go in serious, like interested tourists." She reflected for a moment, then asked, "Was there really an Eris?"

"I think she's part of mythology, but I'm not certain."

The Death Merchant's low voice was amused. "The Romans left a likeness of Eris for posterity. She was shown as a grotesque woman with a pale and ghastly look, her eyes all fire, her single garment ripped and torn, a bloody dagger concealed in her bosom. Actually, most women look pale and ghastly when concealing a bloody dagger in their bosoms."

"Oh-oh, here we go," Linders said, slowing the station wagon.

A female Frimmie waved Linders to a place in the parking lot. After Linders had parked, and the four of them had left the car, three Frimmies—two women and one man, all smiles—herded them gently toward another group, one asking if they were walking too fast for Camellion, who was creeping along with the aid of a cane.

"Don't you fret none about me, young fella," he cackled indignantly. "I may be old but I ain't dead."

Once they reached the designated group of other tourists, a female Frimmie, a small battery-powered bullhorn in one hand, said to the man who had accompanied Camellion and the others from the car, "These four will complete this group. Brother Elwin and I will start them out."

71

The man nodded and, with the two female Frimmies, turned and started toward other vehicles being parked.

The Frimmie with the bullhorn identified herself as Sister Ruth. She identified the male Frimmie standing silently nearby as Brother Elwin. The Death Merchant was quick to notice that Brother Elwin, a man in his thirties, was quietly inspecting the group, his eyes studying each man and each woman. Camellion knew why, and so did Linders and Janet Minnick. The older Frimmie was a recruiter. Not only were there young people within the group, but older couples who, before the day was over, might prove susceptible to the "religious" doctrine of Revered Hannibal Frimm.

The tour was interesting, making even the Death Merchant forget the hellish sun overhead. Sister Ruth, a blonde in her early twenties, pointed out each feature of the camp, speaking in a professional style through the bullhorn. There, she said, were the family cottages, modest frame buildings painted white, each with tiny lawns. Not too far away were the brick barracks where the single members of the church lived.

"Please understand, good people, that the single Brothers and Sisters are segregated. The Brothers live in the white barracks, the Sisters in the gray barracks. I can assure you that there isn't any promiscuity within New Earth Community.

With pride, she pointed out the three-story hospital. "It has the finest of equipment and the best doctors and nurses. Naturally the hospital has certification from the state of Colorado."

Another building was the school, serving both grammar and high school levels.

"All our teachers are college graduates," Sister Ruth said.

One of the tourists asked, "Do you have a regular curriculum, the kind of studies schools on the outside have?"

"Yes, Brother," answered Sister Ruth. "We also have religious studies, in accordance with the teachings of His Oneness and His Onlyness. We have also another feature that schools on the outside do not have—discipline."

Other buildings included garages where cars and trucks and farm machinery were kept in perfect working order.

Three enormous windmills—steel towers almost a hundred feet tall—stood in the northeast corner of the gigantic compound. These were not the conventional kind of windmill with vanes centered in a circle. These windmills were of modern design, each having two sixty-foot blades that drove the turbine. Sister Ruth explained the process of operation. "A mini-computer control starts the turbine when the wind reaches nine point five miles per hour and shuts it down when gusts exceed forty miles per hour."

"Is that your only source of power?" someone in the crowd asked.

"Yes," replied Sister Ruth. "Those windmills furnish ample power for the entire community."

"What about water and sewage disposal?" someone asked.

"We have seven deep wells. I'll show you the pumping station presently, and our sewage disposal plant. Most of the waste is compacted and used as fertilizer in our fields."

Camellion sensed she wasn't telling the whole truth about power. Studying the generator station centered on the ground between the three windmill towers, Camellion could see heavy wires in conduits that led from the powerhouse to high poles. From the way they were grouped together, it was evident that they came from standby generators, no doubt powered by gasoline.

"We are also experimenting with solar power," Sister Ruth said proudly through the small bullhorn. "I will show you our success when we come to the gymnasium and the main dining hall.

Russell Linders leaned close to Janet Minnick and whispered: "From the Book of Uterus, the Honest Book of Truth revealed to Lord Omar. Before the beginning was the Nonexistent Chaos, balanced in Oblivion by the Perfect Counterpushpull of the Hodge and the Podge."

Linders's words were so unexpected that Janet had to go into an act of coughing to keep from laughing.

Sister Ruth and Brother Elwin—he might have been deaf and dumb from the way he acted—led the crowd along wide gravel paths on the sides of the asphalt roads. At one point, she stopped and indicated a narrow concrete walk.

"The walk leads to the home of His Oneness and His Onlyness," she said with reverence, almost with awe—the way a guide in the Middle East would say, "This is the tomb of Christ."

"What does that mean, "His Oneness and His Onlyness'?" a middle-aged woman asked.

"*Oneness* means that Reverend Frimm is one with the Lord. *His Onlyness* means that Reverend Frimm is the only Messenger of God on earth."

A man in the crowd laughed. "I'm inclined to think that

73

half a billion Roman Catholics would disagree. They consider the Pope the right hand of God on earth."

Sister Ruth's reply was a masterpiece of justice: "They have every right to their belief. We have every right to ours. That is why the United States is the greatest nation on earth: because it has complete freedom of worship."

The Death Merchant looked at Frimm's modest, white frame house, which was surrounded by trees and bushes. He didn't fail to notice the small television cameras, mounted in some of the trees, pointed at the house.

Practical. The Protectors in the central station can keep a constant watch over Freak Frimm!

Two men stood in front of the gate at the white picket fence. Dressed in green berets, green fatigues, and Vietnam boots, and standing like statues, they carried a holstered pistol on each hip and held 5.56mm M-16 rifles.

"What are you running here, a military camp?" inquired a man whose voice indicated resentment. "Those guards are carrying automatic rifles. I trust you have a permit for such weapons?"

The man was in his thirties, wore his hair rather long and had long sideburns. The Death Merchant sized him up as a veteran of 'Nam. The woman with him was younger, a slim brunette in a light-blue pants suit. She held up an expensive Yashica camera and started snapping photographs of the two Protectors stationed in front of Reverend Frimm's house.

"We of the Church of the Cosmic Reality comply with all local, state and federal laws regarding firearms," Sister Ruth said calmly.

"In that case you won't mind taking us to where we can inspect your Federal Treasury license for those M-16 submachine guns." The man stepped forward and flipped open a badge case. "I'm Robert Gasjow. "This is Ramona Arnekine." The woman with him opened her badge case and thrust it forward. "We're agents of the Bureau of Alcohol, Tobacco and Firearms—United States Treasury Department," Gasjow said.

Sister Ruth wasn't the least bit shaken. She looked intently at the open badge cases. Brother Elwin came forward, and he too inspected the identification in the badge cases.

"Please follow me," he said mechanically. "The licenses are posted in the Armory." He turned and started to walk away. Gasjow and Arnekine followed.

"Those were agents of the Federal government!" a woman standing close by exclaimed in a shocked voice.

"Yes, they were," admitted Sister Ruth, unruffled. "The Church of the Cosmic Reality is constantly being persecuted by forces that wish to destroy us and stop us from spreading the word of God."

The Death Merchant butted in. "Young woman, how come them fellas over there with them guns have to guard your Reverend Frimm?" His voice cracked just right with age. "There ain't no guns at the Baptist church I belong to back home in Iowa!"

Another man said, "That's right. And I've read in the news magazines that you people have a target range and train in firearms and use karate and all that."

From the back of the group a man called out in a loud voice, "What about the trouble on the highway not far from here a while back? All your people pled guilty and were sent to the penitentiary!"

A murmur of voices rippled through the crowd. Men and women nodded and said to each other, "He's right. Why the guns? Religion and violence don't go together."

Quick to hear the dissent, Sister Ruth spoke to the entire party through the bullhorn: "We do have a target range and each member of the church under forty years of age is instructed in the use of firearms and is trained in karate. This training is vitally necessary because His Oneness and His Onlyness has forseen the black time when any person who believes in Jesus Christ will be attacked by those who work for the Kingdom of Satan. Christians and Jews—for the Father of the Jews is the Father of the Christians—will be hunted down throughout the world and ruthlessly murdered. However, the Church of the Cosmic Reality will be the main target. For that reason, dear Brothers and Sister, we train to defend ourselves. The world is now in its last days and the massacre of Christians and Jews is less than five years away. Already the forces of Satan, the Evil Angel of Light, are gathering against the members of the Church of the Cosmic Reality. That is why our Haven of Truth in Texas was attacked and our people murdered. It was a master agent of Satan that attacked our people on Highway 83. Didn't you read how the Colordao State Police found the devil man named Camellion with a gun in his hand, and how they prevented him from killing more of our Righteous members? These Righteous defenders of the Truth pled guilty in court, because it was the will of God, as revealed to His Oneness and His Onlyness, that they go to prison in order to spread the word among the heathen."

Sister Ruth half turned and pointed at the two Protectors standing guard in front of Reverend Frimm's house. "They are guarding His Oneness and His Onlyness because at this very moment the forces of Satan are planning to kill the Master."

Sister, it's not "Satan" who's trying! It's Richard Camellion—and I'm going to succeed. If the creek doesn't rise!

From the middle of the group, a man laughed nervously. "Thank God I'm an atheist and not Christian or Jewish. The forces of Satan will overlook me!" The speaker had meant his words to be a joke, but he soon wished he had kept his mouth shut. Not only did other members of the group give him dirty looks, but Sister Ruth said in a cold voice, "But God will not overlook you, unbeliever. Your lot for all eternity will be fire and bitterness, with pain and sorrow and maggots crawling in and out of your eye sockets. The very marrow of your bones will boil and blue fire will burn in the center of your brain. But your body will not be consumed. As His Oneness and His Onlyness has proved, the body of the soul is eternal and indestructible." She smiled. "Shall we continue the tour, Brothers and Sisters?"

Sister Ruth took them along a part of the northside fence, to point out the fields pregnant with wheat, sugar beets and vegetables, more than 780 acres that lay beyond the chain-link wire.

"We grow the vegetables for our own use," Sister Ruth said. "The wheat and sugar beets we sell on the public market. Let me point out that we don't undersell or compete with local farmers, but sell on par with their prices."

"The church doesn't have any cattle?" someone asked.

"Yes." She pointed toward the west. "From here you can see the landing strip and the hangar where our planes are kept. Two miles west of the strip we have a large dairy farm. I'm not certain of the figures, but I think we have somewhere in the vicinity of three hundred cows."

Russell Linders caught Camellion and Martinez's eyes and indicated a slowly rotating television camera on a 20-foot-high steel pole. Camellion nodded. During the tour he had noticed more than one TV camera mounted in strategic locations. There were other security devices, such as ultrasonic fence guards, devices to detect cutting, climbing or any kind of penetration. On the sides of various buildings, he had spotted Racon outdoor microwave detectors and outdoor infrared beam-breakers, and here and there a capacitance proximity alarm.

The group came to the Armory, a large white blockhouse kind of building enclosed within a decorative security fence—large, smooth river rocks cemented onto white limestone blocks. The personnel entrance was a seven-foot-high turnstile that contained various barriers. There was a steel ceiling plate to prevent climbing through the barrier; foot guards to prevent crawling under the rotor; and a bottom barrier arm, less than five inches above the concrete, to prevent any intruder from crawling underneath the barrier. Narrow spacing made it impossible for anyone to get through the arms.

First class security, Camellion thought, feeling as gloomy as the downhill side of a thunderhead.

He looked at the Rusco cardentry system that served as the lock. Any person wanted to pass through the turnstile had to insert a Ruscard, the same size and thickness as a credit card, into the slot. The Ruscard contained the invisible magnetic memory that stored the coded information necessary to allow an individual access. After the card was inserted, the person then had to work the coded sequence on the pushbutton console next to the card slot.

Four Protectors—green fatigues and M-16 submachine guns—were patrolling inside the compound. Two more Protectors were stationed in front of the steel door that opened to the inside of the blockhouse.

On the roof were the mounting bumps of two surveillance periscopes, one on the east side, one on the west side. Mounted on a short tower in the center of the roof was a large Modutone continuous sounding alarm, and a 300-watt electronic super siren.

There had to be a central station. Since there were periscope bumps on the roof, there were probably Protectors stationed around the clock in the Armory. But the surveillance cameras and other electronic devices had to be tied in with a master console in a security center.

I can't ask Sister Ruth, Camellion suddenly realized. *She would be suspicious. No telling who might be watching us. Even if I did ask her, I doubt if she would tell me.*

As if God had answered his prayer, a middle-aged woman in the front of the group looked at Sister Ruth. "I have noticed any number of security devices scattered around—cameras and whatnot. Why does the church need these devices?"

What luck! The Death Merchant could hardly believe what he had just heard. He detected a trace of a smile on Russell Linders's face and knew that the CIA man had been thinking along the same lines.

Sister Ruth studied the woman with frankly suspicious eyes. "I would say you have a keen eye for detail, Mrs. . . . Mrs. . . . ?"

"Mrs. Sarah Radak," the woman replied stiffly. "And I should. I'm a guard at the women's penitentiary at Geneva. That's in Illinois. We use similar devices. I was curious as to why your church needs them. I presume this place is not a prison."

Camellion saw almost imperceptible relaxation of muscles in Sister Ruth's face and detected her faint involuntary exhalation of relief.

Sister Ruth replied, "We have alarms for the same reason that the women's prison in Illinois has them—for protection and reasons of security. Night and day our Protectors watch the fence and the buildings from their central headquarters. As I explained earlier, the forces of Satan have already started to attack the Church of the Cosmic Reality. For that reason, the Protectors are on guard. Presently we'll pass their building."

A short man, wearing a silverbelly Stetson and a Western-style suit, asked, "I'd like to know why your church has armored cars, like those five parked outside the Armory?" He laughed, loud and deep for a man of his short stature."

"Those are not armored cars," Sister Ruth said impersonally. "They are surplus U.S. Army personnel carriers. The Protectors use them on occasion to patrol the outside of the fence, in winter when the ground is frozen."

M9 halftracks, to be exact, mused the Death Merchant. *The nice feature about the M9 is that it can be started by only a starter button. One of those babies would plow right through the chain-link fence.*

In the southwest corner of the complex, Sister Ruth pointed out four three-story buildings that housed the business offices. "From these offices the Accounting Department keeps track of the money that is taken in by the church," she explained "As you know, or should, the Church of the Cosmic Reality publishes a yearly report on how much money is received and how it is spent. In 1979 we gave twenty-four million dollars to various charities."

She led them next close to the Tower of Consolation and Heavenly Communication, and, once more in an awed tone of voice, explained that it was at the top of the tower, within "the Dome of Silence," that "God often speaks to His Oneness and His Onlyness."

Russell Linders whispered to Janet Minnick, "Chapter One: *The Epistle of the Paranoids,* by Lord Omar. 'It is written that grasshoppers always are wrong in arguments with chickens, although this is denied by Zarathud the Incorrigible, who is sometimes called Zarathud the Staunch, who was a soft-nosed hermit and Bible banger and the patron of the Season of Bureaucracy.' "

Once more, Janet put her hand over her mouth and pretended to cough. Even Carlos Martinez—a devout Catholic who did not like to hear anyone speak ill of any faith—had to smile.

Sister Ruth steered the group toward the center of New Earth Community. The Assembly Hall of the Ministers of Light was a perfectly round building made of glass blocks.

"It reminds me of a giant igloo," someone said.

In the very center of the dome, at the apex, was an American flag on a pole. Below the national flag, the emblem of the chuch fluttered in the breeze.

"There is the Cosmic Temple," Sister Ruth said proudly, waving her hand at a building which, in any contest in architecture, would have taken first prize in the Monstrosity Division. The Temple was made entirely of varnished wood, the windowless sides seventy feet high, the length two hundred and ten feet. There wasn't any steeple. The roof was of the gambrel type—a curb roof of the same section in all parts, with a lower steeper slope and an upper flatter one, so that each gable was pentagonal.

"It makes me think of an oversized barn," Camellion commented to Linders.

"Yeah, and there's no doubt tons of bullshit inside," the CIA man commented in a hard voice.

Sister Ruth was saying, "I know all of you are wondering why our central Temple is made of wood. The reason is that, unlike other religious organizations, we do not believe in building expensive houses of worship. Christ preached on hillsides. He did not have even a wooden church. Yet today, while people go hungry in this land of plenty, chruches of the various faiths are being built the costs of which are in the millions of dollars. This is not only hypocrisy but an insult to God."

"At last she said something that makes sense," muttered Janet.

Sister Ruth showed them the wooden buildings behind the Temple. Two were a hundred feet long and better than fifty feet wide. "The Reception and Training Center for new members," she said.

The other wooden building was two stories tall and built in the form of a square. On the roof was a large television antenna, half a dozen CB antennae and a high-gain shortwave antenna. Mounted on four steel poles, set in a row, scores of electrical conduits led into the southeast corner of the building. The Death Merchant didn't have to be told what this building was. Indirectly, however, he was.

Sister Ruth searched out Mrs. Radak. "That is the headquarters of the Protectors, Mrs. Radak. The central watch station that monitors all our protective devices is within that building."

Sister Ruth said, "The tour is now over, but supper is waiting for you in the tents. Those of you who wish to stay for religious services are most welcome. The service will begin at six-thirty and will be presided over by His Oneness and His Onlyness."

The tent was not as hot as one would have expected. At each end of the tent were several 36-inch circular fans mounted eight feet above the ground. Too, the welcome aroma of sizzling steaks, of roast beef, of pork roast and of fried chicken took one's mind off the sticky heat. The long wooden tables were loaded with food . . . green salads of various kinds, mashed potatoes, American and German style potato salads. Coffee, tea, milk, soft drinks, and apple cider of the soft variety were available to wash it all down.

The dinner was free, courtesy of the Church of the Cosmic Reality.

"There has to be a gimmick," Linders said, cutting his T-bone with the precision of a brain surgeon. "I'll bet my liver that everyone is supposed to cough up a big donation."

Linders was wrong. When they left the tent, numerous men and women attempted to give money to the Frimmies standing on each side of the entrance. Gently, firmly, the Frimmies refused to accept the money.

"Don't give to us," the Frimmies said sincerely. "Give to the poor."

On their way to the Temple, the Death Merchant gently nudged Linders in the ribs. "Have you figured out yet how you're going to stay alive without a liver?"

Linders merely smiled. "As Lord Homer said in *The Battle Hymn of the Aristocracy*—'Screw you with an assortment of nuts and bolts.'"

"I'm anxious to see the inside of that wooden mausoleum called a Temple," Janet said. "I hope it's air-conditioned."

"You will, in a few minutes," Camellion said. Outwardly, he didn't reveal the concern he felt over the method he would use to remain behind and stay inside the community after the tourists had left. He had to have a place that he could duck into and hide. There were at least four hundred visitors and it was impossible for the Frimmies to keep track of everyone of them. He wouldn't be missed.

So far he had found only one place, some thick hedges and bushes close to the parking lot. No good. While there weren't any lights around the bushes and hedges, they were halfway across the compound from Reverend Frimm's house, and all the way from the Protectors' headquarters. *Nope,* the Death Merchant decided. *I've got to find a place within the Temple. Or give it up for today.*

Going slowly up the wide wooden steps of the Temple— Camellion had to keep up the act and creep along—he leaned closer to Linders and whispered, "Tell Janet that once we're inside, all of us will go to the rest rooms. I want to check out the men's room. Have her pass the word to Carlos."

"Suppose there aren't any rest rooms?" Linders asked.

"Then we won't check them out, will we?"

Upon entering the church through the center door, they were instantly approached by polite Frimmies with hand-held electronic weapons detectors. Carefully, expertly, the Frimmies moved the detectors vertically up and down the bodies of Camellion and his three companions, keeping the instruments several inches from their clothes.

"Please understand," one young Frimmie woman said. "We don't mean to inconvenience anyone, but we must protect His Oneness and His Onlyness from Satan."

"Certainly. We understand," Linders responded seriously.

Finished being checked for weapons, Camellion & Co. found they were in a long foyer, as thick with people as ants on a candy bar. In the front of the vestibule were the three entrances into the nave, or the body of the Temple. Exit signs were at each end of the foyer. Frimmies were stationed not only at the three entrances into the nave but also outside each exit.

Linders addressed himself to one of the Frimmies at the center entrance. "Where are the rest rooms?"

"The exit to your right, Brother."

"The women's, too?" Janet asked.

"To the right, Sister."

With Linders cutting through the wave of people, to make way for poor old Paw, he and Camellion and Janet and Carlos moved across the foyer to the right side exit door. Once they were beyond the door, they saw that the men's room was to the right, the women's to the left.

"Listen, sweets. Meet us on the outside of the exits," Linders said to Janet just as she was about to enter the women's section.

She nodded, pushed on the door and was soon inside.

In the men's room, the stalls were on one side, urinals on the other. A row of lavatories at the end of the room. In front, to the side of the first stall, was a plain wooden door, which Camellion and his two companions were quick to notice. Because of other men coming and going, neither Camellion nor Linders nor Martinez mentioned the door or what might lie beyond it. But it was obvious: the tiny room had to be a closet.

It was not until after they had used the urinals, had washed their hands, and were walking to the hallway that the Death Merchant took the chance. He hobbled over to the ordinary wooden door, opened it and looked inside. *Right. A storage closet.* Mops and buckets. Toilet brushes and various kinds of deodorants. Boxes of Spic & Span. Several large cartons of toilet paper, paper towels and Janitor-in-a-Drum. Bottles of liquid soap for the dispensers over the lavatory sinks. A large canvas hamper.

Men hurrying out of the rest room glanced in surprise. So did others who were lingering to smoke . . . wondering why Camellion was looking inside the closet.

Linders cleverly covered Camellion's unorthodox behavior. He shook his head at a man who was taking a quick drink from a flask. "Paw's getting old." Then, to Camellion, who

82

was closing the door, "Paw, that's the wrong door." Gently he took Camellion by the arm. "Come along, Paw. This way."

"I done knowed it was the wrong door, son," Camellion cackled angrily. "You seen me close it, didn't you?"

"Yes, Paw."

They had to wait for Janet. When she finally met them outside the exit, Camellion whispered, once they were out of ear-shot of the Frimmie, "We'll sit toward the back on the right side."

The rest of them nodded, knowing Camellion had his reasons.

With the other tourists, they entered the main section of the church.

There were three sections of pews, an aisle on either side of the center section. The main Temple of the Cosmic Reality Church resembled a Christian basilica in other ways. The transept, or area in front of where the main altar would have been, contained a wooden pyramid 15 feet tall, the top of the structure a six-foot square, on which was a highback chair and a lectern. On top of the lectern was a microphone, its cable hidden inside the lectern and the pyramid.

On each side of the pyramid, arranged in a semicircle, were more rows of seats—highbacked chairs covered with red velvet. Behind the pyramid and seats—where the high altar would have been in a regular Catholic church—was a large electric organ, its pipes rising halfway to the ceiling. The choir section was to the rear of the organ.

The walls inside the Temple were similar to the outside walls—shiny with varnish of a walnut color. But there was not a single religious item inside the Temple, except for the symbol of the Cosmic Reality church: a giant swirling galaxy with the cross in the center. The emblem was embroidered on a huge tapestry hanging on the wall of the apse to the rear of the choir section.

Linders whispered to Janet, "This place reminds me of the meeting hall of the Legion of Dynamic Discord. A Discordian Society Legionnaire is one who prefers not to create his own sect."

Janet, however, was not in any mood for jocularity. She was tired from walking and, despite the air-conditioning, sticky with perspiration. Before she could speak, the sound of a gong came over the loud speakers scattered throughout the Temple.

The service was about to begin. Voices quieted down. There was almost total silence.

The men and women of the choir, moving in single file from a doorway to the left, entered and took their places. They were dressed in snow-white robes without hoods.

Again the gong sounded. This time, from a door to the right, the Ministers of Light marched in. Their hooded robes were rose-pink, a large white cross on the back. With the cowls pulled over their heads, the Ministers of Light divided into two groups, each group going to a section of seats on the side of the pyramid.

The gong sounded twice.

Preceded by six male protectors wearing white robes with black crosses over the right breast, the Reverend Hannibal Nigel Frimm entered the Temple through the right door. Six more Protectors followed behind, walking slowly. These six were female.

While the twelve Protectors arranged themselves in front and on either sides of the pyramid, His Oneness and His Onlyness walked majestically up the rear steps to the top of the structure. Clad in a bright red robe, with large white cross on the back and small white crosses on each side of his chest, Frimm walked up to the lecturn, raised his arms around over his head and shouted, "*Praise the Lord. God of hosts. God of the universe!*"

Instantly the choir, accompanied by the mighty organ, broke into song—*MARCHING TO VICTORY*, a song that Frimm himself had written.

"Marching to victory,
        Marching to victory,
            Fighting the battle well;
                We'll push old Satan,
                    We'll conquer his minions,
                        And shove them back into Hell.
    Marching to victory,
        Marching to victory . . ."

The volume of voices became a roar when the four hundred white-robed Frimmies in the middle pews joined in.

When the song was finished, Reverend Frimm began his sermon. He didn't read or quote from the Bible. Without any rhetorical preamble, he launched directly into a denunciation of "universal evil."

At once, the Death Merchant saw that Frimm, while he

wasn't a master orator, had both a powerful voice and a persuasive tongue. And the right kind of delivery, the hellfire-and-brimstone damnation style so beloved by Fundamentalists. Frimm did have a certain charisma, that kind of magnetism that appealed not to logic but to raw emotion.

The subject of Frimm's sermon was sex . . . filthy, dirty sex that, according to Frimm, "is sweeping over the United States and the entire world, a flood of immorality that is a tidal wave from Hell."

Reverend Frimm, a look of pure fury on his face, thundered, "Sex is one of Satan's main weapons." He condemned filthy book stores as dens of sin and lust. With a vengeance, he attacked *Playboy*, *Penthouse*, and other publications that he considered inspired by Hell and its fallen angels.

Frimm was especially vicious in his attack of sex researchers and others who refused to condemn homosexuality as "a moral cancer whose seeds have been scattered by Satan himself."

"Those fools who say homosexuality is not a sin are wrong and have been inspired by the Master of all Evil!" Frimm shouted. "I tell you, homosexuals are doomed! With billions of other souls, they are damned to the eternal pit of boiling lava, where there is only physical and mental pain and torment by a trillion evil spirits."

Reverend Frimm continued his vitriolic tirade, his every word dripping with vengeance and a promise of God's wrath, the force of his attack punctuated periodically by "Amen," and "Praise the Lord" from the Frimmies in the center pews.

Authors and the television industry came in for their share of hellfire and the Frimm type of castigation.

"My good friends, I swear to God I experienced culture shock the other day when I tuned in to a radio station in Colorado Springs. On this station, I heard an author being interviewed. This man actually described his book as a work that he hoped would offer help to many people. And what did his pages of slime describe? My friends, his book describes the *therapeutic* and *psychological benefits* of *masturbation!* Look for it to be on the best seller list!

"National television is a disgrace and a spit in the face of God. With few exceptions, prime time has become a plug for the worst kind of sexual openness and freedom. But the plug doesn't stop there, my friends. Oh no! Satan is far too clever. Entertainment television serves us a soft-core, *progressive* statement about love, marriage, drugs, women, blacks and homosexuals. Between the news break and the commercials, the values on prime-time television are consistently proven to be products from Hell.

"Television loves sex. Television gloats over sex. Television dwells on sex—especially sex between 'consenting adults,' who happen not to be married to each other."

"Amen!" shouted the Frimmies. "Praise the Blessed Lord!"

The Death Merchant, who never made the fatal mistake of underestimating an enemy, readily admitted to himself that Reverend Frimm had a method that, with the average listener, was unbeatable: use a few facts for a framework, then proceed to build your mansion of vindictiveness. Toss in some lies and nobody will know the difference. A perfect technique, the kind that demagogues had used for thousands of years, the best example of which, in modern times, was Adolf Hitler. The Death Merchant gave Reverend Frimm a big *C* for credit.

The son-of-a-bitch can take a grain of sand and convince people it's the size of Mount Blanc! he mused.

Reverend Frimm proceeded to other matters that were all true, saying that in the FBI category of major crimes, rape had tripled!

He raved and screamed about the "baby murderers." "Legal abortions in the U.S. have passed the magic mark. Six million! *Six million* murders. What is so horrible is that at this moment, abortions are being performed. Innocent babies are being murdered!"

"Amen!"

"Praise the Lord!"

Reverend Frimm wiped perspiration from his forehead and adjusted the mike on the lecturn. Once more he began, his voice rising for effect, his tone reaching out like a powerful magnet.

"There are fundamental lessons in life, and the first one is that when mortal men try to live without God, they either succumb to megalomania or to erotomania—or to both. Today, that is happening all over the world."

Then came the pitch, the solution, the only way to eternal salvation. Join the Church of the Cosmic Reality. Be saved and escape the final conflagration in which the world and all the universe would be destroyed.

Suddenly, Reverend Frimm stopped speaking and his body began to shake and quiver. His eyes closed. His red robe moved as if pushed by an invisible breeze. Men and women in the audience glanced at each other in puzzlement. Was Reverend Frimm ill? Being seized with some kind of fit on convulsion? However, the Frimmies were poised, their expression one of rapt expectation.

Frimm's mouth began to move, and so did his tongue. At the same time, both tongue and mouth seemed to be removed from him. He began to speak, the look on his face one of ecstasy.

> *Globu tobbi zib lottta lottta libko*
> *Bruga shabrokasgimokko labisbugozumdukahi*
> *Debrosoblihidumodia, bik do akfutibasikomu,*
> *Cillo emfoligiji mosomekondu rik brusavigotum.*
> *Kavinnjidu mi joburostivendokisimi li du elling.*

Filled with the Holy Ghost, Reverend Frimm was speaking in tongues. The spirit of Almighty God had come upon him and the Lord was speaking through him.

> *Tinankets wosibimbo lim trusilidoru fidingha,*
> *Sugiambiloza fedubingmaja op cippilosojakusi. . . .*

With the other tourists, the Death Merchant and his three companions moved up the aisle toward the foyer. The Reverend Frimm had ranted and raved for almost two hours, but his preaching had had the desired effect . . . Camellion listening with amusement to the whispered comments:

"It's the truth what he said about pornography."

"Abortion is murder."

"I tell you the queers are going to take over the country."

"The End of the World by the year two thousand? Ridiculous!"

"And speaking in tongues!"

Janet Minnick said to Linders in a low voice. "You know, there have been mystics who have fasted and prayed and have had visions.

Moving slowly along because of the men and women ahead, Linders was not impressed. "Alcoholics with the DTs see snakes, but we know the snakes don't exist. Why should we believe that people who don't eat and pray see heaven? I think they see what they want to see."

The Death Merchant leaned closer to Linders. "You and I will go to the toilet. Tell Janet that she and Carlos should go to the car and wait for you."

Finally they reached the crowded foyer. Janet and Carlos

87

Martinez continued toward one of the outside entrances while Linders and Camellion moved with other tourists toward an exit door to their left.

Camellion wasn't concerned that the Frimmie at the exit door might remember him. The young man would have to have been a computer to keep track of everyone who went into the rest rooms.

Since the service was over, no one was lingering in the rest room, smoking a final cigarette or just killing time. Camellion and Linders moved to the front of the wash room, their eyes darting about, watching the other men. Slowly they backed toward the door of the storage closet.

Linders lit a cigarette, pretending to ignore Camellion standing between him and the closet door. Camellion slowly backed toward the door. Presently he was only a few feet from the storage closet.

Four men came into the room from the hallway. Several more left. For a moment no one was in front of him and Linders. Very quickly, Camellion opened the closet door and slipped into the tiny room, gently closing the door behind him.

Camellion went to the rear of the large closet, pulled several cartons of toilet paper from the wall and got down behind them. He looked at his wristwatch—8:26. The wait would be a long, boring one. *Unless I'm discovered. If they clean the rest rooms at night, I will be.*

Twenty minutes passed. Gradually the hustle and bustle outside the closet door ceased. Finally there was quiet, except for outside noises in the distance.

At 10:42 Camellion heard the door between the men's room and the hall open. Frimmies. He could tell from the conversation that drifted to him. Two of them.

"The Master's sermon tonight was inspiring," one said.

"I agree," the other man said. "We are fortunate to be members of the church and saved as we are. When the Final Burning takes place, we will be among the ones who inherit the New Earth."

"That's true, Brother. The Master knows. God speaks to Reverend Frimm. He's God's only Messenger on earth."

The Death Merchant smiled. *To become bigger idiots, those two would have to put on weight! Their "Messenger of God" is about to become a member of the Land of the Dead."*

"I'll check the booths," the first man said. "You look in the closet."

"Why bother with the closet? No one's in there."

"Brother, that's not the point!" The speaker was angry. "We must do our duty. Have you forgotten the sin of sloth. For shame."

"Yes, you're right. I'll have to confess at the next tell-all session."

Snug behind the big boxes of toilet paper, Camellion tensed himself. Several moments later, one of the Frimmies opened the door, looked into the closet, and then closed the door.

"Everything's all right," one Frimmie said.

"Sure. Let's go."

Hearing the outside door close, the Death Merchant settled down for the long wait. Crouched in the dark, he knew the only friend he could count on was the Cosmic Lord of Death . . .

Chapter Nine

During the long, monotonous wait, the Death Merchant re-shuffled the various components of the Frimm project and arrived at the conclusion that the Central Intelligence Agency was using him to do its work.

And getting him to do it for free!

Camellion didn't really blame Grojean and the other spooks in Covert Action. It wasn't as if the DD/P and his Q-boys had murdered Everett Padden. The Deputy Director of Plans had only taken advantage of Padden's death, Camellion basing his conclusion on the speed with which Grojean had agreed to help, when Camellion had contacted him to ask if the Agency could spare a "street man" to do some off-the-record moonlighting. Grojean had been all cooperation. Why, certainly! It just so happened that a top man—Russel Linders—was vacationing in the Southwest. Yeah, sure! Grojean was positive that Linders would be glad to help—for a price.

Now, in retrospect, Camellion wondered how Grojean could have been so positive.

There was George McAulay II. When Camellion had phoned him to ask if he had heard of Linders and if he thought he was dependable, McAulay II had been too eager. According to George, Linders was three times better than the whole Russian Army. There had been that subtle inflection and slight hesitation in George's voice, indicating to Camellion that George, while he wasn't lying, was deliberately overemphasizing Linders's capabilities.

Why? Camellion knew McAulay the way he knew the palm of his right hand. The answer was not at all complex. McAulay was only following orders.

It wasn't difficult for Camellion to put together what was no longer a puzzle. The Company had been keeping tabs on Frimm and the Church of the Cosmic Reality. The Moonies, the Children of Jesus, the Hare Krishnas and all the other cults were not a danger to national security. It was different with the Frimmies. They could be a definite threat to the internal security of the nation.

When Padden had been murdered—probably Montroy, too—the Agency had seen its opportunity. *That's how Grojean knew that Padden was one of my best friends—through its Domestic Operations Division.* When Padden had been murdered, Grojean had assumed that Camellion would avenge his murder and had acted accordingly.

Russell Linders wasn't on vacation. Linders was an officer in the Domestic Operations Division and was on assignment. *He had to be.* How else could Linders have obtained the special equipment the Death Merchant needed? From a "friend," Linders had said. *Bunk! Friends* don't have Mertex electric timers lying around, or tiny blocks and small cylinders of cyclonite, the most powerful of military explosives. Nor do "friends" instantly come up with capsules of DM—Adamsite, vomiting gas—and nose filters that could serve as a gas mask.

The "friend" was Linders's backup and supply depot. The Agency probably had four or five agents working with Linders.

The Death Merchant licked his lips and smiled. The cover was Grojean's way of being devious, of obtaining Camellion's services without paying him his usual fee of a hundred grand. *So be it. Let Grojean have his little joke and think he's fooling me.*

Once more, Camellion went over the plan. It would take him 15 minutes to get to Reverend Frimm's house, perhaps longer. He'd have to keep close to the buildings and avoid surveillance cameras, motion detectors and infrared beam-breakers. But before he moved toward Frimm, he would have to plant the cyclonite at the base of the four steel poles at the southeast corner of the Protectors' headquarters building. *I had better time the explosions to go off after twenty minutes,* he thought. *I can't go into Frimm's house until after the blast.*

The rest of the plan was simple but extremly dangerous. Gun the Protectors around Frimm. Put a bullet into His Oneness and His Onlyness. Then smash through the fence with one of the M9 Personnel Carriers. With the cameras and alarm devices cut off from the central watch station in the Protectors' building, getting to the M9s would not be all that difficult. In the first place, there would be a lot of confusion; in the second, there was a minimum of outside lighting within

New Earth Community. Frimm and his leadership had sacrificed electric power for outside lighting in preference for the security devices—a big mistake.

Firearms was another problem, a minor one. Roving Frimmie guards had plenty of automatic weapons.

Killing Reverend Frimm was the only answer. A martyr? To whom? Sure, to the hundreds of thousands of Frimmies. But it would be amusing to see how they were going to explain his murder by an "Agent of Satan" when the Lord was supposedly giving him Divine protection, so that he could be around at the end of the world!

The nation's press would call it murder. And there would be a new cry from the liberals for gun control.

The Death Merchant wasn't concerned about the morality of terminating Reverend Frimm. Morality, like time and eternity, was another unreality that man had created in his avoidance of death, of a condition of no-future. There wasn't any *good* or *bad*, only illusion.

Yet it was necessary for the race to believe in these non-realities, necessary because human beings needed an identity in space and time. It was not for the world to know—*not yet!*—that beyond what it called space and time was a much deeper reality, and that all life in the universe was contained in One Mind, beside which nothing could exist . . . One Mind, which is without beginning, is unborn and indestructible.

Camellion moved from behind the two cartons of toilet paper, went to the closet door and listened. Silence. He couldn't have any light leaking from the closet. To seal the half-inch space between the floor and the bottom of the door, he shoved one of the cartons in front of the door and stuffed the remaining five-inch space with a handkerchief, one side of his mind thinking about man's illusion of time.

Nature does not advance in a line—it happens simultaneously, everywhere-at-once. And because nature does not proceed in a line, it does not proceed in time, but has the whole of its existence simultaneously, and that is the nature of Eternity.

Actually, Camellion thought, *the whole notion of succession, of one "thing" succeeding another "thing" in time, depends entirely and directly upon our precesses of memory, for it is quite obvious that without memory we would have absolutely no idea of time, either of the past or of the future. Okay. The question, then, is whether memory reports a real phenom-*

*enon which we call time, or whether memory creates an illu-
sion of time. Yet in remembering any "past event," we are not
really aware of the actual past at all. I remember what I ate in
the tent hours ago, but this memory won't let me see the meal,
or touch it, or taste it. The truth is, we are never aware of any
actual past at all, but rather only dim mental images of the
past, and those pictures exist only as present experience.*

*The same holds for the "future" as well, for any thought of
tomorrow is nonetheless a present thought. Inescapably, we
know the "past" and "future" only in the present and as part
of the present. The only time we are ever aware of is now.
Mind is always now. There is really no before and no after for
the mind. There is only a now, this instant. The past is literally nothing but a memory and the future nothing but an expectation, with both memory and expectation being a present
fact. Think of the past—that is a present act. Anticipate the
future—also a present act. All done with the mind—a state of
ever-present non-dual awareness wherein the observer is the
observed! The mind and the now-moment, the only true reality for man. . . . But this knowledge won't help me now. The
will to live is the blind panic of not having a future, the panic
that is death, but not having a future doesn't appeal to me.
Call it what you will, dead is still dead. . . .*

Camellion flipped the light switch by the side of the door
and flooded the closet with light. Calmly he went to work. He
unscrewed the handle of the cane and turned the cane upside-
down. Two plastic cylinders, along with five gray cylinders of
a putty-like material, fell to the tiled floor. The five gray cylinders, each slightly less than half an inch in diameter, were
solid cyclonite.

In one plastic cylinder were twelve large capsules of DM
gas and a K17 nose filter. The second hollow cylinder was
filled with several lengths of fishline, three blasting caps, and
three Mertex timers, which were powered by tiny Denoid bat-
teries.

The Death Merchant screwed the handle back onto the
cane, after which he rolled the five tubes of cyclonite into a
ball and then shoved one of the caps into the ball. He attached
the two lengths of wire from the end of the cap to the terminals on the timer and shoved the prongs of the timer into the
ball of high explosive. He put the ball into the left pocket of
his pants, the DM gas capsules into the right.

The K17 nose filter was actually a tiny gas mask, effective
only against those gases that, to do damage, had to be inhaled.

The filter-mask consisted of two small tubes of Pyrene plastic, each about the length and diameter of a filter on the average cigarette. The two tubes were connected by a plastic clip shaped like a T, the vertical part of the T clipping onto the lower part of the nose between the nostrils and the upper lip. He gently shoved each tube into a nostril, carefully attached the clip, clamped his mouth shut and inhaled deeply, smelling a faint odor that resembled cinnamon. The mask worked.

Turning his attention once more to the cane, he pulled the rubber tip from the bottom and, holding the wood tightly in his right hand, while his left hand held the handle, he unscrewed the bottom four inches and pulled off the hollow "cap." The last three inches of the cane was now a plastic "ice-pick."

Camellion consulted his wristwatch—three o'clock on the nose.

All right, you damn fool. Go out there and do it. The odds are in your favor. But only slightly.

He switched off the light in the closet, moved the carton from the door, picked up the handkerchief, opened the door and crept out into the darkened washroom. Like a thief in the night, he moved to the hallway door, paused, listened for a moment, then moved out into the hall, his eyes rapidly adjusting to the blackness. There might be Protectors stationed in the dark Temple, but he didn't think there were. He couldn't take the chance that the Temple was empty. Keeping to the wall, he moved to the exit door. He listened, heard nothing, opened the door and steped into the foyer. Silence. And not a single light. Protectors sitting in the dark? Possible but not very likely.

Within ten minutes, the Death Merchant had crept down the center aisle, had passed the wooden pyramid, and was approaching the side door of the room to his left. He soon found that the anteroon was used for the storage of robes. There were no windows, only a single door to the rear wall. Beyond the door, thirty feet to the north, was the south side of the Protectors' headquarters building.

A piece of cake? Maybe . . .

He tried the handle of the door. Locked. Apparently Reverend Frimm didn't want his flock of fools to come into the Temple unless he was present.

He sat down flat on the floor, and moved the sharp point at the bottom of the cane alond the inside edge of the sole of his left foot. Presently, enough of the sole had opened for him to insert a finger and pull outward on the strip of hard leather. The sole opened like a trap door, with the hinge in front of the heel. There were six carbon steel lockpicks in the sole. Camellion chose a No. 4, and when it failed to click the double tumblers into place, he chose a No. 5 and accomplished the job in less than three minutes. He placed the lockpicks in the sole, snapped the sole into place, picked up the cane, opened the door and looked out into the night. The sound of crickets. The cool night breeze. A small light, attached to the southeast corner of the Protectors' building, was the only light visible. It was the same corner that contained the steel poles and the conduits. It would be a risk, but a slight one. To set the timer and place the ball of explosive in position wouldn't take more than ten seconds. The next step, then, would be to proceed to Frimm's house and make him a corpse. *But first, weapons would have to be obtained!*

Camellion opened the door wider and studied the Protectors' building. Several lights burned toward the center of the second floor. Another light was on in the southeast corner room on the second story—no doubt the monitoring station. A third light was on in a room on the first floor, in the southwest corner of the building.

He looked up and down the space between the rear of the Temple and the side of the Protectors' building. No one in sight. The area was as empty as a Frimmie's mind.

Camellion slipped outside, closed the door and, in the dim light cast by the bulb at the southeast corner of the Protectors' building, hurried toward the four steel poles supporting the mass of cables from TV cameras and the power lines that supplied other detection devices scattered throughout New Earth Community.

Reaching the steel poles, he took the ball of cyclonite from his pocket, carefully turned the pointer-knob of the timer to 25-M and placed the ball between the two inner poles. He straightened up, turned and started to cross the space, to go the the east side of the Temple. At that moment, two Protectors came from around the southwest corner of the Protectors' building and saw him.

"Hey you—stop!" one Protector yelled.

The other guard turned on a hand-held, Q-Beam power-pack spotlight and flashed the bright beam on Camellion, who instantly hunched over and went into his old man act—careful not to lean too heavily on the cane. He didn't want to break off the point.

"What's that you said?" he called back, his voice a perfect imitation of a man closer to death than to life.

"Stay where you are, Brother!" one guard called angrily.

"Why sure," cackled Camellion. "If you fellas want me to."

The two Protectors, clad in berets, green fatigues and Vietnam boots, advanced on Camellion. Yet they didn't suspect him of being an outsider—*or they would have been unslinging their M-16s or pulling sidearms.*

The instant the two Protectors reached him, Camellion cackled, "Either one of you fellas seen my Caroline?" He peered stupidly at the two men as he studied them. Both were in their early twenties. Both wore nameplates over their right breast pockets. The goof with the long sideburns and a mouth like a fish was named Joseph Bayber. The more muscular one was Edward Simms.

Simms and Bayber glanced at each other. Oviously this old Brother was senile. If so, why was he still within the Community. He should have been living at the Haven for the Aged Righteous in Spencer, Iowa.

"Brother, who is Caroline, your wife?" Simms asked in a gentle voice.

"My pet cobra, you moron!" snapped Camellion in his normal voice.

The expressions of astonishment were not fully born on the faces of Simms and Bayber when Camellion attacked with a double strike, his movements a blur.

His left leg came up in a lightning *mae geri kekomi* front thrust kick, the side of his foot striking Simm's chin with such brute force that it was a wonder the man wasn't lifted right out of his combat boots. At the same time that Simm's mandible was breaking and the tip of his tongue was being cut off by his teeth, Camellion's cane was stabbing into the solar plexus of a dumbfounded Bayber. The terrific force of the blow was enough to make the man fall into unconsciousness from shock to his nervous system. As it turned out, the three inches of plastic "ice pick" in the tip of the cane poked through the cloth and flesh and carried the cane halfway through Bayber's body. He sagged with the cane protruding from his body. Simms, unconscious from the karate kick and with blood pouring out of his mouth, fell beside him.

Remarkably spry for a "senior citizen," Camellion pulled the M-16 from underneath Bayber's body, then removed the Colt .45 auto-pistol from the man's belt holster. Camellion jammed the Colt into his own belt and just as quickly took the

.45 autoloader from Simms's holster, shoving it next to the one already in his belt. He was picking up the M-16 when he heard several windows being pushed open in the southeast corner of the Protectors' building.

In the thin slice of a second, Camellion knew his plan had fallen apart. But there wasn't anything he could do about it. All that was left now was save his own life and, somehow, get to the personnel carriers. He threw himself to the right, raised the M-16, switched off the safety, hoped the firing chamber contained a cartridge, and fired by intuitive sixth sense, moving the weapon in a slight left-to-right arc, his finger continuing to pull the trigger of the M-16.

The first sharp cracks of Camellion's rifle mingled into the explosions of another M-16 and a deadly Gwinn Bushmaster auto-pistol* on full automatic fire. Enemy slugs stabbed into the ground only feet from where Camellion had been standing—*zip, zip, zip!* Spurts of dirt even kicked up within inches of his left foot.

His own projectiles broke glass and cut into the two Protectors standing in the windows. Only a minute earlier, one of the three Protectors had happened to look out a window and saw the Death Merchant slamming out Simms and Bayber. While one guard had telephoned the night watch downstairs, the other two had grabbed rifles, pushed out the closed windows and tried for their brief moment of glory. Now they were less than if they had never been born. One man was wedged sideways in the narrow window, most of his face shot away. The second would-be hallelujah hero lay on the floor, stone dead, blood spurting from his mouth and throat.

Brother Harley Rickson, the third Protector, was on the north side of the monitoring room, down on his knees and

*Manufactured by Gwinn Firearms, of Rochester, New Hampshire, and named after the South American snake which herpetologists call *Lachesis muta*, but which is commonly called the Bushmaster. A pit viper, the Bushmaster, about 12-feet long, is very aggressive and is indeed master of the bush country. He'll chase anything that ventures into his domain.

The Gwinn Bushmaster is said to be the most powerful pistol in the world. The weapon—a kind of hybrid between our own M-16 and the Soviet Union's AK-47—fires the 5.56mm or .223 Remington cartridge. Assuming that the Gwinn ammo carries the 55-grain bullet, it would have a muzzle energy of 1128.6 foot-pounds. On the basis of foot-pounds, that puts it in about the same category as the .44 Auto Mag, i.e. shot for shot.)

frantically pressing the emergency button that flashed loud beeps not only to the watch room downstairs and the beepers on the belts of every Protector on patrol, but also to Elmer Peek, the director of overall security, Brother Wilbur Sessons, the Commander of the Protectors, and Frimm himself.

The Death Merchant turned to the south and darted to the north-east corner of the Temple, his momentum almost carrying him straight into three teams of Protectors, who were rushing toward the location of the earlier gunfire.

The six men were as surprised as Camellion, but much slower in their movements. Camellion didn't give them a chance to recover from their bewilderment. He used a *yoko geri keag* left-legged snap-kick to crack the sternum and break several ribs of one startled guard. With a cry of pain, the man staggered back and fell to his left side. Camellion synchronized the kick with a right-handed, four-finger, Nukite spear strike-stab to the right side of the neck of a Protector trying to get behind him. With the M-16 barrel, he attempted to jab a third guard in the stomach. In order to conserve ammo, he didn't want to shoot the man unless he had to. He had to! The man bent over, pulled in his stomach, stepped back and dodged the blow. Camellion pulled the trigger, the M-16 cracked and the spitzer-shaped projectile hit Brother Kigley just above the belt buckle. The impact knocked him off balance against Brother Bertram Higgins, who had pulled a 9mm Colt Commander autoloader and was trying to get close enough to Camellion to swing the barrel against the side of his head.

Simultaneously with Camellion's killing Kigley, he also ducked an intended blow from Brother Dale Bain—a right-handed chop aimed at the bridge of Camellion's nose—and felt both hands of Brother David Cushing, the sixth Protector, clamp around the M-16. At the same time, Cushing tried a Cos-do roundhouse kick to Camellion's stomach.

Ducking the chop from Bain, the Death Merchant used a high fist punch against Brother Bain, the blow landing with a loud thud between Bain's eyes. Dazed, the front of his head exploding with pain, Bain sagged to the ground.

Feeling Cushing jerk the M-16 from his hands, Camellion slammed a right at Cushing, but he had gotten off to a late start and missed when the Protector ducked. Brother Bain, only half-conscious, tried to stagger to his feet, but Camellion broke his neck with a kick to the side of the neck.

Brother Higgins now saw his chance. He didn't know who

or what Camellion was. He couldn't even be sure that he was elderly. Higgins did know that whoever the strange man was—one or young—he could fight with a speed and deadliness that was incredible. Higgins, having no intention of facing Camellion from the front, darted to the Death Merchant's right, in an effort to get behind him.

During those few moments, Brother Cushing did his best to raise the M-16 and use it like a golf club against the side of Camellion's head. Camellion blocked the swinging rifle with his left forearm and used a bottom heel kick that turned Brother Cushing's groin into mush. With a choked cry of excruciating pain, Cushing threw up his arms and fell backward. He was sinking into merciful unconsciousness as the Death Merchant turned his attention to Brother Higgins, who was swinging the butt of the Colt Commander toward the right side of Camellion's head.

"Fool!" hissed Camellion. He turned slightly to the right and wondered if he would live to see the sunrise. His left hand shot out and upward, his fingers wrapping around Higgin's right wrist when the automatic was only inches from his head. As Camellion pushed the arm and Colt upward, he also jerked Higgins toward him and let him have a right elbow in the stomach, the battering ram blow wrapping Higgins's stomach around his backbone. The Colt Commander fell from his hand. Again Camellion pulled on the wrist. Between the tug and the pain in his gut, Higgins doubled over. Once more Camellion powed him with a *hiji* elbow strike, this time in the back of the neck. Higgins went down . . . out cold.

Camellion didn't reach for the Colt Commander on the ground. Knowing he would never live long enough to touch the weapon, he raised his arms above his head. Ten feet in front of him were three Protectors with M-16s pointed at him. Four more were to his left. He glanced over his shoulder—seven more. Camellion sighed. The only reason he was alive was because the Protectors wanted him to remain alive. You can't question a dead man.

The fourteen Protectors advanced on the Death Merchant. . . .

Chapter Ten

"*Heh, heh, heh,*" Camellion sniggered. It appears to me you young 'uns need more exercise. I ain't never seen such weaklings."

He didn't resist as one Protector, staring at him in awe and fear, pulled the two auto-pistols from his belt, then proceeded to search him pocket by pocket. Camellion didn't resist because he couldn't. There were Protectors behind him, one man pressing the muzzle of an autoloader against the base of his skull, the other two keeping the muzzles of their Colts jammed into his sides. Other Protectors were helping the security men Camellion had demolished, except Brother Kigley, who was dead.

Surrounding Camellion on all sides, the Protectors marched him to the Protectors' Headquarters Building, Camellion having noticed on the way that the first two security men he had met had already been picked up from the ground and were gone.

Other than the Protectors, there were three other men in the room, which was on the first floor, toward the center of the building. Camellion recognized only Hannibal Frimm, who stood with folded arms, regarding the Death Merchant with cold, solemn eyes. Camellion could see that Frimm, who wore house slippers, had thrown on a red robe over bathrobe and pajamas.

"This is all we found on him, Commander," the Protector who had searched Camellion said. He handed Wilbur Sessons a white handkerchief, the 12 DM gas capsules, and the K17 nose filter, which the Protector had pulled from Camellion's nose.

Sessons studied the capsules and the nose filter for several seconds, then proved he was far from stupid by saying, "They're some kind of gas." He glanced at Camellion briefly, hate in his eyes. He then turned to Reverend Frimm, who continued to regard Camellion with analytical eyes. "And this is some kind of miniature gas mask, Your Oneness. This man came here to assassinate you, but the Lord prevailed against the Emperor of Hell."

"I can't be killed. I can't die," Reverend Frimm said with great dignity. "It is I who will rule over the New Earth and, before that great day comes, the United States."

There were murmurs of agreement from the serveral dozen Protectors in the large room, which Camellion surmised to be a recreation area.

"This man here—Frimm pointed at Camellion—"is an agent of Satan and is possessed by one of the Evil One's lieutenants."

He motioned with one hand. A Protector hurriedly placed a chair in the center of the room. Several more security men shoved the Death Merchant across the room and pushed him down on the chair, after which most of the Protectors, Reverend Frimm and the two other men, dressed in bathrobes, formed a circle around him.

At least I'm the center of attention! Camellion thought grimly.

At the moment, his only consolation, small as it might be, was that in less than eight minutes the ball of cyclonite would explode.

Even that tiny pleasure went up in smoke, taken from him by Commander Sessons, who said in an even voice, "We discovered the plastic explosives you planted by the terminal inlets. Brother Simms revived long enough to tell us that he and Brother Bayber first spotted you by the terminals. Deducing the rest was not difficult."

"We don't have time for all this now," Brother Peek said nervously. "The Police watching outside the main gate heard the rifle fire."

"We've time enough," Sessons said with a tiny smile that infuriated the Death Merchant, who felt instinctively that Sessons was the sort of joker who enjoyed seeing others suffer. A tall figure and very muscular, the man looked a bit gaunt because of high, deeply tanned cheekbones, but his movements were like a dancer's, quick and sure.

Sessons was saying, "The Community has the same legal status as a private home. The state or sheriff's police can't come in without a search warrant. You know that, Brother."

"And you know there isn't any need to recite the law to

me," Peek responded resentfully. "You also know that if we don't let the police in, they'll suspect we have something to hide."

"Enough!" Frimm sounded like God commanding the sun to shine. "We must let the police into the Community. Have the four corpses been disposed of and the injured men taken to the hospital?"

"The bodies are in the Dissolving Room," Sessions rasped. "The men this devil-man wounded"—he glared fiercely at Camellion—"are in the hospital. The glass from the two corner windows had been cleaned both on the outside and the inside of the Monitor Room. The police won't find a drop of blood. But there's no reason we have to let the police in any of the buildings. We—" Sessions mouth snapped shut the instant Reverend Frimm raised his hand and advanced on the Death Merchant. He stopped six feet from the Death Merchant and stared down at him. Camellion stared right back.

Frimm folded his hands, extended them away from his body, closed his eyes, tilted back his head and his lips moved in silent prayer. After a quarter of a minute, he opened his eyes, moved several steps to Camellion and thundered in a deep, solemn voice, "Spirit of Evil, I, the Messenger of God on Earth, command you to speak. Identify yourself. I, Frimm, command you. I—"

The Death Merchant wanted to laugh, but felt that, given the gravity of the situation, he shouldn't. During the very short time he had been in the building, he had analyzed not only the Protectors but the two other men and Reverend Frimm. The Protectors actually regarded Frimm as some kind of gold-plated god. *Religious fanatics, every one of them! So damned gullible they'd ask Frimm for permission to commit suicide!*

He read Peek differently. *He's intelligent. I think he considers Frimm nothing more than a con artist who's fallen victim to his own con game.*

Commander Sessions? *Power. He's interested only in power. He knows what I know—that Frimm is insane!*

"—the Messenger of God on earth, command you to speak, demon. I command you in the name of Almighty God."

"I am Abraxas, the Prime Minister of the Cult of Discordianism," Camellion replied in a voice even deeper than Frimms. "I will make thee the recipient of a chain letter. Within the next two weeks, you will receive a thousand pounds of chains."

Reverend Frimm drew back, with a look that was half-victorious and half-confused. God had given him great power, but who was Abraxas? There wasn't any Abraxas! The demon within the man was lying.

Brother Peek seemed surprised. Commander Sessons was enraged, finding it difficult to control himself. The Death Merchant was playing the game Frimm's way and Sessons didn't like it.

Before the infuriated Sessons could speak. Camellion cut loose with high-pitched maniacal laughter, hoping that the Protector with the .45 Colt pressed against the back of his head wouldn't become nervous and scramble his brains with a bullet.

Camellion twisted his mouth to resemble a rabbit's, crossed his eyes and yelled, "Onward Christian soldiers, onward Buddhist priests, onward Fruits of Islam, fight till you're deceased. Fight your little battles, join in thickest fray, for the Greater Glory, of Dis-cord-i-a."

Some of the Protectors stepped back in fear, convinced that they were facing a demon. One idiot closed his eyes and began to pray.

"Demon!" shouted Frimm. "We will exorcise this old man and free him from your evil. But before we chase you back to Hell, oh deeply wicked fallen angel, we will force you to reveal Satan's master plan against us!"

Frimm shook with emotion, for this was his moment of triumph. He had forced one of the hierarchy of Hades to reveal himself, and on the first try, too. More proof to Frimm that he was God's chosen spokesman on earth.

"He's not got any demon in him," burst out Sessons, pointing a finger at Camellion. "He's not even old. It's a rubber mask he's wearing, or some kind of makeup. I'll prove it."

He raced to the side of the Death Merchant, motioned for the Protector with the Colt to move back and, with a sideways smirk on his face, hooked a thumb under Camellion's chin and tried to find the edge of the rubber. Somewhat surprised, he tugged at Camellion's cheek with thumb and forefingers, pulling at the flesh, stretching the skin. But there wasn't any rubber mask. Nor was there any way he could loosen the mastoplastic putty, which shaped Camellion's features, or remove the shades and tints of the flesh—not without the proper chemicals. Even then, the job would have taken several hours.

Frustrated in his efforts, Wilbur Sessons stepped back from

Camellion and glared at him, his large hands knotting into fists.

The Death Merchant twisted his face the way a playful chimpanzee would and screeched, "The opposite of the breeze of wisdom is the wind of insanity. The opposite of the breeze of integrity is the wind of arrogance. The opposite of the breeze of beauty is the wind of outrage. Alas, think ye of the Curse of Grayface."

Utterly thwarted, Sessions turned to a solemn Reverend Frimm, who had taken a large gold cross from his bathrobe and was holding it in his left hand, extended outward toward Camellion.

"We can make him talk," Sessions snarled. "We can take him downstairs and beat the devil out of him."

"He that plants too quickly will reap a poor harvest," Frimm said with a touch of annoyance. "Our captive is controlled by Satan. The Master of Hell would not let him feel pain, or let him die if you beat him. You must remember that it is not this poor old man we are fighting, but Satan himself. In order to make the devil talk and expel him, we must first condition the mind of the old man."

Frimm paused at the buzzing of the walkie-talkie in the pocket of Session's bathrobe. Sessions pulled out the W-T, and switched it to full volume so that the others could hear.

"Commander Sessions. Report."

"This is Brother Mercer at the main gate." The man sounded nervous. "The police are here and want to come in. They have a search warrant."

Alarm flashed over the faces of Peek and Sessions.

"They had the warrant made out in advance," Peek said sourly, his brows knitting into an unbroken line above the bridge of his nose. "I don't like that. It means they could force their way in here almost any time they want to."

Reverend Frimm, however, wasn't the least bit disturbed as he took the walkie-talkie from Sessions and pushed the talk button. He lowered the cross in his other hand.

"Brother Mercer, this is Reverend Frimm. Tell the police I shall come to the gate and meet them. I shall personally conduct them through the Community. Remember the Final Burning."

"Yes, Master. The Day of the Final Burning."

Frimm switched off the walkie-talkie and handed the set back to Commander Sessions. "Take the demon-man below and place him in one of the Cells of Attrition," Frimm said.

"Give him the full-cycle treatment. We'll question him in the afternoon. By then the treatment will have weakened the demon's hold on his mind."

"I'll personally take him below." Sesson's former rage had evaporated into eagerness and his eyes glinted with anticipation. "I'll see that he's given the full electronic treatment."

So! It's got to do with electronics! But if that big pig-faced commander had his way, the treatment would be with fists! I've got to get out of this in a hurry, or I'll have breakfast in hell!

"No, Brother. You will come with me," Frimm ordered firmly. "Every time the authorities have come to New Earth Community, I have met them personally, and, as Commander of the Protectors, have always driven the car. If you're not with me now, the police might wonder why." Frimm motioned to the Protectors around Camellion. "Take the demon-possessed man below. Keep your guns trained on him until he's locked in a cell."

"Brother Walles, you take charge," Sessons said stiffly.

Colts .45s pressed against his head and back, Camellion was marched into the next room—an office with several metal desks, filing cabinets, padded armchairs, and a north wall that was one solid bookcase filled with books on the various aspects of security.

There was a barometer—the box-type on a metal base—on the corner of one desk. Brother Walles went over to the desk and turned the small metal knob in the center of the instrument's circular glass face, the knob of the silver pointer that one turned to line up with the red pressure needle of the device.

Silently and immediately, the center portion of the bookcase swung open to reveal an entrance the height and width of a door.

Brother Walles, a thin, bearded man wearing old-fashioned steel spectacles, prodded Camellion in the small of the back with his Colt.

"Keep your hands on your head. Go inside and stand with your face against the wall," the Protector said fiercely. "I know what you are thinking, demon-man. Don't try it. This old man's flesh and blood body can't withstand a .45 bullet. We'll kill him if we have to."

The Death Merchant shrieked with laughter and walked through the opening, saying, "Mr. Momomoto, the Japanese who can swallow his nose is a fake. It has been discovered by the Poee priests of Praw that Mr. Momomoto is really an armadillo."

When the bookcase had swung open, it automatically turned on a light in the space forward, and Camellion, walking to the rear wall, saw that he was in an elevator. Brother Walles and two other Protectors had kept pace with him, their auto-pistols pressed against his head and back. Behind them came six more Protectors, all with weapons drawn. The last man in the car closed the steel accordion-style door and pushed down on the control handle. The car dropped rapidly, Camellion counting the seconds. By the time the elevator stopped, he estimated they had descended between 30 and 35 feet.

The man who had operated the elevator opened the accordion door and got out with five of the other Protectors, all six waiting until Walles and the other two Protectors had backed Camellion out of the car and told him to turn around.

Just before he turned around, Camellion noticed a wooden door to his left, a few feet from the elevator shaft. After he turned, he saw that he and his keepers were in a brightly lighted low room, with walls and ceiling and floor constructed of concrete blocks. Across the bare room, to the south, was a steel door. A tiny speaker was set on a brace above the door.

"Move to that door, sinner possessed of a demon," Walles ordered. "If you make any quick movements, we'll kill you."

The Death Merchant moved over to the door, and Walles made him stand with his nose pressed against the concrete-block wall while another man pressed a button in the steel door.

A voice called out from a tiny speaker above the door, "Give the phrase and code number of the day."

"'The Day of the Final Burning,'" said the man who had pressed the button "Nine. Six. Four. Three. Six."

The electric lock on the door clicked and the Protector pushed it open. Still covered by three Colt .45s, the Death Merchant was pushed inside.

Since Reverend Frimm had mentioned "Cells of Attrition," Camellion wasn't surprised to find himself in an area that resembled the solitary confinement section of a penitentiary. A metal table stood just beyond the door. Ordinary wooden doors were situated to the left and the right of the table. There was a large cross, painted in white, on the door to the left. On the right door hung a red-and-white metal sign—DANGER. Other than those two wooden doors, the long room was nothing more than an 85-foot-long corridor six cells on each side. The only things out of place were the size of the cells and the doors in front of each. The cells were extra-large while the doors resembled the thick insulated doors of old-fashioned ice-boxes. Even the handles were of the pushdown latch type.

Soundproof, Camellion thought. *Each cell is soundproof.*

The Protector sitting at the table got up and stared at the Death Merchant. He had a head of hair that reminded Camellion of a used Brillo pad.

"Brothers, who is this old guy?" the man asked.

"He is possessed of Satan," Walles said dramatically. "He's killed four of the Righteous Protectors and because of him the state police are here. But it's nothing to worry about; the Master has gone out to meet the police. There's no danger from them. The Master wants this demon-possessed old man confined down here. This afternoon, he will chase the devil from the old fool."

The eyes of Brother Gamsen, the guard on duty, widened in terror.

"My God!" he stared at the Death Merchant, sweat glistening in the deep channels of his face. "Demon-possessed. But will a cell hold such a man?"

"There's no danger," Walles reassured Brother Gamsen. "An evil spirit can triple the strength of the creature it possesses. But it can't muster the strength to break down steel walls. Remember, Brother, what the master has taught us: an evil spirit is limited in this world of matter. Come, we are wasting time."

Brother Walles and three other Protectors ushered the Death Merchant to the third cell to the left. Camellion noticed several rows of colored buttons on the wall to the right of the door, the controls to whatever horror would happen inside the cells.

One of the Protectors opened the door, which was a foot and a half thick and, like the walls of the cell, heavily padded.

"Inside, devil-man!" Brother Walles pushed Camellion inside the dark cell. The door shut with a thud. Total silence. Total blackness.

Camellion thought of the four jeeps he had seen parked to one side of the main entrance of the Headquarters Building and wondered what lay behind the door marked DANGER. *And where is the surveillance camera?*

Without any warning, Camellion was suddenly surrounded by hundreds of squealing rats! The walls, the floor, the ceiling, everywhere!—even suspended in the air—were rats, dirty, slimy rats with long tails, some of them only inches from his face. Instinctively, Camellion ducked, throwing up one of his arms which went right through the seemingly "solid" rodents. *It figures! Holography!*

The Death Merchant ignored the rats, moved through them and, in the dim light cast by the hundreds of holographic images, created by sophisticated laser technology, scanned the padded cell for the television camera. He found it in the northwest corner of the cell, a 14K with a wide-angle lens. Amid the angry snarling of the rats, coming from scores of speakers hidden behind the semi-solid padding, Camellion jumped up and jerked the power cable from the back of the camera. Let the halfwitted Protector at the monitoring screen wonder what had happened to the camera. With the state police snooping around upstairs, all the monitors were probably shut off and hidden away. If they weren't, it wasn't likely that anyone would come down to the cells to investigate—*at least not for the next fifteen minutes.*

As suddenly as the rats had appeared, they vanished. In their place were hundreds of squirming snakes—rattlers, the deadly green mamba, huge writhing pythons and boa constrictors . . . every reptile appearing solid and three-dimensional.

Camellion also noticed a strange alien crawling around inside his head, deep within the chambers of his mind, as though a giant maggot were nibbling at his brain cells. With the weird sensation was an intense feeling of anxiety and the beginning of spatial disorientation.

Ultrasonics! The cell is being bombarded with ultrahigh-frequency sound. I'll have to work fast.

Camellion sat down on the padded floor and dug his thumbnail into the heel on his right shoe, at the junction where the top of the heel met the bottom of the sole. The heel finally opened. Camellion took four ounces of cyclonite, two Mertex timers, and two blasting caps from the hollowed heel. He closed the heel, went to work on the left shoe and, at length, took the same number of items from the left heel.

He broke one square of explosive in half, and as he worked, attaching caps and timers to the two halves of cyclonite, he fought the feelings of panic and anxiety caused by the ultrasonic sound waves boring into his brain and the increasing disorientation of his position in space. Like all holier-than-thou fanatics, Frimm knew how to use fear. It was easy to see how a Frimmie, already a religious neurotic, could easily be driven insane or made to confess anything, by being confined in one of the Cells of Attrition. The Spanish and the Italian Inquisitions, and the witch-hunters that had been the curse of Europe for hundreds of years, had torn people apart on the rack to make them confess. Not His Oneness and His Onlyness. Frimm used mental torture.

His senses reeling, snakes crawling all around him, the Death Merchant completed the two bombs and dropped them in his pocket. He picked up the second block of cyclonite and pinched off a piece of explosive the size of his fingernail and no more than a half-inch thick. He attached the blasting cap to the timer and pushed timer and cap onto the smidgen of explosive. He then pasted timer, cap and explosive against the outer edge of the door, at about the same height of the pushdown latch on the opposite side. The remainder of the cyclonite block he made into a bomb and placed in his left pocket.

The problem now was concussion. The concussion from an explosion in a soundproofed room would be terrific. Logically, there wasn't anything to worry about. The only way to do it was just to do it and hope for the best. There wasn't any other way.

He was about to turn the knob of the timer when the snakes vanished and were replaced by demons—short devils, tall devils, fat and thin devils . . . red, black, green, blue, and orange devils . . . complete with horns and cloven hooves . . . devils that danced and grinned and reached out for him. And with the dancing devils boomed the solemn voice of Reverend Frimm: "Ye have sinned against the Church of the Cosmic Reality and against God. Repent, sinner, and know that the truth is only in my words. Repent, sinner, or for all eternity you will be at the mercy of the demons ye now see. Repent! Repent! Repent! Repent!"

Well, it's good of Frimm to put his "church" ahead of God, Camellion conceded. *The "devils" aren't bad. Damned good theatrics.*

The demons being picked up by the lasers weren't paintings, but men in costumes, very realistic costumes, perfect in every way as to what devils are supposed to look like. *But no tails. Tails would hang limp. They figured it would be too complicated to make tails that moved.*

Thinking that some smoke of Satan was about to seep through a crack in the Cosmic Reality Temple, Camellion turned the timer to what he thought was two minutes—it was difficult to tell in the dim light—rushed over to the northeast

109

corner of the cell, jammed the tips of his trigger fingers into his ears, and began yelling "*Hayyyyyyyy*" as loud as he could.

The explosion resembled a grenade going off inside the giant pillow of the Jolly Green Giant. The Death Merchant felt invisible hands slam him against the padded wall and sky-rockets spit fire in his brain. He jumped up, staggered for an instant, and looked through the smoke, and cloud of bits of rubber and cotton padding torn off by the blast. A two-foot hole had been blown in the edges of the door and the wall. The door was half-open, part of the outside pushdown latch hanging loose.

He stormed through the door like a whirlwind and streaked toward Brother Cecil Gamsen, the Protector who had been at the desk reading the latest issue of *Cosmic Truth* magazine. The sudden explosion had thrown Gamsen into mental and emotional confusion, but he had recovered by the time the Death Merchant was headed straight at him.

The Frimmie might have had a chance if he'd kept his senses and pulled the .38 Colt automatic from the flapped holster on his belt. But he was rattled and so terrified he could hardly think. After all, wasn't the "old man" possessed by an evil spirit?

In blind panic, Brother Gamsen jumped from the chair and tried to grab the M-16 leaning against the wall in the north-west corner. He was three-fourths successful. By the time he had the rifle and was swinging it around, the Death Merchant was all over him.

Camellion's right hand grabbed the barrel and shoved the weapon up and away from him, while his left knee came up in a vicious groin smash and the fingers of his left hand grabbed Gamsen in a "face clutch." Gamsen screamed, dropped the M-16 and sank to his knees, almost blubbering with agony.

Camellion flipped open the flap of Gamsen's holster, jerked out the .38 Colt, shoved off the safety, and jammed the auto-loader under the man's chin. Brother Gamsen kept muttering, "Jesus save me from the hands of Satan! Jesus save me from the hands of Satan! Jesus save me from—"

"Satan's been unchained, Brother," whispered Camellion. "I might take you back to the Kingdom with me, if you don't tell me what I want to know!" He then cut loose with a frenetic laugh that almost frightened him! It scared the living bejesus out of Brother Gamsen who was positive he would soon feel the roaring flames and smell the stink of brimstone.

"What's behind the door with the DANGER sign?" demanded

Camellion. "And the door on the other side of the desk. Talk, slimy human being!"

"W-Weapons and g-grenades in the room marked d-danger," said Brother Gamsen, his voice shaking more than his body. "The other door is to the Master's personal meditation room."

"And the door beside the elevator up front?"

"To a f-flight of s-stairs, escape stairs."

"The top of the stairs open where, into what?"

"Into a t-toilet, a toilet in the recreation r-room on the first floor. Jesus, Jesus! Save me!"

. The Death Merchant shrieked again with insane laughter. "Get up and open the door with the electric lock. Make one false move and I'll take away your soul and stuff it into the tail of a swine!"

His entire body trembling, Brother Gamsen got up, rubbed his painful face, staggered over to the outside steel door and pressed a button set in the concrete-block wall. The locked clicked open. To be on the safe side, Camellion opened the door several inches.

Four seconds later, Brother Gamsen was sagging unconscious from the rap on the head Camellion had given him with the .38. Camellion pulled two spare magazines for the .38 from a leather cartridge case on Gamsen's belt, then raced over to the corner and picked up the M-16. Now it was touch and go . . . experience and some luck versus Fate.

He rushed out into the anteroom, the rifle slung over his left shoulder, the .38 auto-pistol in his right hand. He pulled open the door next to the elevator shaft, took a quick look at the twisting flight of steel steps and started upward, stepping lightly.

It was a moot question whether the explosion inside the cell had been heard above ground. The cell had been soundproof; thus most of the sound had been absorbed by the thick cotton and rubber padding. Too, there was almost 40 feet of solid earth overhead, plus the lining of concrete blocks. It was possible that the explosion could have been heard as a distant rumble. *But by the time anyone figures out what really happened*, thought the Death Merchant, *I'll either be dead or on my way to escaping through the fence.*

He reached the top of the stairs and found himself in a small area the size of an average clothes closet, at one end of which was another door. Carefully, he opened the door and found himself in a john. He moved to the outer door, listened and heard a familiar sound. Feeling meaner than two bootfuls of barbed wire, he opened the door and stepped out into the recreation room.

Four Protectors were playing ping-pong, stopping and jerking back in surprise when they saw Camellion. Two of the goons were so stupid that they tried to drop down and pull their holstered pistols. The first freak went down with a .38 projectile in his upper chest. Camellion aimed deliberately low at the second boob. Instead of the slug hitting the man in the chest, the bullet caught him high on the left side of his forehead and killed him instantly.

Brothers Hale and Frobine, the two Protectors who were left, proved they had the IQs of retarded frogs. Frobine tried to throw himself to the side of a soft-drink machine while his right hand tugged at his holster. Hale made a frantic effort to dash to the hall door. Camellion's automatic roared twice. Frobine went down with a bullet in the right hip. He had not yet hit the floor when Hale stopped a slug between the shoulder blades. The Protector stopped, staggered, did a faltering one-two step and slipped dying to the floor.

The Death Merchant felt like the big red bull's-eye in the center of a target. *Frimm might be a fraud and a liar, but my fat's in the fire,* he thought. *Those shots have alerted the entire camp, including the state police.*

He raced across the room, sped through the door to the hall and headed for the main entrance, shoving the .38 into his belt and unslinging the M-16 on the way.

He was only 50 feet from the doors when he met Brother Koerber coming out of a side room with one of the new 16-shot Berettas in his hand. The Death Merchant jerked sideways and fired the M-16 just as Koerber snapped off several shots, one of which came within several inches of Camellion's left side. Richard's own bullet knifed into Koerber's stomach, went all the way through his body, and buried itself in the wall. The man doubled over, fell, and began dying.

Camellion stopped, scooped up the Beretta, turned the corner, ran north down the hall, came to the entrance and shoved open the double doors with his left shoulder. He was now on the outside, on a small porch constructed in a 7′ X 5′ inset.

Damn it, the four jeeps were gone. No doubt the Protectors had used the vehicles to escort Reverend Frimm and Commander Sessons to the front gate.

The Death Merchant was saved by several other jeeps roaring in from opposite directions. The one from the east was still

112

half a block away while the driver of the other jeep was braking 30 feet in front of the building, all the Protectors, except the driver, reaching for their M-16s when they saw Camellion.

Camellion ducked to the corner of the short wall, brought up the M-16, switched the firing lever to full automatic, and fired at the four men in the jeep ahead. The Protectors didn't have time to get off a single shot. All they could do was jump and jerk and fall like rag dolls.

By this time, the jeep from the east was so close that Camellion was certain several of the gunners were aiming in on his position. He executed the only manuever possible under the circumstances, hoping he could dodge before the damned jeep ran over him.

He jumped from the small porch, threw himself flat to the ground and, as two M-16s cracked from the jeep, opened fire. Slugs from two Protectors—Brothers Lesco and Forester, both in the rear seat—chipped the concrete blocks on the northwest corner. A blink later, Lesco and Forester were stone-dead, the front of their shirts ripped from Camellion's .223 projectiles. Brother Morrison, the driver who had also been blinded by glass from the windshield, was also a corpse, blood from his shot-out throat splattering all over the dash.

A corpse can't drive a jeep. Out of control, but with Morrison's foot wedged down on the gas pedal, the jeep swerved to the right and headed for the northwest corner of the building as Camellion jumped up and sprinted toward the jeep. Reaching the vehicle, he quickly pulled the four dead men from the jeep and let them fall to the ground. He got in, put the M-16 on the floor, and took the three cyclonite bombs from his pockets and placed them on the seat next to him, wedging them into the crack between the vertical and horizontal sections to keep them from sliding off.

He glanced toward the east. Dawn had just been born, the eastern sky tinged with light, the night itself having changed to a deep twilight. He shifted gears, pressed down on the gas and headed west, quickly increasing speed, aware that several other jeeps had turned and were a block behind him. He glanced to his left and saw four more jeeps coming in fast from the south, along the road by the inside of the fence. But they were still a long way off, and the fence was only a few hundred feet away.

With a little luck, I might make it, thought the Death Merchant. *I know I'll get beyond the fence. And if Carlos hasn't*

113

failed me with the car, I might make it to full safety. I hope Russ didn't goof with the makeup job.

From a southeast direction, he heard three or four police sirens, the very same sirens of the cars that had come to the front gate. Ironic! If the state police hadn't come to the gate, he would never have had the chance to effect his escape.

Only 20 feet from the fence, he gradually applied the brakes and expertly turned the steering wheel to the right, the dual move making the rear end of the jeep swing around in a half-circle, so that the front of the jeep was facing north.

The Death Merchant picked up the largest hunk of cyclonite and, by the light of the dash, turned the timer to 1-M, the minimum setting. He threw the small package by the fence and, ignoring the seconds ticking off on the timer, picked up the M-16, aimed carefully at the nearest jeep coming from the east and triggered off the remainder of the magazine. Projectiles ripped into the driver and the man next to him, and by the time Camellion had shifted gears and was starting to move north, the jeep had rolled over once. It rolled over again, struck the side of a barrack building, and exploded.

Camellion's jeep had moved 53 feet when the cyclonite exploded with a flash and a thundering roar, the blast tearing out a 15-foot-wide section of the fence. He immediately swung the jeep around and headed for the gap in the fence, slowly just before he came to the small but still smoking crater below, where the section of the fence had been. He went through the gap at 18 m.p.h., the jeep bouncing up and down from the unevenness of the crater. He stopped on the other side of the fence, picked up another blob of cyclonite, turned the timer to one minute, and tossed it back into the large depression in the ground. He then gave the jeep the gas and headed into the cornfield, the big crash-bumper of the jeep knocking aside the stalks.

Rifle fire erupted from behind him as several of the jeeps drew closer to the tear in the wire-mesh fence. A bullet hit the windshield frame and ricocheted. Several more loud whines sounded as slugs ricocheted from the rear of the jeep. *Pingggggg!* A rifle bullet buried itself in the top of the dash, to Camellion's right. More projectiles passed close to Camellion's body. Moments later, the jeep was lost in the corn.

The driver of the first jeep that arrived at the fence was slowing down and just starting to drive his vehicle through the tear in the fence when the cyclonite in the crater exploded and flipped the jeep over on its right side, spilling out the four Protectors, none of whom had been injured.

The Death Merchant drove with a definite route in mind. In fact, he told himself, he was better off with a jeep because he could make better time. He drove at an angle through the cornfield, moving in a southwest direction. Behind him, straight east, was State Highway Number 94, which moved in front of New Earth Community.

There was a side road that intersected 94, the near lane laid out in an east-west direction. Camellion had to reach that two-lane road and cross the bridge over Dewberry Creek before he could really feel safe. Past the bridge, a few miles to the west, was another road, a dirt deal moving north and south and, three miles to the north, terminating into a Y. The left arm of the Y moved toward Colorado Springs; the right arm went on to the northwest and intersected 94.

Camellion increased speed, the jeep groaning and bouncing up and down, Richard dodging and ducking swishing cornstalks. Finally, there it was—the side road. The jeep was on smooth asphalt within a matter of minutes. He pressed down on the gas and roared up to 80 m.p.h.

Police sirens screamed a mile behind him; yet only half a mile ahead, to the west, was the bridge. Sweat rolling down his back and sides, he came to the bridge, slowed, drove to the center of the single-lane structure, turned the timer of the last cyclonite bomb to two minutes, and dropped it in the center of the bridge. He then roared off to the west. The only danger now was that the state police at New Earth Community had called reinforcements, and Camellion would run into one or more of the police cars before he could turn off onto the north-south dirt road. He had covered a tenth of the distance when the cyclonite exploded and blew an eight-foot hole in the floor of the bridge, the blast effectively cutting off pursuit.

Half as fast as God can make a handful of wishes come true, Camellion came to the side road and turned to the left. As fast as he could go on the dusty road, he drove north.

Carlos had better be there, he thought. *If he's not, I've had it. This jeep will stand out like a boil on the tip of the nose. Within the next half-hour this entire area will be sealed off.*

He saw the grove of Ponderosa pines and silver firs to his left, the newly risen sun glistening off dew-wet, snow-on-the-mountain flowers on each side of the road. He slowed, swung left into the road, which was a lovers' lane for young studs and hot boxes, and honked—two shorts, one long, then three more shorts.

Presently a cream-and-red two-door Chevy Citation came from around a mass of trees and tall poinsettia shrubs, and parked next to the jeep. The driver had straw-colored hair, a thick straw-colored mustache, and a small goatee. He wore rimless eyeglasses.

The Death Merchant got out of the jeep and got into the Chevy Citation hatchback.

"God was with you, *mi compadre*," Carlos Martinez said.

Chapter Eleven

From where the Death Merchant sat in the Silver Ranch motorhome, he could see the rays of the mid-afternoon sun glittering from the Diamond-T Trailer Ranch's swimming pool. His face reflected deep thought. Money's a wonderful thing, but it's possible to pay too high a price for it. It's the same with revenge. Terminating Frimm wasn't worth the time and effort—unless he could do a con job on the CIA. . . .

He leaned back in the leather swivel recliner, put his bare feet on the flat hinged ottoman and thought about his narrow escape from New Earth Community. Several miles from Colorado Springs, he and Carlos Martinez had met seven police cars, four from the sheriff's police of El Paso County and three state police cruisers. But the authorities were looking for a blue jeep, not a Chevy Citation. By the time the police found the jeep and were poking behind bushes and trees, on the premise that Camellion had fled on foot, the Death Merchant and Martinez were in Colorado Springs. Miles to the east, when the police were concluding that the one-man army had probably changed cars, Camellion was sitting next to Janet Minnick, in the Dodge Challenger that "Mr. and Mrs. Barry Robbinette" had rented from Hertz on a monthly basis. Twenty minutes later, "Mrs. Robbinette" was walking with her "father-in-law" in Palmer Park, both killing time until the better restaurants opened.

After a leisurely breakfast at the Ramada Inn on Prospect Avenue, Camellion and Janet had picked up Carlos, who had left the Chevy several blocks from Hertz Rental. There was that slight possibility some of the police might remember passing the Chevy and, as a result, might be watching Hertz. Later in the day, Carlos would call Hertz and tell the company where the car would be found, saying he had left the Chevy there because he had been drinking and had become confused.

117

On the slow drive back to the Diamond-T, Carlos removed his blond wig, blond mustache and blond goatee.

The news reports described the shoot-out at New Earth Community as "a massacre committed by a crazed gunman." Eighteen men had been "gunned down by the man who is described by members of the Cosmic Reality church as being a stocky individual about thirty-five years of age." The police had found the jeep parked off Old Bunker Road. "The latest report is that the gunman has vanished. Captain Marvin Dowdy, of the Colorado State Patrol, and Sheriff Edgar Bunsen have stated that they have no clues as to the identity of the lone gunman."

The various newscasts, describing Camellion as "about thirty-five years of age" astonished Janet and Carlos, but not Linders and the Death Merchant, both of whom knew why Reverend Frimm and his associates had lied to the police: they didn't want the world-at-large to know that an "old man" had been able to create such carnage at the very heart of the Cosmic Reality church. With the sinister cleverness often exhibited by mentally deranged persons, Frimm knew to tell the police, who had not seen Camellion except at a great distance, that the kills had been made by "an old man possessed of an evil spirit" would not only have sounded foolish but would have branded him an idiot to the entire world.

Camellion glanced at Russell Linders, who was inspecting the 16-shot Beretta Camellion had taken from the dead Protector. Carlos Martinez was listening to a Spanish broadcast from Mexico City, using headphones plugged into a Drake SL60 short-wave set.

Camellion's eyes turned appreciatively to Janet Minnick, who was in the kitchen section making a salad for dinner. Just looking at her was distracting, making him think of creating life instead of destroying it. If only she wouldn't go around showing all her natural assets. She wore a red T-shirt with cap sleeves, a western front and a back yoke. Her creme knit shorts were so short that almost every inch of her long suntanned legs showed.

Suddenly hungry, Camellion called out, "Jan, how about putting a small steak in the microwave—well done, please."

"Okay." She finished cutting up the cucumber, wiped her hands, and flushed the peelings down the garbage disposal.

Linders got up, walked past Camellion and, placing the Beretta in a drawer, said in a low questioning voice, "You told us what happened out there at New Earth, but you haven't said anything about our next move."

The Death Merchant sat up on the recliner. "I haven't because there isn't going to be a next move. I'm canceling the project. We've done all we can do. We'll hang around a week yet, then pack up and go home."

Linders, sitting down across from Camellion, glanced at the Death Merchant, a startled expression on his urbane face. Camellion's announcement didn't set well with Janet either, who gave him a momentary look of alarm.

Also barefooted and in walking shorts, Linders scratched his hairy chest. "From what I've heard, it's not like you to throw in the towel. What's your reason?"

"We don't have enough professional help," Camellion explained, forcing a note of finality into his voice, "and we don't have the proper equipment. I've got to be realistic. We tried the impossible."

"Not necessarily," Linders said hastily. "We have Buttons and Hardtack and their choppers at Yoder. They can supply us with automatic weapons. Anything we need."

"Your 'friends' seem to have a horn of plenty," crowed the Death Merchant, not failing to notice the peculiar looks that Janet and Russell were giving him. "You mentioned 'from what you've heard' about me," continued Camellion. "Heard from whom, I'd like to know?"

The Death Merchant knew he had hit home base. Linders had been caught off guard, his eyes showing stress, the pupils enlarging with anxiety. Quickly, Linders became his normal self.

"A figure of speech," he said evenly, acting unconcerned while he reached for his cigarettes and lighter on a small table.

"How long have you been a Case Officer in the Agency's Domestic Operations Division?" asked Camellion in an easy manner.

Not expecting such a blunt question, Linders stared at Camellion, his face a mirror of confusion. He couldn't decide whether Camellion was serious or pulling his leg. For the moment, he was saved by Janet who, bringing Camellion his steak, handed him the tray. She, too, had a nervous look in her eyes.

Russell Linders breathed in deeply and noisily. "What makes you think I'm with D.O.D.?" It was apparent he was going to try to bluff his way through. "I'm beginning to think you think I'm hiding something." He exhaled smoke, maintaining his calm as much as possible.

With the tray resting on his lap, Camellion cut into the steak. The meat was red. Camellion put down the knife and fork and looked at Janet, who had returned to the kitchen. "Damn it! I said well done. This steak is almost alive. If I waved a handkerchief in front of it, it, it would charge!"

Only with effort did Janet control her temper. Without a word, she came back, picked up the plate, returned to the kitchen, and put the steak in the microwave oven. She then gave Camellion a go-to-hell look and turned the dial.

"You're not hiding anything," Camellion said to Linders, a slight mocking tone to his voice. "You're only following orders. I'd do the same thing were I in your position." He called to Janet. "I suppose you're also with the Company?"

"I don't know what you mean!" Avoiding his eyes, she pretended unconcern.

Linders smiled crookedly, realizing the game was over. "How long have you known about Janet and me?"

"Ever since I had my first pow-wow with Grojean," admitted the Death Merchant. "A man as tough as he is doesn't give in so easily. And the fact that you just happened to be 'vacationing' in the Southwest seemed to be almost too convenient. I don't blame Grojean either. He was only trying to save money and have the last laugh. That's his style."

"But now you're calling it off," countered Linders, leaving the most sensitive part for last, "or is it that you're going to demand your hundred grand fee before you continue."

The Death Merchant smiled at the loaded statement, leaned forward and put his folded hands between his knees.

"Grojean is only going to have half a laugh, provided I get the job done. But forget the dough I was going to pay you and Janet and the two with the choppers. Furthermore, I'm charging the Company for this palace on wheels."

"It's no bucks off my nose," Linders said harshly. "What the hell! Any money from you we'd turn into the Center. You know how those things work. But let's stop this talking in shadows. Where do we go from here?"

"Home—unless the Company can give me what I need." Camellion was frank. "Other than you and I and the two chopper pilots, we need six more men, three to back us, three to keep the police from coming through the main gate when the show begins."

Linders, turning his lighter over and over in his fingers, remained calm and unruffled. His voice was very serious. "At all costs, the Company is not involved in the Frimm project." He then reconsidered. "It won't hurt to put your proposal to the brass." He lighted another Kent III and expelled the smoke forcefully, as though giving birth to a fresh thought. "There's one problem from my end of the boat. The higher-ups won't be happy that you're wise to the real facts."

"You're afraid you'll get the blame," Camellion said, noticing that Janet was coming toward him with the plate. He picked up the tray and placed it on his lap.

Linders nodded. "Somebody has to take the heat. The division chiefs can't admit to any mistakes."

The Death Merchant accepted the plate from Janet, put it on the tray, and picked up the knife and fork.

Janet smiled wickedly at Camellion. "I would say you're underestimating Grojean and especially the Director of Central Intelligence himself. There isn't any way you can force them to pay for this motorhome."

Camellion cut off a piece of meat. The outside of the steak was almost burnt, the inside well done. He winked at Janet, who had sat down next to Linders, crossed her legs, and was watching him tranquilly.

"They'll pay," was all he said, thinking of part of the conversation he had had with Grojean. As soon as the Frimm operation was completed, Grojean wanted him to go into the Caribbean on a mission that, in Grojean's words was "of vital importance to this country. I can't tell you right now, except that you'll see action in the Bermuda Triangle. Be prepared for anything. There's something very odd going on down there and we want you to find out what it is."

"The Company will pay," Camellion said again. "The Company has no choice."

He cut off another piece of steak. "Russ, when you make your report, explain that I told you I was wise to the double-dealing from the very beginning. After all, whoever heard of a case officer free-lancing for pay, and with the permission of the Company to boot? Tell them that I laid it on the line to you when I got tired of playing the game."

"Well, that's the truth," admitted Linders.

"How do you contact your Control Center in this area?" asked the Death Merchant. He put another forkful of meat into his mouth and glanced at Carlos Martinez who, sensing that something important was being discussed, took off the headphones, switched off the short wave and joined the small group.

Janet Minnick surveyed Camellion critically. "Six men you said, besides you and Russ. What will Carlos and I be doing?"

"I'm no amateur with a gun," Carlos said with a crinkly grin. Remember the *Sangre de Cristo**, Richard?"

"Only too well, *amigo*," replied Camellion. "But this is a different ball game. If all goes as planned, I'll want you and Janet outside the fence at New Earth as backups. Rather I should say that you two will scratch any police helicopters that might come to the scene."

Three pairs of eyes stared at Camellion in disbelief.

"Just Carlos and I! We're going to shoot down helicopters!" Janet repudiated indignantly. "Would you mind explaining how we're going to accomplish such a feat?"

"Will small missiles, fired from a bazooka launcher," Camellion explained. "Believe me, a child could do it."

Linders head snapped up as though a spring had been released.

"Have you considered that the police are only doing their jobs?" The sharp edge of his voice did not surprise the Death Merchant. Camellion had anticipated some resistance to the idea that officers of the law might have to be smoked.

Camellion swallowed, put down his knife and fork, and patted his lips with a paper napkin.

"I don't like killing cops either," he said quietly. "But tell me of a war in which the innocent don't die. Better yet, tell me how to get the job done without maybe having to terminate a dozen or so cops?"

No one commented. Linders's blue-green eyes darted suspiciously to Carlos Martinez. It was easy to know what the Company man was thinking: Carlos wasn't a member of the Company. Could he be trusted? Perhaps in a month from now, or ten years, he would reveal bits and parts and pieces of the operation.

"I brought him into the project," Camellion said. "Trust him."

A very perceptive individual, Carlos instantly deduced the prime reason for Linders's caution: the CIA's reputation had to be protected and kept as pure as the Virgin Mary.

Linders leaned back and crossed his legs. "I was only think-

*The "Blood of Christ", a range of the Rockies in northern New Mexico. See Death Merchant #32. *The Deadly Manhunt.*

122

ing of the old saying that three may keep a secret if two are dead. What's the difference at this point. He's on it, so that's that."

"There is also an old Spanish saying, *mi amigo*," Carlos said. "When three men discuss secrets, two are police agents and the other is a fool."

Linders said good-naturedly, "In this case, two are police agents, in a manner of speaking. But I wouldn't regard you or Camellion as fools. It takes a lot of guts and discipline to do what you're doing."

Camellion shifted the conversation. "Russ, can you obtain the equipment I need?" He put plate and tray on the floor.

"I'm glad our true positions are out in the open," Linders said idly. "I was wondering how to sneak the Com-C-Box* out of my duffle and compose a report to Control in Denver. Now that our cards are on the table, my task of Rivest coding will be a lot easier."

"That doesn't answer my question."

"Damn it, you know the answer, Camellion. Draw up a list of what we need and I'll put in the request. The stuff can be delivered to Buttons and Hardtack after we detail logistics. I can get the request out today. Figure on a week before delivery."

"We'd better make that two weeks." Camellion was thoughtful. "I want some unusual items, ergot fungus for one; however, a pint of LSD will do just as well. I'll also want equipment that can be carried above one of the choppers, equipment that can produce a 'flying saucer' a hundred feet in diameter. This will necessitate someone in the Company making a damn good model that can be photographed."

Janet smiled sweetly while uncrossing her legs. "I gather you're going to give Frimm a taste of his own medicine in holography."

---

*Computer-Cryptography-Box, a code machine slightly larger than a portable typewriter. There has been a revolution in the ancient art of cryptography—codes and decoding. Now, anyone with a computer can "talk" to anyone else with a code that definitely is unbreakable. The techniques, known as "Rivest coding" and "trap-door functions," involves mathematics. By using some familiar properties of large prime numbers and a computer to perform the calculations, it is now possible for two persons, who exchange in advance a numerical "key" (or password). to exchange messages with perfect security. The National Security Agency is trying to suppress this kind of math in public life.

Linders scowl proved his skepticism. "Since we're apparently going to terminate everyone at the camp, why not just bomb New Earth." His voice grew more serious, more determined. "Why go in by helicopters and even look for Frimm? After what happened last night, we've no assurance that he'll even be there. He has Havens and Abodes all over the U.S. He might be at any one of them!"

Carlos Martinéz said quickly, "Frimm is not leaving New Earth. He said he intends to remain and destroy the evil that is attacking him and his people. He made the announcement this afternoon. I heard it on the news from Mexico City. By the way, NBC is having a special on Frimm and his church tomorrow night. Such a program should be a lot of free publicity for the madman."

"And maybe generate a lot of sympathy for him and his cult," Janet said mournfully. "I was never in favor of trying to assassinate him."

"I think you're missing the point," Camellion said with a twinkle in his eye. "The point is that Frimm can't leave New Earth Community. How would it look to all the thousands of simple-minded Frimmies if their 'Messenger of God' deserted his post, if he fled the church's national headquarters? God is supposed to be on Frimm's side. How can His Oneness and His Onlyness flee in retreat from Satan." The Death Merchant laughed in amusement and triumph. "No, we're not going to exterminate Frimm. We're going to expose him and his Ministers of Light for what they really are—psychopathic sadists, 'religious' Hitlers who'll destroy anyone who gets in their way. For that reason we're going to have the helicopters drop us off within the fence, inside the Community."

Fast on the trigger of deductive reasoning, Linders instantly guessed the core of the Death Merchant's plan. "The *Cells of Attrition*. A good idea if we can pull it off."

Camellion nodded. "The Cells of Attrition and the Dissolving Room. It's underground with the Cells. I noticed that at the end of the corridor, between the cells, was another steel door. I think the Dissolving Room is behind that door."

"But you had no way of knowing if anyone else is in the Cells?" asked Linders.

"How could I? Each Cell is soundproof. As it was, I was extremely pressed for time. I had time only to get out of there and escape."

Carlos Martinez said in a thoughtful voice, "It's not important to the project, but after we succeed, provided we do, the liberals and head-in-the-clouds scholars are going to bring in situational ethics and flatly call any deaths cold-blooded murder."

Linders and Janet Minnick exchanged glances. It had never occurred to them that Carlos might be an educated man.

Linders became uncomfortable and defensive. "There's no such thing as ethics when it comes to protecting the United States, and believe you me, the Frimmies represent a clear danger to internal order. Can you imagine what it would be like if a couple of hundred people rose in rebellion, each one trained in the use of firearms? Just think about it, how they could strike at communications and our defense systems! Such a coordinated effort could seriously cripple the nation."

He glared at Carlos. "We know that Frimm's a megalomaniac. It's only natural that, sooner or later, 'God' will tell him to take over the country. We've got to stop Frimm before he tries it."

The Death Merchant said, "Standards of moral conduct are all relative, like time and space. The Inquisition, or the systematic pursuit of heresy, was not only 'moral' and 'ethical' in the 15th century, it was considered the 'will of God.' Can any of you picture the present Pope advocating torture and burning at the stake of anyone who happens to be non-Catholic? The mere thought is insanity."

"You're right, of course," Janet said. "But after several hundred Frimmies are stretched out dead, the general public isn't going to be much interested in ethical considerations."

Camellion leaned back on the recliner and relaxed his lean, hard body. "What the three of you apparently are forgetting is that society as a whole regards the Church of the Cosmic Reality as a cult; and society makes a definite distinction between cults and mainstream religions. The public is right. Cults are nothing more than big business, enriching their founders and making saps out of thousands of men and women who should know better, but haven't the guts to stand on their own two feet and fight the battle of life."

Carlos cut in, "It's a sticky problem, one that involves freedom of religion. What constitutes a genuine religion? That's the problem."

"Not much of a problem," Linders said crisply. "The worship and adoration of God, or gods. Worshiping a flesh-and-blood man, a leader of a cult, is definitely not religion. It's stupidity."

"A pinch of applied common sense can show us the difference," Camellion said brusquely. "We know what actual religion is. But take a look at some of the cults, the Children of God for example. They also call themselves the Family of Love. David 'Moses' Berg, the leader, *instructs women converts to overwhelm men sexually—all in the name of Jesus!* Berg fled the U.S. in 1974, just before the New York attorney general published a highly critical report on his activities." He paused and cleared his throat. "Then there's the cult of Iso Zen. It's 'religious' members not only *worship UFOs* but *practice homosexual love-making in public.* You call that religion?

"Another cult as useful as a comb to a baldie is the Age of Enlightenment. At each meeting, members are supposed to *levitate* twice—from one and a half to two feet. They even give lessons to people who are even more halfwitted than they are—at rates up to $2,400 for a full course of levitation. I don't have to tell you they're as phony as Jim Jones, who forced his followers to find 'salvation' in a vat of poisoned punch. None of it is religion. All of it is dangerous to society. All of it should be destroyed."

Linders, Minnick and Martinez drew back slightly, not only from the sinister quality in the Death Merchant's voice, but from the eerie glow that suddenly flared in his deep blue eyes, a mysterious luminescence which was as alien as some distant planet in a far-off galaxy.

"I'm not the least bit concerned about the Frimmies who will die," Camellion went on in a brutal tone. "The world will be better off without such weaklings. Normal people face ilfe and do the best they can. The spineless sickies join cults. When they wise up and leave the cults, or the cults boot 'em out, half of them wind up on some funny farm, the other half on Skid Row or on welfare."

Linders stood up, hooked a thumb over the left side of his shorts, looked at the Death Merchant and announced, "We're wasting time. Get your list made out. I'll transmit your needs into code and include it in my report. I'll go into Colorado Springs this evening, use a public phone and phone the numbers into Control."

He turned and headed for his blue nylon weekender.

Camellion got to his feet and started for the desk built into the wall, hearing Janet remark to Carlos, "Camellion's plan is so fantastic and ridiculous, it might work."

Unless Fate sticks out a foot! Camellion sat down at the small desk and reached for a ballpoint and a pad. No matter how carefully an operation was planned, one could scheme

126

only so far and only up to a certain point. After that, one was always at the mercy of Factor X—the unexpected and often the totally unexplained. The entire operation could collapse from any number of strange coincidences—seriality, or what Carl Jung, he Swiss psychologist-philosopher-mystic, called Synchronicity.

Either way, it's the Cosmic Lord of Death who will win, the Death Merchant mused grimly. *He always does.*

Chapter Twelve

Thomas Edwin Pepperinni liked his job. Each day brought something different. There never was any monotony, even if a lot of the work was routine. For thirteen years he had enjoyed the prestige of being a Special Agent in the Federal Bureau of Investigation. He didn't even mind when fellow agents called him "Pepperone" or "Pepper-Pot." There were, however, those times when parts of the job irked him. Waiting half a day to testify before a grand jury was one. Having to go back the next day was even worse. Worst of all were persistent bastards like Marvin Dowdy. They were real pains in the butt . . . old-time Wyatt Earps who put more faith in instinct than in modern methods of criminology.

This was the fifth time in less than a month that Pepperinni had driven down from Denver to have a conference with Dowdy. The Denver office of the F.B.I. would have liked to ignore Dowdy. But Dowdy was an official of the Colorado State Highway Patrol, and when he called and requested an agent, the Bureau sent one—always Pepperinni, who had the least seniority in the Denver office.

Ralph Hines, the Agent-in-Charge, always cautioned Pepperinni. "Listen to the old fool. And for God's sake, don't argue with him. All we need is for someone like him to put in a complaint to D.C."

". . . Somehow I know that this Camellion is tied in with those eighteen men who were murdered almost a month ago," Dowdy was saiyng. "Goddamnit, the fact that he's been missing all this time should indicate something to even the F.B.I.!"

Pepperinni, sitting in front of Dowdy's desk, forced himself to be polite and speak in an even tone of voice.

"Captain, as I explained before, you have failed to consider Camellion's lifestyle. We've checked him upside-down, inside

128

out and sideways. We've talked to any number of people in the Big Thicket region of Texas, and they all tell the same story: that he often disappears for months at a time. He's been doing it for years. This is not the first time Camellion has done a vanishing act."

"Well, damn it, man! That in itself should make you Feds suspicious!" Dowdy sat back in the chair with a jerk. "What the hell does he do when he takes off? Where does he go? I don't have the men and the facilities to keep track of him!"

Pepperinni treated Captain Dowdy to a blandly disarming look and responded in measured tones. "Captain, the Bureau doesn't have a reason to keep track of Richard Camellion. As far as the Bureau is concerned, he's not a suspicious character. There isn't any law that says an individual must make his whereabouts known to the public. It's not against the law to disappear, as long as the person isn't running out on his wife and kids, or the vanishing act isn't a part of some crime. None of this fits Richard Camellion. All right! So he's a loner and lives a secluded life. But that's not a crime either. And he does make money in the stock market. We checked with IRS. Last year he grossed sixty-five thousand dollars in the stock market. Captain, Camellion's clean. He's an oddball, but clean. No priors . . . nothing."

Dowdy sighed, bent forward, folded his leather-like hands on the desk and stared at Pepperinni beneath shaggy brows. "And I suppose you people are still convinced that it was all a case of mistaken identity when the Frimmies tried to kill him?"

Pepperinni kept a straight face. "What else? Even if the Protectors were trying to kill Camellion, the case is not within our jurisdiction. We can't come in on the interstate factor because there were witnesses—half a dozen of them—who saw the Protectors attack him. They're the ones who started it on the highway, not Camellion. After all, Captain, it's not a violation of any federal law for a man to defend himself."

"On the basis that you put it—no," conceded Dowdy. "But I'm talking about why the Frimmies attacked him in the first place. They never did admit in court that Camellion wasn't the man they were after. They only pled guilty. Now doesn't that seem strange?"

"Captain, anything a member of the Frimmie church does is strange!" Pepperinni remarked judicially. "Naturally the Bureau keeps tabs on Reverend Frimm and his people, not only here in Colorado but all over the United States. The son of a—I mean, Reverend Frimm—hasn't broken any laws involving federal statutes. As you know, the Bureau must be very careful in all matters involving freedom of religion."

"Bull crap!" snorted Dowdy angrily. "Frimm and his freaks are a damned cult and you know it. If Washington did something about all these cults, we wouldn't have such a mess in society."

Pepperinni's face remained noncommittal; yet his voice was slightly coated with admonition. "Captain, the Federal Bureau of Investigation is an investigative agency. We don't make the laws. We only reinforce them."

"Those eighteen murders at New Earth Community," retorted Dowdy. "Naturally you people investigated them!"

There he goes with that "you people" again! Pepperinni's expression did not betray his thoughts. Looking exasperatingly genial, he folded his arms and said suavely, "Yes, we did. There weren't any federal laws broken."

"The hell with federal laws!" raged Dowdy. He got up, put his hands on the desk, palms down, and glared furiously at the FBI agent. "I want you college boys to tell me how one man—only one man, mind you—could get into New Earth, murder eighteen crackpots, and then escape? We've concluded that the assassin must have posed as a visitor and somehow managed to hide on the grounds before the gates were closed. We know he had at least one accomplice, or had a car stashed on a side road, but—"

"There had to be more than one assassin," interrupted Pepperinni. "We've concluded that there must have been three or four men. One man could not have—"

"I was there, damn it!" stormed Dowdy, bitter anger and frustration making the blue veins in his neck throb. "None of us saw more than one man in the jeep. It was fairly dark, and we saw him only at distance—the back of him anyhow—but we know what we saw!"

Pepperinni quickly raised a restraining hand and gave Dowdy a brief look of warning. *Control your temper! Control your temper!*

"Captain, I didn't say that you and your men didn't see one man. I do mean that it's possible that two or three other assassins, who were with the individual you saw, were killed by the Protectors and dragged out of sight before you and your men arrived. Have you thought of that possibility?"

"You damn well better believe we did!" Dowdy bit off each word. "We searched every building, even the barracks, and found nothing. We even searched their damned 'Temple,' and found nothing. Your theory is all cock-eyed."

Pepperinni nodded. "I know, Captain. I know," he said sympathetically. "But the case is not within the Bureau's jurisdiction. We can't enter it." He abandoned his lazy pose and sat up straighter.

Dowdy shifted the unlit cigar to the other side of his mouth and spoke around it. Anything new on the explosive analysis?" he demanded tersely.

Pepperinni shook his head. "No. We told you weeks ago that the particle test revealed that the explosive was cyclonite. It's a common military explosive but never sold commercially. It's too powerful."

"Could this cyclonite be obtained from a military installation, or made in a home lab?"

"Possibly from a large military installation, but forget the USAF Academy, if that's what you're thinking. And forget a home lab. It would take an expert and a lot of lab equipment to make cyclonite. The Bureau's opinion is that the murders were committed by ex-Frimmies who may have been Vietnam vets at one time. But where they could have gotten the cyclonite . . ." Pepperinni hunched his shoulder and spread his hands. He looked at his wristwatch. "Captain, if there isn't anything else, I am pressed for time . . ."

Chapter Thirteen

A first rate executive is always very careful about his personnel. The Death Merchant, watching the half-moon through a portside window of the helicopter, didn't have any doubts about the capabilities of the 13 men helping him. Linders was a pure professional, with a CIA mentality that enabled him to believe, without troubling his conscience, that a successful result always justified the means employed to obtain that result.

The two pilots, Merle "Hardtack" Jausel and Virgil "Buttons" Draves, had flown numerous search-and-destroy missions in Vietnam and could fly the two Westland Lynx helicopters the way the Death Merchant could handle a pair of Auto Mags. Three years previously, Draves and Jausel had established the Rocky Mountain Air Transport Service five miles northwest of Yoder, a spit-in-the-road near Ellicott on Highway 94. The air transport service was nothing but a front, a base from which to spy on New Earth Community, although Jausel and Draves, both of whom were officers in the CIA's Domestic Operations Division, had turned the small flying service into a halfway paying proposition by taking hunters and other people into the Rockies.

The two copilots, mild-mannered men who said little but saw everything, had to be experts or the Company would not have sent them. The same could be said of Vander and Kirchhoefer, the two technicians from the Company's Office of Science and Technology, who would operate the holographic and sound equipment in each chopper.

The six combat men looked hard enough to chew railroad spikes. None past 25, all were muscular and very sure of themselves, including their leader, Captain Dickinson.

On first meeting Camellion, Dickinson had stuck out his hand and growled, "I'm Captain Dickinson—John. My orders are to follow your instructions to the letter. Only one thing: don't ask what unit we're attached to. I can't tell you."

"I couldn't care less," Camellion had replied. "But you'd better be expert killers."

"We are."

Black Berets! Camellion had thought at the time. *Good! They're the best.*

The six Black Berets, the two copilots and the two technicians and their equipment had come to the Rocky Mountain Air Transport Service over a period of eleven days, arriving in twos and threes.

There had been drawbacks. The Company refused to "buy" Camellion's motorhome. Grojean had sent word through Linders—"Tell the subject we'll discuss it before he starts cherry blossoms."

"Cherry Blossoms" was the code name of the Bermuda Triangle Action. . . .

A wisp of cloud passed over the face of the half-moon, and Camellion mused, *If I don't get killed on this mission, weeks from now I might get my share of eternity down in the waters of the Caribbean. So why worry about meeting Old Rattle Bones on this strike. It's all relative. . . .*

The Company's Deputy Director of Planning would not OK the use of missiles to knock down any possible police helicopters. Too sophisticated! the DD/P had said. Sophisticated weapons might make someone think of the CIA and point an accusing finger. However, the DD/P had given permission to use rifle grenades. Accordingly, the Death Merchant had made some changes in his plans regarding Janet Minnick and Carlos Martinez. Janet and Carlos would wait with the motorhome 10 miles northwest of Royal Gorge Bridge, a toll bridge that was 1,053 feet above the twisting Currant River, 48 miles southwest of Colorado Springs. Should Janet and Carlos not make the rendezvous point in time—there could be engine trouble, or rain could slow them down—Camellion would continue on his way with the rest of the force. Janet and Carlos would then drive to Pueblo and, later, contact him by phone. Camellion would then fly from Topeka, Kansas to meet them.

After the strike was completed at New Earth Community and Camellion and his men lifted out, one of the choppers would drop Camellion off in the isolated area where the motorhome was parked. Assuming that the motorhome arrived on schedule, Camellion, Carlos and Janet would then start the drive back to Texas, Carlos taking a plane from Pueblo to New Mexico.

The two helicopters would continue on their way and then land in a deserted area 14 miles east of Salida. There a van would be waiting. A short drive of 3.7 miles to a level stretch of ground that could be used as a runway by a small transport, in this case an IAI-201 Arava marked Glencoe Plastics, Inc., Los Angeles, California. There was a "Glencoe Plastics, Inc.," but the company was only a phone and a P.O. Box number. The Arava would make a straight flight to Topeka. From Topeka, the men would take separate commercial flights for their final destination.

Ten minutes after the Arava took off, the two Westland Lynx helicopters would explode and scatter into a hundred thousand pieces of junk.

At 1:15—just about the time the two eggbeaters were settling down toward New Earth Community—the buildings of the Rocky Mountain Air Transoprt Service would start burning, would go up in smoke with the speed of gasoline-soaked cellophane. The quick burn would not be done with thermate—too sophisticated—but with rags and furniture doused with gas, the big blaze touched off by three books of matches attached to "sparklers." The latter were essentially tiny incendiaries that could be set to explode like large firecrackers. By the time the Yoder Fire Department arrived, there would be only ashes. Laboratory analysis would definitely reveal arson, a fire started with gasoline. But—so what? Buttons and Hardtack would be long gone and in no danger since—so Camellion suspected—they were DBIs.*

The Colorado police would quickly link the fire and the disappearance of Buttons and Hardtack with the wipe-out of the New Earth Community, but without Buttons and Hardtack, the case would come to a standstill for lack of evidence.

The Death Merchant turned and looked out the starboard window and across the aisle. The other Westland Aérospatiale Lynx** was several hundred feet to the right of the chopper in

---

*Deep-Black-Internal. Only rarely do Case Officers of the CIA's Domestic Operations Division go into deep cover for any length of time. Case Officers who do are almost always single and without families or any close attachments. Later, they are given new identities and, if necessary, new faces, with the aid of plastic surgery.

**Made by Great Britain in partnership with Aérospatiale, France.

which Camellion rode—and slightly lower. Closed bands on special transmitters enabled the pilots to communicate with each other. Camellion and his men would carry four radios, which would let them communicate on closed bands with the pilots and copilots. After the attack force was dropped, the two choppers would whiz off and land several miles from the center of the Cosmic Reality church.

"Another six and one-half minutes until descent," Hardtack called over the speaker.

While Camellion and Linders and three of the Black Berets put on very heavy leather gloves, the palms of which were coated with what looked like steel wool, Lawrence Vander turned on the long laser tube, then began checking the various mirrors and the 35mm movie projector of the multiplex holography equipment.

The only object on the film was a fly, a common, ordinary housefly, which when projected outside the helicopter, would appear five times the size of an elephant and glow red and orange.

Watching Vander throw analog switches and make adjustments, the Death Merchant and Linders knew that Herman Kirchhoefer, the other technician, was going through the same check-list routine in the other Lynx chopper—only Kirchhoefer's laser would project the three-dimensional photograph of a flying saucer, the plastic and wooden model having been constructed by the Company's Office of Science and Technology.

Vanders irked Camellion, not the man himself but one of his habits. The technician was forever smoking Tijuana Smalls and dropping ashes, either on himself or the floor.

"Do you think it will work?" Linders asked, lighting a final cigarette. "I mean the picture of the fly."

Camellion's smile was one of relish. "Why not. Rev Frimm teaches that Beelzebub is one of Satan's major lieutenants and that he often appears as a large fly. Coupled with the sound, the image of Beelzebub should drive the Frimmies into a panic."

One of the Black Berets got up and went over to the winch

Powered by two 900shp Rolls-Royce Gem 10001 three-shaft turbines. Maximum speed is 207 mph. Range 473. Ceiling, well over 25,000 feet. The Lynx is the world's most maneuverable helicopter. It has been rolled at over 100 degrees per second and flown backwards at 80 mph.

mounted to the right of the portside door, wanting to make sure that the cable was ready to be lowered.

"The only trouble with an operation of this nature is that if you get killed, you don't even get your name in the paper," Linders murmured as he made a final check of a Wildey 9mm Winchester Magnum auto pistol.* "Not even in the obituary column!"

The Death Merchant didn't respond.

Vander began checking the sound equipment.

Toward the rear of the helicopters, back of the sliding doors on both the port and starboard sides, a tri-axial stereo speaker was mounted to the aluminum fuselage and connected to an amplifier inside each helicopter. Combined, the four speakers could deliver a piercing shriek of 740 decibels.

"Four minutes!" Hardtack called out. "Go overboard when you see the flashing green light. Good luck."

"Gentlemen, insert your ear plugs and put on your ear muffs," Vanders said. He then reached for his own plugs and ear protectors, the latter of which resembled oversized headphones.

Ahead, to the west, were the lights of New Earth Community.

---

*A brand-new stainless steel, gas-operated autoloader. Chambered for the potent 9mm and the .45 Winchester Magnum cartridge, the Wildey is a chunky 60 ounces in weight. The first magnum gas-operated pistol in the world, the Wildey is truly stainless as all parts are crafted from stainless alloys picked for their particular usage. The only screws in the pistol are those in the adjustable rear sight and the single screw which clamps the vent rib to the barrel extension.

Chapter Fourteen

All was not well in New Earth Community. Ever since the "demonpossessed old man" had destroyed 18 Protectors, conditions had not been the same, disorder replacing order. There had been more defections, not only of single men and women but of entire families. The number of police watchers outside the fence had increased. The Ministers of Light had begun to argue among themselves. Brother Wilbur Sessons, the Commander of the Protectors assumed greater authority as Reverend Frimm started to spend more and more time in the Tower of Consolation and Heavenly Communication.

Frimm was in the Tower now, at 1:17 in the morning . . . all alone on his knees, his arms outstretched, his face looking up to the heavens through the eight-foot circular opening in the roof of the plastic dome.

He got to his feet when he heard the two helicopters approaching, intense alarm on his face when he realized that the eggbeaters were not merely flying low and passing over, but sounding as if they were going to land within the grounds of the Community.

The screaming blast of sound hit Frimm when he was halfway to the phone to alert Brother Sessons—a piercing shriek of noise that became a million needles stabbing at the very center of his brain. He screamed but couldn't hear his own voice. His hands pressed against his ears, he wobbled like a drunk, the tornado of sound interfering with the semicircular canals of the middle ear.

Frimm sank to his knees, the ear-piercing blast permeating every cell and nerve of his body. He was attempting to crawl to the door of the stairway when he saw the enormous fly and the flying Saucer, The fly was to the left of the Tower, the saucer to the right, both glowing reddish-white, with a brilliancy that illuminated the entire area.

137

In spite of the vibration of sound trying to shake Frimm apart, he stared in hate and bitterness at the gargantuan fly.

Beelzebub! The Lord of the Flies and the Prime Minister of Hell—one of Satan's chief lieutenants.

"Ye of Hell cannot fool me!" screamed Frimm. He could feel his mouth and lips forming the words. He knew he was shouting them but still could not hear his own voice. "Satan! I know that ye have sent Beelzebub to destroy me and the Righteous. I know that the saucer is filled with lesser demons who will try to sow lust and discord, but ye shall not succeed. Lord God! Cast Beelzebub and his legions back into Hell with Satan, their master!"

Either the Lord was out to lunch, wasn't listening, or didn't give a damn. Fly and saucer didn't vanish. Slowly, the fly moved off to the south, the saucer to the east, both gradually drawing closer to the ground.

The blast of sound suddenly stopped, and there was nothing but the roaring of the two helicopters and shouts of terror and panic from all sides of the Tower.

Frimm stood straight and tall, trembling all over. He looked up at the sky and screamed, *"Lord, why hast Thou forsaken me! Tell me, Lord God of the Universe. Tell me, Your Messenger."*

For once, Frimm did not hear the voice of God coming in on the beams of moonlight. Heaven remained silent.

Dreadful visions exploded in Frimm's mind—blobs of alien somethings covered with blood and leering sentiently at him with phosphorescent red eyes. Sharp ensanguined fangs snapped and clicked in mockery, and there was deep, sardonic laughter from long well-like throats filled with slime and maggots. He saw claws and teeth kept razor-sharp on centuries of decaying corpses. Always there was the laughter, and in it the overtones of the totally insane, who can do nothing but laugh day and night at their own dreadful and horrifying aberrations, at their total violence, their treasured filth, their own self-murder. And in the universe of roaring laughter, Frimm could detect an echo of Satan's own reasonless crackling, the mocking of his own self-destruction and deliberately chosen state of positive evil, which was hate and more hate and still more *hate*.

A great light of understanding dawned within Frimm. *Yes! God was testing him.* God was permitting the legions of Hell to torment him. Had not St. Anthony and other great saints been tempted and tormented by the legions of Hell? Jesus

Christ Himself had been tempted by Satan! And there was Elijah! God had taken him into Heaven alive.

Yes, it was all a test. God was all wise. God was all good. God was permitting Beelzebub and his infernal legions to destroy New Earth Community because the Righteous were not worthy of His blessing. *The Righteous have sinned. They have doubted me, the Messenger of God, and the Lord is punishing them. But saved I shall be.*

Frimm lifted his arms and looked up at the sky. "*I am ready, God!*" he shouted. "*I am ready to ascend!*"

He hurried across the room and pulled a small table to the center of the floor. He placed a chair on it, then climbed up on the chair so that he could reach the rim of the opening in the center of the dome. Slowly, with great effort, he began to pull himself through the opening.

For measures of security, the seemingly solid fly and the equally dense saucer were being projected 30 feet above the helicopters—not that it was completely impossible for anyone on the ground to see the two Westland Lynxes. The sky was dirty with scattered clouds, but there was a half-moon. Even when clouds passed over the moon, there was still enough background light by which one could see, after his or her eyes were adjusted to the darkness. At this hour of the very early morning, the majority of the Frimmies were asleep. The only people wide awake were the 100 Protectors on night duty. All this under normal circumstances!

As it was, there weren't any eye adjustments to be made. The glowing fly and saucer were lighting up the entire area with an eerie reddish radiance, with a cold sheen that was unearthly. Nonetheless, the light was in Camellion's favor, being one of two factors he was counting on to help him and his men get to the ground in safety. The first was that each helicopter, 30 feet below the bright images, was in a "blind spot" as far as sight from the ground was concerned. Put another way, this meant that the light radiating out from the laser projected images more-or-less blinded the the viewers on the ground to the area directly below the fly and the saucer. Add to this blindspot 740 decibels of sound, plus the factor of the unexpected, and the odds became 95 to 5 in favor of the Death Merchant.

While Vander swung the Westland Lynx to the left and two of the Black Berets began tossing out M 34 WP smoke grenades, Herman Kirchhoefer took his "saucer" and helicopter north. He would descend over the parking lot. Captain Dickinson and his two boys would then slide down. But they would not attempt to advance in any direction. From the parking lot, they could easily employ rifle grenades to destroy any car that that might attempt to come through the main gate.

In the Death Merchant's whirlybird, the green light began flashing above the door of the pilot's compartment. *Go!* Vander had brought the Lynx to within 25 feet of the ground, in an area between the Temple to the east, and the target range to the west.

Time to go out and do it! A 9-millimeter M4 submachine gun, with flash-hider, across his back, Camellion moved to the portside opening, put both hands around the cable to the right, swung outward into the air and started down. Even though he and the other men wore Pirsin ear plugs and "muff" ear protectors over their heads, the blast of sound, which could be compared to bees buzzing inside one's head, was annoying.

With the sharp odor of phosphorous smoke in his nostrils, Camellion slid down the cable, controlling his speed with the heavy leather gloves, by gripping the cable tightly and digging in the steel-wool covering with which the palms of the gloves were coated. No sooner had he started down than Linders swung outward on the cable, a 5.56mm Armalite assault rifle, with a CGL-4 grenade launcher attached, over his shoulder. The three Black Berets followed.

The slide to the ground took less than a minute. The instant the last Black Beret was on solid ground, Vander shut off the sound equipment and Hardtack began to rotor the Lynx straight upward, the turbines roaring with increased power. It wasn't until Hardtack was a thousand feet in the air that Vander turned off the sound and holography equipment. Instantly, "Beelzebub" vanished. Without running lights flashing, the two choppers headed off, for Buttons, too, had let out his cargo of three Berets and Kirchhoefer had switched off the sound and holography equipment.

Brother Wilbur Sessons had been fully clothed and sleeping in his office in the Protectors' Building when the screaming wall of noise had awakened him. With scores of other Protectors, he had held his ears and stared in astonishment at the images of the fly and the saucer. Many of the Protectors were religious psychopaths and actually thought they were seeing the demon Beelzebub, but Sessons wasn't fooled. Nor was he

140

actually afraid; his rage left no room for fear. For any number of years, he had envisioned himself as the Supreme Commander of the United States Federal Protectors, which would have replaced the FBI and, under his leadership, become a ruthless national police force—all this after the Church of the Cosmic Reality ruled the United States and that idiot Frimm was installed in the White House.

Now, Sessons saw his dream of becoming an American Himmler falling apart. Somehow, he sensed that the end was rapidly approaching and that the image of the fly and of the saucer, as well as the sound, were only diversionary tactics for the landing of men from helicopters.

By God! They hadn't won yet. It was still possible to save New Earth and perhaps salvage his position.

"Every one of you, get out there!" Sessons screamed at his men. "Show that evil trash that you're the best fighting men in the world."

Chapter Fifteen

Convinced that delay is usually the forerunner of defeat, the Death Merchant instantly swung into action. First slipping the leather gloves into one of the Musette shoulder bags, he removed the M4 sub-gun from his back, made sure the narrow straps holding the Auto Mags in their holsters were secure, and all the while urged the others to hurry. They did—Linders taking off his assault rifle and placing a grenade in the launcher.

Sergeant George Griffith, who carried a sack of nine shaped charges, took an M4 machine gun from his back. Watson and Golmis carried ARs, with attached grenade launchers. They would work their way northeast and help Captain Dickinson and his men hold the front fence and the main gate. Sergeant Griffith would accompany Camellion and Linders. Contact between the three groups would be maintained by walkie-talkies with closed side bands.

Watson and Golmis, dressed like the others in night-patch camouflaged suits, were soon running northeast through the smoke, triggering microwave and capacitance proximity alarms on their course. Camellion, Linders and Griffith ran to the west side of the Assembly Hall of the Ministers of Light.

"Give the Armory three of the grenades," Camellion said, his eyes scanning the west, "just to let goofy Protectors know we're here. We might even make them lose their faith in Cosmic Realitism."

"You know what I've always said," Linders growled and raised the AR. "A man without religion is like a fish without a bicycle."

"Yeah, friends come and go, but enemies are around forever," Griffith said. "Where do you suppose Frimm is?"

"Who cares," Camellion said. "We're not after him."

The first shaped charge blew out a wide section of the decorative brick fence in front of the Armory. The second went off in a brief pattern of red and orange flame and tore a large hole in the east wall. The third rifle grenade demolished the steel door of the entrance, throwing parts of steel plate inward and outward like chunks of large shrapnel. A loud scream came from inside the building. However, the Death Merchant and his two companions did not see the two Protectors who staggered through the smoking entrance, their uniforms ripped and torn, their faces black from burnt powder. Camellion, Linders and Griffith didn't see the two Protectors because the Death Merchant & Co. had turned and were racing in the direction of the Temple, dodging and ducking, running at acute angles, first one way and then another, to avoid slugs that, by now, were coming in their direction. If Camellion had seen the two Protectors, he wouldn't have been surprised. After all, heroism is accomplished by fools who have not yet reached their level of incompetence.

Toward the north, Camellion & Co. could hear shots and terrified screams coming from the family cottages and the barracks housing single men and women. Behind them, sirens shrieked and modutone vibrating horns blared as their moving bodies triggered microwave motion detectors, pulsed infrared detection beams, and even buried seismic outdoor intruder systems that had been turned on after midnight.

Camellion, with Linders and Griffith on either side of him, reached the south side of the Assembly Hall of the Ministers of Light, stopped and looked around. To the northeast and due east there was the roaring of gunfire, pistols and automatic weapons.

Fifty feet south of the Assembly Hall was the Tower of Consolation and Heavenly Communication, the 176-foot-tall stainless steel "needle" reflecting the lights of the community and the flames of the fire that had been started in the Armory by one of the rifle grenades. But because of the height of the needle and the darkness and Camellion's proximity to the tower, he and the other two men couldn't see the domed top.

Russell Linders, thinking of the COM-B-2 charges* he and Camellion carried, glanced expectantly at the Death Mer-

---

*COMPOSITION B-2. A military explosive. Composition B refers specifically to a mixture of 52.2 percent RDX, 40 percent TNT, 4.8 percent bees wax. COM-B-2 is an unwaxed composition of 60 percent RDX and 40 percent TNT.

chant. "Are we going to blow the Tower or this glass block igloo?"

"We don't have the time," Camellion said. "We're here to expose Frimm and his Cosmic Reality church, not blow up every building in sight. Let's move. The water filtration plant is our next stop; then we'll hit the Protectors' Headquarters Building. Watch yourselves."

They zigzagged southeast toward a long flat-roofed building east of the Temple. They were halfway between the Temple and the side of the filtration plant when two enclosed jeeps roared around from the south side of the Protectors' Headquarters Building and came straight at them, quadriflash superlights flashing blue at 90 pulses per minute. A third jeep—this one open—roared in at them from the west, a Protector standing up in the front seat, firing an Ingram submachine gun. The Protectors in the two other jeeps didn't have it as good. They had to lean out the side windows to trigger Ingrams.

Slugs cut the air on all sides of Camellion. One hot bullet tweaked his left ear in its passage. Several more nipped at the outer sleeve of his right forearm. He wasn't worried about his chest, back and stomach, since he and the other men wore Kevlar body armor,* but their arms and legs and head were not so protected.

Linders and Griffith were in the same dangerous fix as the Death Merchant. Griffith's fatigue cap was knocked sideways when a 9mm missile clipped the bill. A muffled richochet was heard when another slug struck the barrel, just behind the sight, of his holstered S&W .44 stainless steel Magnum. A slug tugged at Linders's left shoulder, going through the tough cloth and just missing the skin. Another pulled at the right side of his collar.

Within the next second, Camellion, Linders, and Griffith were on the ground and firing. One of the jeeps coming from the south exploded in a sound of thunder and with a brief, bright flash of flame when Linders slammed a heat grenade into the cab. Parts of engine and half of the body went flying in one direction, tires and dismembered limbs in another. Pieces of metal struck the windshield of the second jeep at the

---

*Kevlar is the trade name. The material is actually ballistic nylon. Not so strange when we stop to consider that Kevlar was first introduced by the Dupont Company as a long-wearing material for automobile tires. But Kevlar will not stop a .44 Magnum projectile.

same instant that the Death Merchant's stream of 9mm projectiles dissolved the glass and tore into the driver and the machine-gunner next to him; at the same moment that Griffith's chain of 5.56mm Armalite projectiles ripped into the driver and the shooter of the jeep coming from the west. Instantly the jeep went out of control, swerved to the right and tried to climb the front steps of the Temple. It couldn't, so it did the only other thing possible: the jeep turned over on its left side, the right wheels spinning furiously as the vehicle lay there with its two bloody corpses. The jeep that the Death Merchant had taken out veered to its dead driver's left and crashed into the side of the Temple.

"Let's make tracks," said Griffith who, with his long dark hair and beard, reminded Camellion of a young-old prophet dressed up in a combat uniform. "The Frimmies aren't at all friendly."

"And they're psychopathic to boot," put in Linders. He got to his feet and ran after the Death Merchant, who was sprinting toward the water filtration plant, firing the M4 as he ran. A line of his slugs stabbed through the window next to the door, two of them finding the man on duty, the Frimmie who was too nervous to even get a halfway bead on Camellion. Unconscious and dying, the man dropped the .38 Rossi revolver and fell to the floor.

Camellion reached the building, sprayed the lock with slugs, kicked in the door and raced in, Linders and Griffith right behind him.

"Russ, from the southwest windows you can see part of the Protectors' Building," Camellion said. "Put a couple of grenades into the corner and shake them up. Griff, watch the door."

"We've already got company," Griffith said drily. "Two more jeeps. One has stopped in front of the church. The other's at the northeast corner . . ."

The Frimmie on the floor moaned. Griffith put a slug into the man's head, then got to the side of the window and began firing short bursts at the corner of the church. Immediately, the Frimmies began returning the fire, high-velocity projectiles from automatic rifles and submachine guns thudding into the outside brick wall and coming through the window to whine off various pieces of equipment.

The Death Merchant looked around the long room and saw that New Earth Community used standard filtration to turn its hard water into soft water. The water was first filtered through rock salt and charcoal; the water was then sent through four "washers"—the machines in the center of the floor. Finally, the water was washed a final time and chlorine added.

Camellion found the fifth washer and hurried toward it, glancing at Linders who was about to fire the first rifle grenade at the east end of the Protectors' Headquarters Building.

Whooschhhhhhh! The first shaped charge left the launcher on the Armalite assault rifle, struck the northeast corner of the building and exploded with a loud roar and a bright flash. The smoke cleared to reveal a gaping rent in the wooden structure, the widest part—where the ceiling of the ground story became the floor of the second story—almost fifteen feet.

Linders's next charge did the same kind of damage to the corner of the second story, the big blast sending shattered boards stabbing through the air like enormous splinters, as well as three bodies which turned over and over as they fell back to the wreckage below. Two hit the ground. The third struck the flat roof, bounced, then fell to the ground.

"Hey Linders," yelled Griffith. "Over here! Those guys in the jeeps were waiting for a halftrack. Knock the damned thing out for me."

The Death Merchant, standing by the chlorine additive machine, unscrewed the cap of the tube on the roll-drum. He next removed two green plastic bottles from his left shoulder bag and poured the contents through the tube into drum— enough LSD to make everyone in New Earth Community flip his religious lid . . . and then some! He recapped the green bottles and, not wanting to leave any evidence behind, returned the bottles to the bag. He then screwed the cap back onto the tube and headed to the side of the door, thinking that Linders and Griffith were good men on a quick hit job of this nature.

Linders sent a shaped grenade at the clanking M9 halftrack, whose driver was aiming the front of the cab directly at the door of the building. Just as he pulled the trip-trigger of the launcher, the enemy gunner started to rake the side of the waterworks with a 30-caliber machine gun mounted on a swing-swivel on the rim of the turret.

Blammmmmm! The halftrack dissolved in a huge flash of fire, the sloping roof of the cab, the turret and the mangled gunner soaring upward as if shot from the mouth of a cannon.

The doors of the cab jumped sideways and clanked to the ground.

The seven Protectors still alive in the rear of the now-burning halftrack stumbled to the ground, their senses numbed by the explosion. Dazed, five of them forgot where they were and staggered out into the open—right into the 9mm slugs of Griffith's machine gun. The five cultists died without really knowing what had hit them. The two still alive stayed behind the end of the halftrack, wishing they had never heard of Reverend Frimm and his church of the Cosmic Reality.

There was a loud, screaming ricochet as a projectile hit one side of the barrel of Linders's Armalite, the force of the impact knocking the assault rifle to the right. Another bullet passed through the very top of his fatigue cap, knocking it off his head. Several Protectors were firing from the southeast corner of the Temple and the projectiles were far too close for comfort.

Linders dropped down and crawled to a new position on the other side of the window, picking up his cap and calling out to Camellion and Griffith, "If we don't get out of here, we're going to find ourselves pinned down. What's all that yelling and chanting?"

"Frimmie 'civilians,' " the Death Merchant called back. "We'll leave here as soon as I and Griffith put them to sleep. Griff, don't fire until they're closer."

"It's like they want to commit suicide," said Griffith at the sight of the dozens of Frimmies running toward the waterworks from the northwest, young men and women shouting, *"Frimm! Frimm! Frimm!"* and waving pistols, revolvers and rifles. Not a single man or woman was making any attempt at concealment, nor was there any kind of order. The Frimmies were nothing but a crazed mob bent on vengeance, determined to kill the agents of Satan invading their sacred city, convinced that the power of God's Messenger on Earth would protect them.

Frimm couldn't and didn't!

"Terminate!" hissed the Death Merchant.

The mentally deranged, fanatical Frimmies were destroyed faster than a wheat field in a raging fire. They jerked and jumped, screamed, twisted and died. In less than a minute, the slaughter was over, and all that was left were scores of corpses lying in mounds.

Camellion smiled bitterly. Those Frimmies will never take

147

part in any cultist revolt to take over the government. All they will ever do now is walk forever in the dark world of Belial.*

As if to stamp *finis* to the deaths of the Frimmies, there was suddenly a series of popping explosions from the northwest. The fire in the Armory had reached the cases of stacked ammunition.

Thrusting a full magazine of cartridges into the M4 chopper, Camellion called to Linders, "Russ, come over to the north wall."

"Sure, in just a second!" yelled Linders, who was carefully aiming at the corner of the Temple. Muttering, "You crazy sonsabitches," he pulled the trigger. *Woschhhhhhhh.* The grenade whizzed from the launcher, struck the southeast corner of the Temple and blossomed into the most beautiful explosion Linders had ever seen. A ten-foot section of the Temple was turned into kindling, the several Protectors into large chopped-up chunks of bloody flesh, a leg falling here, an arm there . . . a head hitting the ground and rolling to a stop, eyes open like tiny headlights.

A puzzled Griffith soon joined the Death Merchant and George Griffith by the side of the north wall. "Why here, by this wall? What's going on?"

"Aim for the southwest corner," ordered Camellion, pointing with a finger. By going through the hole in the corner, we'll be fifty feet closer to the Protectors Building. Before we leave, you can slam a few more grenades into the Protectors' Headquarters to shake them up."

"Good idea," Linders agreed. "But I used my last charge on the Temple. Give me your bag of goodies, Griff."

Griffith was handing Linders the canvas bag of nine heat charges when there were two loud explosions, one after another, to the northeast. The lights in the ceiling flickered, went out, came on again, flickered and went out again for three or four seconds. Then the lights came on and stayed on. No one said anything. They knew what had happened: Watson and Golmis had sent a couple of rifle grenades into the powerhouse, and automatic relays had switched on battery power in all the vital sections of the city.

"Won't the explosion damage the water equipment?" asked

---

*The most vicious of all evil spirits, Belial is named in the Book of Revelation which calls him the "Beast." In apocalyptic writings, Belial is the cosmic power of evil, identified with death and the evil impulse in mankind.

Linders, who adjusted the bag to his hip. He reached into the canvas, pulled out a grenade and fitted it securely to the launcher.

"The first washer is twenty feet from the corner," Camellion said. "The blast will shake hell out of the machines but won't damage them."

"Let's get over by the last machine," Linders said and started toward the chlorine additive drum. He reached the drum and, with Camellion and Griffith standing behind him, aimed and pulled the trigger of the launcher attached to the underside of the Armalite assault rifle.

A huge blossom of flame, a crashing explosion and a ball of smoke.

Before the smoke could clear, Camellion and Linders and Griffith were racing toward the huge gap . . .

Chapter Sixteen

Captain Dickinson and the two Black Berets with him had worked their way to the south side of the parking lot and had taken positions behind the windows of a small concrete-block building, which was used as an emergency first-aid station for any visitor who might suddenly become ill. From this building, Dickinson, Purr, and Tolbert had a clear view of not only the main gate—several hundred feet to the southeast—but also the north, west, and south sides of the Community. Oddly enough, the Protectors at the main gate had not fired at them. The answer why was simple enough: the Protectors had not seen them; neither had any of the Frimmies in the barracks, some distance away. Now, with the street lights no longer burning, it wasn't likely that anyone would spot the three Black Berets, not until they started firing. The lights over the main entrance were still burning; they were using battery power.

The three waited. When they heard Watson and Golmis blow the generating station, Dickinson contacted them on the TEX 10-8 walkie-talkie. "Have you found positions in the station?" he asked, looking down at a carefully drawn to scale diagram of the Community, with the aid of a penlight.

"Affirmative," Frank Watson's voice floated back metallically. "We have full-field vision of the gates and can see both sides of the east road. Dave's watching our flanks and the rear. Any news from Polywog-One?"

"Negative. My instructions are to give them thirty-five minutes max. If I don't hear from them at the end of that period, I'm to presume they've bought it and contact the choppers. Anything else?"

"I—hold on! I can see red and blue flasher lights coming down the road from the south. It has to be the police."

"Affirmative," said Dickinson. "You and Dave know what

to do. Take out any vehicles that come through the gate to your right. We'll take the left. Polywog-Two out."

Dickinson switched off the walkie-talkie, placed the set in its case on his belt, picked up the Armalite assault rifle and sighted in carefully on the main gate. Just in case the lights over the main gate might go out, he switched on the Star-Tron night scope mounted to the carrying handle of the Armalite. He had been in situations similar to this one and knew that death was just around the corner, only a short step from nowhere.

Commander Wilbur Sessons didn't have time to think about his misery; if he had, he would have concluded that he was suffering the worst day of his life. The Protectors were brave, even fanatical, but they had been trained to deal with individuals and with sneak-in attacks. What they were facing now was open warfare. To further complicate the defense, fires had been started by the two grenades the enemy had lobbed into the east end of the building. It was only with great effort and a lot of luck that the Protectors had managed to put out the flames. It was even more fortunate that the grenade which had struck the corner of the Temple had not started another fire.

Sessons, his face smudged with wood smoke and fumes from burnt cartridge powder, turned when a Protector touched him on the arm.

"Commander, we are still unable to make contact with the Master in the Tower of Consolation and Heavenly Communication," Brother Melnor whispered, a frightened look on his freckled face. "He doesn't answer the phone."

Sessons laughed scornfully. "You might as well stand there and tell me that the present is now, you idiot! Of course he's not answering the phone, or you would have made contact with him."

A sudden explosion, 125 feet to the northeast, prevented an embarrassed Brother Melnor from giving any kind of reply. Sessons ran from his office and almost collided with a Protector, who was coming to tell him that the enemy had blown an enormous hole in the corner of the waterworks building.

"It don't make sense," Brother Kramm said, a dumb look on his sweaty face. "Why would they destroy part of the building they're in?"

A worried look crossed Sessons dirty face and his nostrils flared with the intensity of rapid thought. Suddenly he knew.

"Get the men back," he roared at Brother Kramm. "Get them back here to the—"

The explosion—this time only 35 feet to the east—cut him short and made the entire Headquarters Building shake and shudder. Listening to confused yells and screams of agony, Sessons and the two Protectors dropped to the floor. Four more Protectors staggered through a doorway to the east, their uniforms torn and black with smoke. No sooner had they got down beside a row of black filing cabinets than there was another huge blast, followed by the strong fumes of burnt explosive and a few screams, as well as the crashing of boards and demolished furniture.

Sessons knew he had been right: the enemy was about to attack. He jumped to his feet, pulled one of his 14-shot Smith & Wesson autopistols from its Bianchi holster on his hip, and said tight-lipped, "We can't fight them here on the first floor, or on the second floor. There's too much danger of fire. We'll go below."

Brother Gene Gibney, one of the Protectors who had just come from the east end, was startled. "Commander, what about the rest of the men in the west end?"

Unable to say *Let them look out for themselves!* Sessons turned, hurried into the next room, and went to the barometer on his desk, the six Protectors trotting after him like the trained dogs they were.

The last explosion had not started to echo back and forth across the Colorado countryside when the Death Merchant, Linders and Griffith dashed the distance from the corner of the filtration plant to the totally wrecked east end of the Protectors' Building. The end looked like a bulldozer had gone through it. Both the first and second floors were exposed— flooring, crossbeams and joists splintered and wrecked, plasterboard smashed and hanging in large sagging patches. Now and then a beam or board fell. Or a piece of furniture, at the end of the building, slid along the sagging floor and tumbled to the area below.

There were still five Protectors in the east end of the building on the ground floor, and while they had been badly jolted by the two grenade explosions, they hadn't sustained any serious injuries. Time, however, was against them. It took almost a minute for them to recover their senses and to reorganize their thoughts. By then it was too late. The Death Merchant and his two companions were practically on top of them.

Brother Ferbend, crouching behind a desk, came very close to whacking out Camellion with a short burst from a SIG-AMT automatic rifle, some of the round-nosed missiles almost kissing the Death Merchant's right temple. A micromoment later, Brother Ferbend had only half an instant of agony as Camellion blew his chest open with the M4 submachine gun, then stitched the right rib cage of Brother Matsler who, unable to free his Thompson submachine gun pinned by a heavy beam, had fired pointblank at Linders with a .38 Colt Commander pistol. Both hollow-pointed projectiles had struck Linders in the center of the chest and then flattened out against the Kevlar body armor, knocking him backward toward the floor. Linders had been zeroing in on Matsler when the Death Merchant fired and sent the Frimmie Protector into the dimension of timelessness. Bits and pieces of Matsler's uniform, chopped off by the projectiles, were still fluttering to the floor as Griffith swung his machine gun from left to right and hosed Brothers Tonn and Sverson with a hot wave of slugs. The two men fell with a wild, horrified look on their grimy faces.

Synchronous with Griffith's raking Sverson and Tonn, Brother Felix Brosch made the greatest mistake of his 23 years on Earth. He leaned out from the end of an overturned filing cabinet and nervously tried to draw a bead on the Death Merchant, who was darting from side to side and jumping over splintered boards and other debris. Spotting the short-bearded Brosch, Camellion ducked to the left at the same time the Protector pulled the trigger of the Armalite-18 auto-rifle.

The Death Merchant fired on instinct, by experience based on the run-together crackings of the AR-18's exploding cartridges, a long burst of missiles that literally dissolved Brosch's face, exploded his skull into several dozen bloody pieces, and left pieces of his gray matter sliding down the filing cabinets like gigantic, slow-moving amoebae.

Far to the northeast there were several loud explosions! The other Berets had just destroyed several police cars trying to enter the city.

The Death Merchant and his two men didn't stop to admire their handiwork. Moving quickly, they darted through the thick smoke and rubble, raced through several empty rooms, and came to the large room that Camellion remembered so well: the recreation area where he had first met "His Oneness and His Onlyness." This room, too, was empty.

"I swear to God," mumbled Linders. "When we get out of this, I'm going to take to drink."

"Where in hell are they?" Griffith was alarmed. "We didn't kill that many of the scum."

The Death Merchant thought of the stairway in the hallway. He remembered seeing the stairs when he was captured.

"They've either fled the whole building," he said, "or have gone upstairs or to the Cells below."

"Make it upstairs, 'cause now they've come down," Linders hissed, hearing men moving around cautiously from several rooms ahead.

Instantly, he and Camellion and Griffith made themselves small behind the largest pieces of furniture. The Death Merchant jerked a thumb to the left and whispered, "Watch that door. It's to the hall. At the end of the hall are the stairs to the top floor. Cover me. I'm going ahead."

Camellion was almost to the west wall when Linders and Griffith opened fire to keep the Protectors from coming into the recreation room, their high-powered projectiles nicking splinters from the doorway. The Death Merchant, knowing that the Protectors were not aware of his presence, pulled out one of the five MK-2 fragmentation grenades he carried. For a moment he listened to the Protectors who were firing short bursts at Linders and Griffith. Three were firing from the doorways, but there should have been more. He pulled the pin from the frag grenade and pressed down firmly on the handle, then pulled one of the M-200 International Auto Mags, crept to within three feet of the left side of the doorway and, as Linders and Griffith quit firing, flipped the grenade around the edge of the opening into the room beyond. Quickly, he jumped to his feet and ducked back.

1-2-3-4-5 . . . the explosion was deafening! There were sounds of pieces of furniture striking the walls, sharp, piercing screams, and bodies hitting the floor. Camellion swung around as Linders stitched the doorway to his left with Armlite slugs. The door swung open and a dead Protector, his uniform full of black bullet holes, fell face down into the room. Several men behind him sagged like wax melting in the hot sun.

"Blow those stairs at the end of the hall," yelled Camellion, "and keep an eye on the door to the right. It's a toilet. In the back wall is the door of the steps that lead to the Cells below."

As Linders darted to the hall, Camellion picked up the M4 submachine gun, struggled into the strap and slung the weapon across his back. Pulling the second Auto Mag, he clicked off the safety, took a deep breath, and darted low into the next room, into what had been Commander Sessons office, but was now a wrecked, bloody mess. Suddenly the room shook violently from the explosion at the other end of the hall. Linders had demolished the stairs with a heat charge. A huge photograph of Reverend Frimm, already hanging crookedly on the wall, fell to the floor, the glass smashing. Dust from blood-splattered plasterboard walls and ceiling drifted through the blue fumes.

Seven bodies were on the floor, one without a face, another without a leg, several minus arms. All had been riddled with shrapnel, some more so than others. The eighth man was on his hands and knees trying to crawl from the room. Another man, lying on his stomach, moaned loudly. The man who was crawling jumped when Camellion broke his spine with a .357 bullet, jumped, fell flat on his face, and lay still.

The Death Merchant went over to the man who was moaning. The poor fool's belly looked as if it had been run twice through a meat grinder. Evidently the explosion had demolished a chair and sent a huge jagged splinter slicing across his abdominal region. A mess! Part of a ropey colon protruded like an overinflated gray balloon through his bloody clothes. The man was slowly dying, but still conscious, his cloudy eyes flickering in fear.

Camellion bent down and asked in a soft but ominous voice, "Where are the others—upstairs or in the rooms underground. Talk or you'll never put your hand in the hand of the man from Galilee."

"I-I don't know." The man was losing strength and Camellion could barely hear him. "There was no one h-here when we c-came from upstairs. I-I th-think they went to the Cells to u-use the escape tunnel."

The Death Merchant felt as if he had just been doused with scalding lye water.

"Tunnel! What tunnel?" His glare was twice as sharp as his voice. "Tell me or I'll send you straight to hell!"

"The t-tunnel from the D-Dissolving Room to the front of the Tem-p-ple. The entrance in the Temple is under . . . is u-under the sacred pyramid of the M-Master. It . . ." The man closed his eyes. He was dead.

A terrible look on his lean face, Camellion stood up and glanced at a worried Russell Linders, who had just entered the wrecked office. Backing in behind Linders was a careful, observant Griffith.

"Smell that smoke?" Linders tossed a black look at Camel-

155

lion. "The east end is starting to burn and I think another fire has started in the stairway wreckage."

"We have time. That joker there"—Camellion glanced at the dead Frimmie—"told me there's an escape tunnel below that comes out underneath the pyramid in the Temple. I'll bet a mess of the sickies are hiding below, maybe even Frimm and Sessons."

Linders turned away and looked unhappily at the closed bookcases. He turned back to Camellion. "Why not blow a hole in the floor?" he suggested. "The police will find the Cells when they get here."

"Griff, get on the TEX 10-8 and inform Polywog-2 that we're okay and that I'm extending the schedule another twenty minutes. Have P-2 repeat for confirmation. Russ, how many heat charges do you have left?"

Linders blinked in puzzlement. "Five. Why?"

As Griffith moved off slightly to contact Captain Dickinson, Camellion explained that since they could see the rear of the Temple, "It should be comparatively easy to blow up the back of the Temple, which will give you a view of the pyramid. All you have to do then is demolish the pyramid. The wreckage should provide sufficient weight to hold the trap door down."

"And we use explosives to blast our way out," said Linders, putting a charge in the launcher. "We'll have to. By the time we're dead or done down there, this place will be an inferno. Personally I think we're nuts for trying such a dangerous stunt."

"Naturally—or we wouldn't be here," Camellion readily agreed.

While Griffith acted as lookout, Camellion took out a half-pound of COM-B-2 and Linders went to one of the windows on the north side of the office. He adjusted his night-sight Star-Tron scope, aimed at the back of the Temple and fired. The first heat charge exploded and tore a hole in the rear wall large enough to drive a small automobile through. The second and third grenades expanded the hole.

Meanwhile, Camellion had fastened electric timer-detonators to the two small blocks of COM-B-2. He placed one block in the center of the floor. Thirty-five feet straight down was the anteroom between the elevator, the stairway and the Cells of Attrition. He did some thinking, mentally measuring where the electric-lock steel door was locked. It should be—*just about here.* Camellion placed the COM-B-2 about eight feet north of where he had placed the first block.

Linders had a clear, unobstructed view of the pyramid. He was adjusting the luminosity of the Star-Tron and the Death Merchant was attaching one end of a long nylon rope around 2′ x 4′ in part of the exposed north wall when Griffith yelled at Linders, "Get on with it, or can't you smell the smoke?"

Linders did not reply. He centered the crosshairs of the scope at the base of the pyramid and pulled the trigger of the launcher. A *whoossch!* The *HEAT* charge left the launcher, shot through the open window, rocketed through the hole in the rear of the Temple wall and hit the target. *Blammmmmm!* For a twinkling it appeared that the entire rear of the Temple had erupted in red-orange flame. When the smoke cleared, the pyramid was gone and in its place was a huge pile of the structure and the pyramid had fallen in on itself.

By now, the crackling of flames was very loud, the smoke so thick that the three men could hardly breathe. Camellion quickly explained his plan to Linders and Griffith who, coughing, nodded.

"Good deal," Linders said. "If any of them are directly below, a few grenades will do the job and save us the trouble."

The Death Merchant, who had picked up both packages of COM-B-2, waited in the center of the wrecked office. Griffith and Linders raced into the next room to the west and took cover by the side of a north-south wall.

Humming "Fat Bridget and Mournful Ben," a little known country-music tune, Camellion turned each timer to 1-MIN. He placed the first pack of COM-B-2 six feet south of the center of the floor, the second pack about four feet from one of the windows. He ran across the room, hurried through the door and got down beside Griffith and Linders, the latter of whom had placed the fifth and last charge in the launcher.

The twin explosions crashed against their ears and shook the protective wall with such force that the three men suspected it might cave in on them. The Death Merchant looked around the side of the doorway. Almost all of the floor was gone, and so was a large section of the north wall and practically all of the furniture. But the rope tied to the 2′ x 4′ was secure. The sad part was that there was only a narrow strip of flooring on the west side of the room, five feet at the widest.

"It's no good," Camellion said in disgust. He turned to Griffith. "Griff, see that turn-wheel on the wall safe across the room? Fasten the end of your line to the wheel, and we'll slide down from here."

Camellion and Linders got down on their knees and crawled to the splintered edge of the hole and looked down. Camellion was elated. He had gambled and won. He had gambled that Frimm and his close aides, in excavating the space for the chambers below, had built the Cells of Attrition and the Dissolving Room surreptitiously, since the existence of the cells was only a rumor. Camellion had further reasoned that the easiest way would have been to dig a shaft straight down, then to proceed sideways from the bottom.

"All I can see is the roof made out of concrete blocks," Linders said slowly. "But grenades will turn that roof to powder.

"We're lucky there wasn't solid ground under the floor," Camellion said thoughtfully, "or we would have had to leave the strike uncompleted."

Linders gave him a quick, scrutinizing look. "What do you mean—*fortunate*? You mean to tell me you didn't know there was a shaft underneath the floor?"

Camellion grinned. "What gave you the impression I knew?"

"You did, goddamnit!" raged Linders. "From the way you talked, I assumed you knew there was a shaft. So did Griffith."

"When they had me down there, all I saw were concrete walls and ceiling, but logic told me there had to be a shaft. All we have to worry about now is that when the ceiling collapses, it won't affect the concrete sides of the shaft. I don't think it will. The walls of the shaft probably extend downward to form the walls of the anteroom."

George Griffith crawled out and announced that the nylon line was secure. "All we have to do now is blast through the ceiling."

They blasted. They dropped seven grenades down the shaft, scattering them out and anxiously listening to them explode. To the loud sound of broken concrete blocks crashing against the floor of the anteroom, gray-white dust and fumes rolled upward. The sides of the shaft shook and shuddered. In the rooms to the east of the hole in the floor, burning boards and other flaming material were falling to the floor. In the office, smoke was rolling where ceiling joined the top of the walls, long dirty gray-black caterpillars that indicated the path of the eventual flames.

Leaning over the edge of the floor and looking downward, they could see a dim light emitting through what had to be the opening in the steel door to the Cells of Attrition. There was just enough light for them to see that the ceiling had been turned into rubble that lay on the floor of the anteroom.

"Russ, can you see the door to the cells?" Camellion asked.

"I'll see it clearly through the night scope." Linders raised the rifle and looked through the Star-Tron. "Yeah, I've got it. Say when."

The Death Merchant picked up the nylon rope and tugged at it.

"It's as tight as a virgin's twat," Griffith said. His eyes jumped to Camellion. "Do you think they're down there?"

"I don't know." Camellion pulled the line tight and tossed the coiled length into the shaft. "I think they are, if they didn't escape through the tunnel before we destroyed the pyramid. We'll know in a minute." He tapped Linders on the shoulder. "Let her fly."

Linders pulled the trigger. The grenade left the launcher, shot at an angle down the shaft, and struck the floor several inches in front of the steel door, the bone-banging blast tearing a hole in the concrete and smashing the door inward.

Linders and Griffith didn't watch as Camellion took the nylon rope in his hands stood up and swung himself outward over the side of the shaft. Seconds later he was on his way down. Linders and Griffith kept their weapons trained on the smoky rectangular of light where the steel door had been. In less than a minute, Camellion reached the bottom and shook the rope as a signal that he had made it safely down.

"Wish me luck." Linders shouldered his assault rifle, picked up the line, and soon disappeared within the shaft.

A minute and a half more and Griffith was going hand over hand down the nylon. He was only a very short distance from the jumble of torn concrete on the floor and was about to let go of the line when burning rubble, falling from the ceiling in the room containing the wall safe, set the rope on fire.

Filled with hate and bitterness, Commander Sessons stood at the end of the half-opened steel door of the Dissolving Room, every nerve and muscle quivering with pent-up tension. He looked down the length of the long, dim corridor and impatiently waited for Brother Melnor to return. Everything had backfired. He had stationed Brothers Bialk and Mumbower at the door, instructing them not to fire until the enemy dropped to the floor of the anteroom. He might as well have told them to use spit balls, he thought bitterly. The grenade had slammed the steel door against the two Protectors and killed them. They lay still at the end of the passage, the heavy door on top of them.

"Commander, I hear him coming back," Brother Harry Cramm said uneasily. He glanced uncertainly at Brother Gene Gibney, whose face wore a stunned expression.

Sessons turned just as Brother Ralph Melnor stepped through the low opening of the tunnel and switched off the flashlight.

"Well?" demanded Sessons sharply. "Is the other end clear?"

"It's blocked," answered Melnor in a choked voice, wiping sweat from his dirty face. "The entire pyramid must have collapsed on top of the trap door." Red-eyed, he looked straight at a desperate Sessons. "Commander, we're trapped down here."

"What are we going to do?" Brother Kramm sounded like a small child crying in the darkness for his mother.

"We'll wait for them here," Sessons said hoarsely. Now he wished that he had wired the ammo, grenades and bazooka shells in the arsenal room to explode. Another mistake! Now there wasn't anymore time.

"Maybe Brother Atkins and Brother Chiprin will get them?" Gene Gibney said hopefully.

Sessons closed the steel door, threw the top and bottom bolts, and opened the top viewing port. "They'll have to use explosives to get in here," he said, glancing around at the three Protectors. "Melnor, get over here with me. We'll kill them when they come down the corridor. The rest of you get over by the east wall."

Brother Melnor hurried over to Sessons, the cutting stink of sulphuric acid strong in his nose. He had always hated this room of death with its "pond" of acid.

The Death Merchant, Russell Linders and George Griffith moved through the wrecked entrance into the corridor. Linders and Griffith, their weapons trained on the steel door of the Dissolving Room, thought they could see several heads behind the door, on each side of the square viewing port. They couldn't be sure. The light was too dim, the passage too smoky.

To the rear, the ceiling of the office was falling into the shaft, burning boards and other blazing debris hitting the concrete rubble on the floor of the anteroom.

160

"Slow down," Camellion whispered. "I want to check the door of the explosives' room. The room could be wired to explode."

"The door certainly took care of those religious crackpots," Linders said, staring down at the blackened door on top of the two corpses. "Concussion probably killed them before the door crashed into them."

"Who gives a fiddler's fuck!" snapped Griffith. "They're dead."

The Death Merchant went over to the door and checked the steel hasp below the red and white DANGER sign. Two stainless-steel combination locks secured the latch to the hasp. No one was in the room, which meant that there wouldn't be any Protectors coming at them from the rear as they proceeded down the corridor.

The Death Merchant, crossing behind the two other men, went to the other side of the corridor and saw that the lock was secure on the door of Frimm's meditation room. For a moment he looked at the large white cross on the door. A mockery! Christ stood for justice. Frimm preached only his own weird brand of "religious" Hitlerism.

Camellion looked at the latch of the Cell next to Frimm's room. The pushdown handle was raised! He looked at the latch of the opposite cell across the corridor. *Well now, that handle is down,* he thought.

He tapped Linders and Griffith on the shoulders, pointed to the raised handle and, using sign language, indicated what he wanted them to do. Linders moved back ten feet and sighted in on the steel door at the end of the very long corridor, this time using the Star-Tron. Camellion shoved the Auto Mag into a holster, took out a grenade, pulled the pin, and clamped his hand down on the handle. He again pulled the Auto Mag and moved to the side of the wall just ahead of the door. He then nodded to Griffith, who had shouldered his M4 chatter box, and had a 9mm Browning auto-pistol in his right hand. His left hand was on the raised handle of the Cell door. He pulled back on the handle, stepping back with the door as it opened.

The door was three-fourths open when two submachine guns roared from inside the Cell, the streams of projectiles ripping into the leather covering the rubber-and-cotton padding on the inside of the door. Came that split-second lag time on the part of the Protectors inside the Cell and Camellion flipped the grenade around the molding through the opening.

161

Immediately Griffith pushed the door shut and pushed down on the handle. At the same time, Linders yelled *"Down,"* and triggered a long burst at the far-end steel door as he ducked to the right.

Camellion and Griffith, hearing a muffled *whooommmm* from inside the cell, dropped in time to avoid a hail of 9mm Ingram projectiles from the viewing port of the door of the Dissolving Room. Some of Linders's slugs knifed through the opening, but Sessons and Melnor had ducked to the side. A dozen other 5.56mm missiles struck the steel door and set up a loud screaming symphony as they ricocheted.

The Death Merchant shoved up on the latch of the cell, pushed open the door and crawled through the opening. By the time Linders and Griffith had crawled in behind him, he had switched on a Kel-lite flash.

The three men were actually kneeling in blood. Even Camellion gagged slightly at the hideous sight. The grenade, within the closed soundproof cell, had had the effect of a firecracker exploding in a can of sardines! The padding of the walls, ceiling, and floor was ripped and shredded and covered with blood, long strips of rubber and cotton hanging like grotesque stalactites. Everywhere, bits of flesh and clothing were blood-pasted to the padding. The two heads of the Protectors were on the floor, one lying on its right temple, the other upside-down with its eyes wide open! Next to the upside-down head was half an arm and a leg. Next to the other head was another leg and a hand. The explosion had even thrust a dozen long pieces of rib bones into the padding. Over the mess hung the clawing stink of blood, smoke and death.

"Put in full magazines," Camellion said lazily. "You two can keep them busy. I'm going to rush that door and place a charge against it."

"We're going to have a hard time taking any of them alive," Linders commented. He shoved a fresh magazine into the Armalite.

Camellion took a block of COM-B-2 from one of his shoulder bags.

"I know. I'd like to find out where Padden and Zettker are buried, but I doubt if I ever will. The *Dissolving* Room could mean that there aren't any bodies."

George Griffith asked, "Any Frimmies in the other Cells?"

"We don't have time to let them out," Camellion said. "Besides, I want the police to find them."

"If we don't get the anvils out of our tails, the cops will find *us!*" grunted Griffith. "We've got only ten minutes left on the extended time."

Camellion didn't argue. "So let's do it. Russ, you go first. You have the Star-Tron."

Linders crawled out in the passage, scampered to the far wall, stood up, sighted in on the opening in the steel door, then said, "Go!"

The Death Merchant went! He plunged through the partially open Cell door and sprinted along the left side wall, an AMP in his right hand, the block of COM-B-2 in his left. He was four-fifths of the way to the door when Linders spotted Sessons and Melnor once more thrusting the stubby barrels of Ingrams through the port and triggering off a stream of 5.56mm missiles.

None of the slugs touched Sessons, but one bullet struck Brother Melnor in the back of the left hand and, for all practical purposes, tore it off. Melnor yelled with fear and shock, dropped the Ingram, staggered back and stared at his half-torn-off hand dripping blood.

Sessons cursed, ducked, and jumped to the side of the door. For a moment or two, he toyed with the idea of taking refuge in the blocked tunnel, but couldn't force himself to appear as a coward in front of the three other Brothers. Anyhow, it was better to die standing straight and tall.

The Death Merchant reached the end of the corridor and jumped to the wall by the left side of the steel door studded with rivet heads, an area three feet wide. He turned the timer on the COM-B-2 to 3-MIN, placed the block of explosive on the floor, at the bottom center of the door, then turned and raced back to Linders and Griffith.

Brother Ralph Melnor had dropped into unconsciousness and lay face down on the concrete floor in a pool of blood. Sessons had moved to the east wall and was crouched on one knee with Brother Harry Kramm and Brother Gene Gibney, the latter two so nervous that their Ingrams shook.

"Commander, do you think Brothers Atkins and Chiprin are dead?" Kramm asked. "There's no way we can be sure."

"They're dead," Sessons snapped. "What do you think that explosion meant?"

"But it's—"

"Shut up, Kramm," muttered Sessons. "Keep your sights

centered on the door." Sessions own sight seemed to waver before his eyes.

The only protective barrier between them and the enemy was the ten-foot-square pool of sulphuric acid. The pool wasn't really any protection. There was an eight-foot space, to the south and the north, on either side of the pool of death. And acid below could stop bullets from above. Damn Frimm! Sessions hoped the son-of-a-bitch was dead and that he had died slowly.

The colossal explosion sent waves of concussion that could actually be felt by Sessions and the two other Protectors, the blast of such force that it ripped the heavy steel door off its inner hinges and slammed it across the room. With a loud clang, one corner of the door struck the concrete-block wall with such force that several blocks crumpled. The door then crashed to the floor.

An enormous ball of smoke rolled through the space where the door had been.

"Don't fire!" yelled Sessions. "Wait until they charge."

Several minutes passed. Three grenades sailed through the door.

"Get down!" screamed Sessions, fear clutching at his mind.

The grenades hit the floor, rolled a foot, and exploded with enormous flashes of fire and the *ping-ping-pings* of vicious shrapnel, some of which struck the east wall but passed over the three Protectors face down on the floor.

Sessions, Kramm and Gibney were trying to scramble to their feet and swing their Ingram submachine guns toward the door, but the lag-time on their part had given Camellion & Friends time to storm into the room.

A blast of Armalite projectiles from Linders dissolved Brother Harry Kramm's face, head, and chest. Griffith's hollow-pointed 9mm bullets flowed all over Brother Gibney. The powerful slugs chopped his shoulder bones into splinters and tore out his back. Others exploded his skull with such force that pieces of brain and bone struck the east wall.

Commander Sessions's finger never touched the trigger of his Ingram. The Death Merchant's bullet hit him high in the chest and rocketed out his back, leaving a hole large enough for a mouse to crawl through. Dead, Sessions fell to his back and lay still, his sightless eyes staring at the ceiling.

" 'The candle of the wicked shall be put out!' The Good Book says so!" The Death Merchant looked around the room. As Griffith pulled out the TEX-10-8 and extended its whip antenna, Camellion walked over to the pool and looked down at the colorless sulphuric acid. He had his answer. Padden and Zettker would never be found. . . .

He turned, raced toward the entrance of the tunnel that led under the Temple, and called over his shoulder, "I'll set the charge by the trap door and we'll get out of here."

In another 14 minutes, they had left the Temple by way of one of the front doors and were crouched by bushes a hundred feet northwest of the building. The back wall and rear roof were blazing and the Temple would be ashes within the hour.

All around Camellion and his men was fire and destruction. They could see Frimmies running in the distance, hysterically running nowhere, like blindfolded chickens. Everywhere was black smoke and the sweet smell of violent death.

The most welcome sights and sounds were the two Westland Lynx helicopters—one lifting off from the northeast. The other chopper had been hovering high, not too distant from the burning Temple. It began to settle several hundred feet to the west.

"Let's move," Camellion said. "I need a steak . . ."

Three Weeks Later . . .

Richard Camellion was in the file room underneath the barn of his *Memento Mori* Ranch in the Big Thicket region of Texas, reading a newspaper. For the past two and a half weeks, the Church of the Cosmic Reality had continually been on the front pages. The latest news was that the seven Ministers of Light of New Earth Community had been indicted by the federal government for illegal possession of automatic weapons and explosives. In the Arsenal, police had found not only dynamite but various kinds of military explosives, as well as hundreds of submachine guns and automatic rifles. The police had also found grenades and World War II bazookas.

The police had also found the Cells of Attrition. Every occupant was insane. . . .

All over the United States, the FBI and the ATF, with the help of local police, had raided Frimmie camps and homes. In every raid, more illegal firearms had been found.

Numermous Protectors had confessed to murder, including five Protectors in Mesa, Arizona. Everett Padden and Roger Zettker had been shot and their corpses dissolved in acid.

One hundred and sixty-three Frimmies had been killed at New Earth Community by "dissident ex-members of the Cosmic Reality church"—including Commander Sessons and his aides. On the same day of the strike, 410 Frimmies had been hospitalized . . . due to shock and to mass hallucinations induced by LSD.

Camellion put down the paper and, thinking of the FBI, smiled.

He had resurfaced and the Feds had swarmed all over him. Where had he been? Pretending great reluctance, he had told them. He was a secret alcoholic and had spent weeks in a rest home that specialized in treating alcoholism.

Could he prove it?

166

He could and did.

Reverend Hannibal Frimm was the biggest joke of all. His broken body had been found at the base of the Tower of Consolation and Heavenly Communication. He had either fallen, jumped, or been thrown from the Needle.

According to the media, Frimm's death did prove two things: the first, that he was not "immortal;" the second, that he would not be around to see the end of the Universe.

The local FBI in Colorado Springs was feuding with the state police. Captain Marvin Dowdy had said about the FBI on television: "They're a bunch of know-it-alls who couldn't find their own two feet with a magnifying glass."

The Church of the Cosmic Reality had been smashed.

Drumming the fingers of his left hand on the polished table-top, the Death Merchant frowned when he thought of Grojean, who was still refusing to pay Camellion for the motor-home.

But I've got him over the well-known barrel! Camellion thought. *He will either pay or I'll refuse to go to the Bermuda Triangle. . . .*

Dear Reader:

The Pinnacle Books editors strive to select and produce books that are exciting, entertaining and readable . . . no matter what the category. From time to time we will attempt to discover what you, the reader, think about a particular book or series.

Now that you've finished reading this volume in *The Death Merchant* series, we'd like to find out what you liked, or didn't like, about this story. We'll share your opinions with the author and discuss them as we plan future books. This will result in books that you will find more to your liking. As in fine art and good cooking a matter of taste is involved; and for you, of course, it is *your* taste that is most important to you. For Joseph Rosenberger, and the Pinnacle editors, it is not the critics' reviews and publicity that have been most rewarding, it is the unending stream of readers' mail. Here is where we discover what readers like, what they *feel* about a story, and what they find memorable. So, do help us in becoming a little more knowledgeable in providing you with the kind of stories you like. Here's how . . .

WIN BOOKS . . . AND $200! Please fill out the following pages and mail them as indicated. Every week, for twelve weeks following publication, the editors will choose, at random, a reader's name from all the questionnaires received. The twelve lucky readers will receive $25 worth of paperbacks *and* become official entrants in our Pinnacle Books Reader Sweepstakes. The winner of this sweepstakes drawing will receive a Grand Prize of $200, the inclusion of his or her name in a forthcoming Pinnacle Book (as a special acknowledgment, possibly even as a character!), and several other local prizes to be announced to each initial winner. As a further inducement to send in your questionnaire *now,* we will send the first 25 replies received a free book by return mail! Here's a chance to talk to the author and editors, voice your opinions, and win some great prizes, too!

READER SURVEY

1. Are you glad you bought this book, and did it live up to your expectations?

   _____

2. What was it about this book that induced you to buy it?
   (A. The title_____) (B. The author's name_____)
   (C. A friend's recommendation_____)
   (D. The cover art_____)
   (E. The cover description_____)
   (F. Subject matter_____) (G. Advertisement_____)
   (H. Heard author on TV or radio_____)
   (I. Read previous books in this series_____ . . .
      which ones? _____)
   (J. Bookstore display_____)
   (K. Other? _____).

3. What is the book you read just before this one?

   _____
   And how would you rate it with this volume in
   The Death Merchant series?_____

   _____

4. What is the very next book you plan to read?

   _____
   How did you decide on that?_____

5. Where did you buy this volume in *The Death Merchant* series? _____

   _____

(Name and address of store, please):

_____

_____

6. Where do you buy the majority of your paperbacks? _____

7. What seems to be the major factor that persuades you to buy a certain book?

_____

8. How many books do you buy each month?

_____

9. Do you ever write letters to the author or publisher . . . and why? _____

_____

10. About how many hours a week do you spend reading books? _____ How many hours a week watching television? _____

11. What other spare-time activity do you enjoy most? _____ For how many hours a week? _____

12. Which magazines do you read regularly? . . . in order of your preference _____,

_____, _____,

_____

13. Of your favorite magazine, what is it that you like best about it? _____

_____

14. What is your favorite television show of the past year or so? _____

15. What is your favorite motion picture of the past year or so? _____

16. What is the most disappointing television show you've seen lately? _____

17. What is the most disappointing motion picture you've seen lately? _____

18. What is the most disappointing book you've read lately? _____

19. Are there authors that you like so well that you read *all* their books? _____
    Who are they? _____

20. And can you explain *why* you like their books so much? _____
    _____
    _____

21. Which particular books by these authors do you like best? _____
    _____

22. Did you read Taylor Caldwell's *Captains and the Kings*?____ Did you watch it on television? ____ Which did you do first? _____

23. Did you read John Jakes' *The Bastard*? ____ Did you watch it on TV?____ Which first?____ Have you read any of the other books in John Jakes' Bicentennial Series? _____ What do you think of them? _____

24. Did you read James Michener's *Centennial*?____ Did you watch it on TV?____ Which first?____

25. Did you read Irwin Shaw's *Rich Man, Poor Man?* ____ Did you watch it on TV?____ Which first?_____

26. Of all the recent books you've read, or films you've seen, are there any that you would compare in any way to *The Death Merchant*? _____

27. With series books that you like, how often would you like to read them . . . (a) twice a year _____? (b) three times a year _____? (c) every other month _____? (d) every month _____? (e) other _____ ?

28. What is your favorite book character or series of all time? _____
And why? _____

29. Do you collect any paperback series? _____
Which ones? _____

30. What do like *best* about *The Death Merchant* series? _____

31. And what don't you like about it . . . if anything? _____

32. Have you read any books in *The Destroyer* series? _____ And what is your opinion of them?
_____

33. Have you read any books in the Nick Carter *Killmaster* series? _____ Opinion? _____
_____

34. Have you read any books in *The Executioner* series? _____ Opinion? _____
_____

35. Have you read any books in *The Penetrator* series? _____ Opinion? _____
_____

36. Have you read any books in *The Edge* series? _____ Opinion? _____
_____

37. Have you read any books in *The Butcher* series? _____ Opinion? _____

38. Have you read any books in the *Louis L'Amour* western series? _____ Opinion? _____

39. Have you read any books in the *Travis McGee* series? Opinion? _____

40. Have you read any books in the *Matt Helm* series? _____ Opinion? _____

41. Have you read any books in the *Carter Brown* mystery series? _____ Opinion? _____

42. Rank the following descriptions of *The Death Merchant* series as you feel they are best defined:

	Excellent	*Okay*	*Poor*
A. A sense of reality	_____	_____	_____
B. Suspense	_____	_____	_____
C. Intrigue	_____	_____	_____
D. Sexuality	_____	_____	_____
E. Violence	_____	_____	_____
F. Romance	_____	_____	_____
G. History	_____	_____	_____
H. Characterization	_____	_____	_____
I. Scenes, events	_____	_____	_____
J. Pace, readability	_____	_____	_____
K. Dialogue	_____	_____	_____
L. Style	_____	_____	_____

43. What do you do with your paperbacks after you've read them? _____
_____

44. Do you buy paperbacks in any of the following categories, and approximately how many do you buy in a year?

A. Contemporary fiction _____

B. Historical romance _____

C. Family saga _____

D. Romance (like Harlequin) _____

E. Romantic suspense _____

F. Gothic romance _____

G. Occult novels _____

H. War novels _____

I. Action/adventure novels (like *this* book) _____

J. "Bestsellers" _____

K. Science fiction _____

L. Mystery _____

M. Westerns _____

N. Nonfiction _____

O. Biography _____

P. How-To books _____

Q. Other _____

45. And, lastly some profile data on *you* the reader . . .

A. Age: 12–16_____ 17–20_____ 21–30_____
31–40_____ 41–50_____ 51–60_____
61 or over_____

B. Occupation: _____

C. Education level; check last grade completed:
10_____ 11_____ 12_____ Freshman_____
Sophomore_____ Junior_____ Senior_____
Graduate School_____, plus any specialized
schooling _____

D. Your average annual gross income:
Under $10,000_____ $10,000–$15,000_____
$15,000–$20,000_____ $20,000–$30,000_____
$30,000–$50,000_____ Above $50,000_____

E. Did you read a lot as a child? _____ Do you
recall your favorite childhood novel? _____
_____

F. Do you find yourself reading more or less
than you did five years ago? _____

G. Do you read hardcover books? _____ How
often? _____ If so, are they books that you
buy? _____ borrow? _____ or trade? _____ Or
other? _____

H. Does the imprint (Pinnacle, Avon, Bantam,
etc.) make any difference to you when considering a paperback purchase? _____

I. Have you ever bought paperbacks by mail
directly from the publisher? _____ And do
you like to buy books that way? _____

J. Would you be interested in buying paperbacks via a book club or subscription program? _____ And, in your opinion, what

would be the best reasons for doing so? _____

... the problems in doing so? _____

K. Is there something that you'd like to see writers or publishers do for you as a reader of paperbacks? _____

L. Would you be interested in joining a *Death Merchant* fan club? _____

M. If so, which of the following items would interest you most:

	GREAT IDEA!	DEPENDS ...	FORGET IT!
Monthly Newsletter	_____	_____	_____
Membership card	_____	_____	_____
Membership scroll (for framing)	_____	_____	_____
T-shirt	_____	_____	_____
Sweat shirt	_____	_____	_____
Windbreaker jacket	_____	_____	_____
Poster	_____	_____	_____
Decal	_____	_____	_____
Other ideas?	_____		

(On those items that you *do* like, indicate what you think a fair price would be.)

THANK YOU FOR TAKING THE TIME TO REPLY TO THIS, THE FIRST PUBLIC READER SURVEY IN PAPERBACK HISTORY!

NAME _____

ADDRESS _____

CITY _____ STATE _____ ZIP _____

PHONE _____

Please return this questionnaire to:

The Editors; Survey Dept. DMS
Pinnacle Books, Inc.
2029 Century Park East
Los Angeles, CA 90067

the EXECUTIONER by Don Pendleton

☐ 40-027-9	Executioner's War Book		$1.50
☐ 40-299-6	War Against the Mafia	#1	1.50
☐ 40-300-3	Death Squad	#2	1.50
☐ 40-301-1	Battle Mask	#3	1.50
☐ 40-302-X	Miami Massacre	#4	1.50
☐ 40-303-8	Continental Contract	#5	1.50
☐ 40-304-6	Assault on Soho	#6	1.50
☐ 40-305-4	Nightmare in New York	#7	1.50
☐ 40-306-2	Chicago Wipeout	#8	1.50
☐ 40-307-0	Vegas Vendetta	#9	1.50
☐ 40-308-9	Caribbean Kill	#10	1.50
☐ 40-309-7	California Hit	#11	1.50
☐ 40-310-0	Boston Blitz	#12	1.50
☐ 40-311-9	Washington I.O.U.	#13	1.50
☐ 40-312-7	San Diego Siege	#14	1.50
☐ 40-313-5	Panic in Philly	#15	1.50
☐ 40-314-3	Sicilian Slaughter	#16	1.50
☐ 40-237-6	Jersey Guns	#17	1.50
☐ 40-315-1	Texas Storm	#18	1.50
☐ 40-316-X	Detroit Deathwatch	#19	1.50
☐ 40-238-4	New Orleans Knockout	#20	1.50
☐ 40-317-8	Firebase Seattle	#21	1.50
☐ 40-318-6	Hawaiian Hellground	#22	1.50
☐ 40-319-4	St. Louis Showdown	#23	1.50
☐ 40-239-2	Canadian Crisis	#24	1.50
☐ 40-224-4	Colorado Kill-Zone	#25	1.50
☐ 40-320-8	Acapulco Rampage	#26	1.50
☐ 40-321-6	Dixie Convoy	#27	1.50
☐ 40-225-2	Savage Fire	#28	1.50
☐ 40-240-6	Command Strike	#29	1.50
☐ 40-150-7	Cleveland Pipeline	#30	1.50
☐ 40-166-3	Arizona Ambush	#31	1.50
☐ 40-252-X	Tennessee Smash	#32	1.50
☐ 40-333-X	Monday's Mob	#33	1.50
☐ 40-334-8	Terrible Tuesday	#34	1.50

The Destroyer by Warren Murphy

Remo Williams is the perfect weapon—a cold, calculating death machine developed by CURE, the world's most secret crime-fighting organization. Together with his mentor, Chiun, the oriental martial arts wizard, The Destroyer makes the impossible missions possible.

Over 13 million copies sold!